# About the author

Claire Allan has worked as a reporter for the *Derry Journal* for the past eight years. Aside from work, she has a passion for reading, buying inexpensive handbags in Tesco and blethering on the phone. She has been married to Neil for six years (she was a child bride) and they have one slightly hyper three-year-old, Joseph. Claire also has a time share of a serial-killing goldfish called Dorothy. *Rainy Days and Tuesdays* is her debut novel. You can visit her website at www.claireallan.com

# Acknowledgements

First and foremost, I would like to thank my family and friends for their unwavering support. Thanks to the two men in my life, Neil and Joseph, for putting up with a wife and mammy who spends all her free time attached to a laptop.

To my parents, thank you for always believing in me. Lisa, thanks for that special first edition. To Emma and Peter, I'm sure it won't be long until you give me a run for my money. And Abby, thank you for being my perfect little Lily. And to all the Davidson/McGuinness connections – thank you.

Special thanks go to my reading team, for support and encouragement and loads of white wine. Nora, Erin, Amanda, you are stars and I'm very blessed to have your friendship.

Special mention has to go to my VBF Vicki: you know this book would never have been written without you and Mabel pushing me along every step of the way.

Thanks also to the wonderful support network at Writewords.org, especially the chick-lit ladies and the site experts. In particular I must mention Luisa Plaja, Keris Stainton and the wonderful Kate Long for reminding me it's all just a bit of craic.

Special mention must also go to the staff and management of the *Derry Journal* for their fantastic support and encouragement and copious free plugs.

And finally thanks to those people who believed in me and this book enough to take a chance. To Ger Nichol, my agent, a big thank-you for her friendship and support. To the team at Poolbeg, especially Paula Campbell, Niamh Fitzgerald (for saving copies of everything!), Lynda Laffan and Gaye Shortland for her keen eye and encouragement.

*For Siobhan McEleney*
*Always remembered*

# 1

I used to be glamorous once. Honestly I was. I went to the hairdresser's every six weeks and had my roots done. I wore boot-cut jeans, suit jackets and fitted T-shirts which hugged my contours perfectly. I had a dressing-table overflowing with Clarins and L'Oréal and a selection of funky jewellery to jazz up any outfit. I was a babe – but somewhere between being a babe and having a baby I lost my mojo. Now I'm the ultimate slummy mummy.

This thought dances through my mind as I wake up – hair damp with sweat, skin greasy from last night's takeaway. I toy with the idea of hiding under the duvet, ducking my responsibilities and going back to sleep, but then it dawns on me – I'm a grown-up. I can't just do that. It's not like when I was at school and I could feign a cough or grab my stomach and perform my dying-swan routine for my unimpressed mammy who would eventually give in to my pitiful whinges and allow me a day under the blue blanket on the sofa. You can't just refuse to go to work – not when there are bills to pay and stories to write.

You can't go back to sleep when you can hear a wee voice from the nursery next door giving a rather amusing rendition of 'Jingle Bells' (despite it being July), letting you know that your toddler is awake and will soon be demanding breakfast. The dream I had been having was so nice too. It was sunny and bright and I felt gloriously relaxed. I was cycling to a local dress shop to pick a dress to wear to accompany *dish-du-jour* Dermot Murnaghan, TV News Presenter Extraordinaire, to the BAFTAS.

Himself is snoring beside me and I realise this is my reality. A stuffy, too bright room. A snoring husband, who bears not even a passing resemblance to the delectable Dermot, and a child who has started to reach fever pitch with his singing.

Oh yes, and there is work. I have to go to work. I pull myself out of bed and blearily reach for the cow-print slippers which are hiding on the floor. After pulling on my dressing-gown, I give a cursory glance at the mirror. T – minus 60 minutes (in NASA-speak) until I have to be dressed and out of the house. T – minus 60 minutes to make this face, this crumpled, wrinkly, bed-headed vision before me, respectable enough to face my public. It almost makes me laugh.

When I walk into the nursery I am greeted with a "Mammeeee!". Jack is grinning ear to ear from his cot. "My want breakfass!" he cheeps, and I smile again, realising that when my son looks at me he sees nothing but his very own mammy and he loves me.

He is not one bit bothered about my bed-head and the saggy pyjama bottoms I'm wearing. He thinks I am the bee's knees, one yummy mummy, a foxy mamma. He reaches out his chubby arms and I reach in to lift him up, envelop him in my arms and feel his cuddly body against mine. Until, of course, he tries to bite me and the spell is somewhat broken.

This morning, like almost every other, I manage to get myself and Jack out the door in time. At least, I manage to get out the door ten minutes after I wanted to, which is a record for this year. Aidan is still snoring comfortably, having worked long into the night, and I have spent my precious sixty minutes trying to entertain my two-year-old, getting us dressed and getting into the car without totally losing my cool.

I choose to ignore the Weetabix stain I know is on my trousers. It's not that I don't care about my appearance but I know no one gives me a second glance any more anyway, so they are hardly going to notice one wee stain. Grooming is a thing of the past when you have to get a child to the childminder and yourself to work on time.

Where once I would practically dance into the office, throw my (designer) handbag onto my desk and set about working on the features for next month's issue, now I saunter in the back door, sit down, bury my head in organising my desk and offer to cover all the boring, respectable features that don't actually require me to leave the office or speak to anyone face to face.

This morning is no different. I say a few hellos to the team before plonking myself down with my morning coffee and sausage roll to open the post. Somehow in the proper daylight the Weetabix stain on my trousers has morphed from an eeny-weeny mark to one not too dissimilar to that birthmark on Gorbachov's head.

Running my fingers through my hair, I realise, not for the

first time, that I have forgotten to brush it again before leaving home. No wonder Susie, the normally very friendly childminder, had looked at me in an alarmed way as I dropped Jack off. Searching through my tatty Dunnes Stores Better Value handbag for a mini-hairbrush, I am needless to say more than a little dismayed to find the bottle of Calpol I keep for emergencies has sprung a leak and, yes, I can still brush my hair, but only if I don't mind it being strawberry-flavoured and slightly pink in colour all day.

I give my hair a quick detangle with my fingers, hoping that everyone is thinking I'm trying the new just-fell-out-of-bed look, and go back to my hiding place behind my monitor. From the other end of the office I can hear Louise laughing uproariously. She was at some launch or other last night and apparently everyone who was anyone was there. It was a scream, she says, and she had a hundred admiring comments for her new dress which she bought in some boutique in Belfast. I try to look interested but all I really want to do is staple her head to her desk so I don't have to look at her smug and gorgeous face any more.

I shouldn't be jealous. I attended a launch myself yesterday. One of the local supermarkets was launching their new improved Mother and Baby Club and I was invited along to find out all about their groovy new parking facilities and padded trolleys. All the best mummies were there. And I stress, they were *mummies* – the posh version of mammies. The post generates its usual share of gems. At least, being Parenting Editor, I can always expect some interesting samples. There is a book on raising your toddler to be politically correct, some toilet wipes and a dummy which promises to soothe even the most fractious of children.

And for the glamorous mummy-on-the-go, well, there was a sample of Tena Lady because we all know the busy working mum can't smell of wee. I switch on my computer and smile as an image of the lovely Dermot flickers onto the screen. Dermot is my escape – my little fantasy where I can pretend I am still me and not just a mammy or Grace Adams, Parenting Editor of *Northern People* magazine. Amid the cute pictures of Jack grinning at me from the gaudy-coloured frames proclaiming '*I love Mummy!*', beside the piles of parenting magazines, nappies and nipple-creams (again, samples) which clutter my desk, there is Dermot – all be-suited and handsome. He looks at me, his eyebrow raised in that quizzical and sexy manner of his, and I wish, oh really wish, we really were heading out to the BAFTAS for a date. I sigh, sip my coffee and finish the sausage roll. I cannot lose myself in another daydream today. There is work to be done. I have to come face to face with thirty screaming toddlers at Cheeky Monkeys Day Care Centre for a feature on 'Messy Play'. And when all that is done, I have to find the answers to the parenting problems submitted to me by overwrought mummies and daddies all across Ireland. Oh, if only my readers knew that Jack had cheese and ham for breakfast this morning because today his favourite Weetabix was "Icky, Mammy, icky!" or that I'd let him watch *CBeebies* videos until nine thirty last night just to get some peace and quiet. I already know this is one of those days when I will need two Nurofen and a power nap in the toilets before lunch-time. If Louise keeps on screeching in her high-pitched giggle, it might even be before tea break.

I open my email and find my daily reminder from *lifecoaches.com* to take each day as a new challenge, relax, breathe and remember: **"I am a strong, confident woman. I can do this!"** Breathing in, holding for five and breathing out, I feel myself relax and get ready for another day.

And then the phone rings.

I would say it is a pretty poor reflection of my ability to be an award-winning journalist that I mentally cringe when the phone rings at my desk. I frequently toy with the idea of not answering it and doing that oh-so-American thing of screening my calls. I imagine that wouldn't go down the best with the powers that be.

"Good morning, Grace Adams speaking!" I trill down the phone.

"Hi, Grace."

Sighing with relief, I realise it is only Aidan – fresh from his slumbers and ready for another day of scratching himself on the PlayStation before heading out for his bar job in the evening.

"Do you know where my phone is?" he asks.

"No," I reply. "Where have you looked for it?"

"I haven't yet. I thought you might know," he says.

My blood pressure rises.

We have this conversation every morning. Sure enough, it might not be the phone we are talking about – it might be the keys, the bills that need paying, the wee doodah you use to bleed the fecked radiator in the front room – but the premise is the same. He asks, I tell him to look, he looks, he finds. Why he can't realise he would be better served to just cut out the middle-woman and look himself is beyond me.

But this morning, in a remarkable turn of events, I don't need to answer. By now he has looked around him and found said item two feet from where he is standing. He informs me of this and I get ready to hang up and go somewhere to faint with shock.

However, just then an unexpected noise comes shooting down the phone-line.

"Do you want to go out tomorrow night, Grace?" he asks and I start to wonder if my cholesterol-stuffed heart can really take the impact of two such shocks in one day.

We don't go out. Not any more. Not since we became parents. We tried it once when Jack was one and it was an unmitigated disaster. I spent the whole night worrying about whether or not Jack would settle without me, and himself spent the whole evening telling me why we needed to get out more. Both of us drank ourselves silly, talked shite about the wee man, ignoring the real issues in our relationship, before going home and falling straight to sleep. As I threw my considerable guts up the next day, I vowed never again. Seeing my whiter-than-white pallor, himself agreed that was not a sight he ever wished to see again either so we became Mr and Mrs Bottle-of-Wine-on-a-Saturday-Night. In other words, we became so boring we even bored ourselves.

Soon the bottle of wine would involve him on the PlayStation and me watching a chick flick on my own in the other room, and even that went by the wayside when he got the bar job. So, if I'm honest, I've become a sad old wino on a Saturday night on my own and he has become the life and soul of the staff-party scene at Jackson's Bar.

How we manage to survive as a couple is slightly beyond me so I guess, if I'm trying to operate in the spirit of willingness to save what's left of our marriage, I'll have to say yes to his night out – even though I have nothing to wear.

"Okay then," I mumble, closely followed by a litany of

7

who, what, where questions that any woman needs to know the answer to before she can even think about picking out an outfit. For one brief moment I wonder if we are going somewhere nice, just the two of us.

"It's one of the new bosses at work," Aidan replies. "He wants to talk to me about my job prospects. He thought it might be nice for us to go out for dinner."

I agree, hang up and contemplate suicide. You see, I don't like going out for dinner with strangers. (Strike Two against my ability to be a fabulous journalist.) There is always a great deal of awkwardness when deciding whether or not to have that extra garlic bread or dessert, and I inevitably end up choosing the most unappetising salad on the menu as I don't want to appear a greedy gulpen.

And of course, the menfolk will be talking business – of which I know nothing and care even less for. (Strike Three against my ability to be a renowned journalist – apparently I should be very interested in business and politics etc.)

As I get in the car and leave for Cheeky Monkeys, I'm already frantically trying to figure out what to wear. I have two problems. The first is that when it comes to suitable evening attire, I'm pretty limited to cosy pyjamas and, second of all, even if I do find some treasure lurking in the back of my wardrobe, I'm not sure how to get out of the door without Jack leaving a special food-stain reminder on it.

I think about this, while driving along the Foyle Road towards Cheeky Monkeys. I have approximately twenty-three pairs of tatty tracksuit bottoms and a million T-shirts, but when it comes to glamming it up I realise it will have to be the RBTs again (Reliable Black Trousers), some killer heels (as we will be in a restaurant and therefore not required to walk any further than the toilet and back) and perhaps my nice turquoise satin vest-top would finish it off nicely. (I don't know why I say 'perhaps': it is in fact the only dressy top I have that still fits.)

Congratulating myself on my quick outfit-choosing decisions, I park my car, head inside and immerse my arms in a bowl of jelly.

Whoever said being a journalist wasn't glamorous?

Apparently I am growing too fond of my evening glass of wine. Mammy is concerned. She has been surfing the net, reading about working mums under stress and has even suggested in her ever-so-subtle-as-a-brick way that perhaps I might want to "write a wee feature on parents who hit the sauce".

It was never this way in her day. Oh no, you made do and you survived on a fiver a week and you were there for your children and you didn't want it all. You didn't need to drink and, even if you did, you couldn't afford it anyway. As I listen to The Speech, as my friend Daisy has dubbed it, I pour myself another glass and start to fill the bath.

This is my salvation – my Me Time. A glass of wine, a bubble bath, a good book or, if I'm feeling too tired to read a book, a cheesy weekly magazine to soak away my troubles and forget about the stresses of the day that has passed.

It has only been in the last few months that I've actually been able to get away with a soak. Before then it would be almost guaranteed that no sooner would bum hit bubbles than Jack would wake screaming and I would run, soaking and dripping, to his room where he would then stare at my nakedness with a strange mixture of curiosity, disgust and humour. By the time he was settled the bath would be cold, the wine would be warm and the magazine would be soggy so I'd opt for a quick shower before climbing into my jammies. I don't drink too much, honestly I don't. Well, not unless Daisy and I have dumped the children for the night and we are on the proverbial piss. But I suppose mammies will always be mammies and mine is as prone to worrying as I am. It is a genetic curse.

Aidan, for those who are interested, is working tonight. He doesn't normally work on a Thursday but, as he isn't working tomorrow night for the big dinner meeting, he has to make up his hours. I decide to make the most of the peace and quiet and climb into the bath and try to lose myself in the latest Marian Keyes while trying to de-fuzz, exfoliate and moisturise all at the same time. I realise that, much as I am not used to pampering myself, I'm actually quite good at multi-tasking and I even manage to tidy that delicate bikini area without clipping a vein.

Climbing out of the bath I start the arduous task of applying self-tanning lotion. Trust me, when you are on the larger side it takes some time to smooth it into your skin. The smell is cloying, but then I tell myself it will all be worth it when I look like a tanned goddess as I step into the restaurant tomorrow night.

Checking the RBTs are clean, and the turquoise top is back from the drycleaner's I find myself then faced with an array of shoes of various heights, styles and colours and the real decision-making process has to start.

"Three-inch, four-inch, sparkly or black?" I ask down the phone without even saying hello.

"Occasion? Location? Water-retention levels?" Daisy counters – she knows me so well.

"Dinner with Aidan's bosses," I reply. "Swanky new Italian beside the river, mid-cycle-ankles decidedly unpuffy."

"Outfit?" she counters.

"RBTs," (Daisy knows all my code words as I do hers) "and satin top."

"Three-inch sparkly, with that silver cross I bought for your birthday and your hair swept up at one side with that wee sparkly clip."

"Love you," I answer.

"Love you too," she replies, and hangs up.

The thing with Daisy is that there is no bullshit. She knows me, I know her and there is no need for small-talk – no need to pepper every sentence with pauses and niceties. She is like the modern-day ghostbuster: she comes, she sees, she kicks my arse.

I've only known Daisy two years. We met when I was heavy with child as opposed to being just ordinarily heavy. She was the little ray of Scottish sunshine who phoned the office one day to ask me to feature her nursery in the magazine. We met for coffee, swapped pregnancy stories and became friends.

She assures me she is not merely my friend for the copious amounts of free publicity I can offer her – and, after feeling hormonally paranoid for the first year of Jack's life, I now believe her.

Lifting the sparkly shoes out of the cupboard, I realise Daisy has indeed made the right decision and I could look half-respectable after all.

I climb into bed, close my eyes and drift off to sleep, hoping that Dermot and I get to go to the BAFTAS again tonight.

11

# 2

Friday is a fairly relaxed day at *Northern People* – unless of course it's pre-publication week and then it all gets a bit edgy. People scream, slam down phones, cry in the toilets and chain-smoke out the back door as if there is no tomorrow. At such times we are grateful for our out-of-town location. No one can hear you scream in Springtown.

Thankfully, we have another week until the bell tolls for the September edition so we can sit back and relax – sort of.

As usual I say good morning to Dermot and go through the motions with the post. I decide no one is going to put me in a bad mood today because, even though we have to go with Aidan's boss, Aidan and I are actually going out tonight. Perhaps, after his boss leaves, we can sit down and talk about us and regain some of that old magic.

I feel butterflies rise in my stomach. In so many silly little ways this feels just like our first date. I was so nervous back then. I didn't dare believe that Aidan, tall, brooding and gorgeous, wanted to go out with me. Even though I was a lot slimmer then, and even though I had a promising career, a wardrobe of fascinating clothes and a repertoire of witty and intellectually stimulating one-liners tucked up my sleeve, I also had the utter lack of self-confidence so common in twenty-one-year-olds, especially Irish twenty-one-year-olds.

My friend had introduced us a few weeks before at a work mixer. Aidan was at that stage working in advertising and while his jokes about column inches and the size of his packages weren't as funny as he tried to have me believe, I found myself laughing anyway. There was something about him that pulled me in from the start.

There followed at least half a dozen phone calls whereby we both tried to ascertain from my friend whether the other was interested or not. When it was firmly established that both parties were raring to go, we set about arranging a night out.

Now usually I had a strict policy whereby the first date should always be a trip to the cinema. This would mean that pressure would be off for conversation, and afterwards we could always break the ice by talking about the film. If it was going well (i.e. he hadn't stolen half my popcorn or dared to drink from my cup) we would retire to a wee bar down the road and chat for a few hours.

But with Aidan something stupid in me made me opt for a dinner date. As I've already said, I don't normally like dinner with strangers, but I wanted so desperately to come across as a sophisticated young thing that I guessed inviting him to a screening of *The Bodyguard* would seem terribly naff.

We arrived at the restaurant and took our seats. Already my mind was ticking over. Yes, I would love a nice glass of wine, but if I ordered a bottle would I look like a desperate drunk – even though it was obviously cheaper than paying by the glass? Garlic Potatoes were my favourite but would I be wise to order them on a date? What if our kiss was a smelly mess and he never wanted to see me again? Lord knows, even though we hadn't actually had our date at that stage, I knew with 99% certainty that I would want to see him again.

You see, when I met Aidan, I had one of those heart-stopping moments of clarity I'd only ever read about before. I just knew something was going to happen. I didn't know, admittedly, if that something would be that we slept together and he dumped me like a shitty sandwich, I only knew that something was meant to be. I don't want to say it was love at first sight, so I'll stick to saying, in this instance, it was 'like' love at first sight.

In the end, I threw caution to the wind and ordered the bottle of wine. We shared it, then another, before we walked tipsily home to my flat. He kissed me, gently and tenderly – but with enough passion that I knew he felt for me just as I did for him – and then we said goodnight. If something really was going to be that good, it was worth waiting for.

Sighing, I realise it has been four months since we've shared anything 'worth waiting for'. Perhaps tonight could be the night? When Louise comes and stands by my desk she finds my eyes closed, sighing in a dirty little daydream.

"Are you okay?" she asks, plonking herself on the corner of my desk and feigning fake concern.

I sense she smells scandal and is afraid of missing one iota of gossip.

"It's just you look very flushed."

I can see already that she assumes I am with child. Louise,

15

you see, tends to assume this about once a month because, as far as she is concerned I've already sprogged once, so I'm now a walking liability to the office's full quota of staff.

After assuring her that I'm most certainly not with child, despite the copious amount of mother and baby magazines littering my desk, I note that she is not moving. Usually with Louise, she says hello, asks how I am and clears off before waiting to hear the answer. But today is different. Today she is sitting on my desk, looking to all intents and purposes as if some kind of a thought is forming in her head – which, if you know Louise, is so very unlike her. I'm almost afraid to ask, so I sit there . . . waiting, until I can take it no more. "Can I help you?"

"I'm in trouble," she replies and suddenly I wonder if she could be pregnant herself. She looks around my desk and picks up a sample of nipple-protectors, starts playing with them between her fingers, and continues. "Really big trouble and I figured you could help me."

Suddenly I feel important. I feel useful. I could help her. We could shop for baby things together. I could tell her when to expect her first fluttering kicks, how to do her pelvic-floor exercises and what pain relief is best in labour. Unless, of course, she wants me to be her birth partner, which would be gross. Miracle of birth or not, I'm not up for dealing with that hysterical hyena in the throes of labour. Not for all the tea in China. No, sireee. Not me.

But, hey, every baby is a miracle, every pregnancy a joy, every birth an experience to be treasured (or recalled to terrified expectant mums with a degree of glee).

"I need you to lose weight," Louise says, cutting through my thoughts and leaving me, perhaps for the first time ever, speechless.

I'm mouthing my response, forming words which won't come out and trying to make sure the ground doesn't open up and swallow me whole, when Louise continues.

"It's for the magazine. We want to change people's lives and we were talking in the tea room the other day and realised you would be a great guinea pig. Sinéad has told me if I don't have you signed up soon then the feature falls on its face and I really, really want to do this. So, you see, unless you help me, I'm buggered."

My brain tries to process this information. First of all, I'm fat – which I kind of knew anyway – I mean, it wasn't today or yesterday my arse fitted into a Size 14. Second of all, they talk about me in here. They sit in the tea room and dissect my life – feeling sorry for me, pitying me, feeling disgusted by me. Apparently even Sinéad talks about me, and I thought she was my friend as well as my boss. And finally, I'm a pig – okay, a pig of the guinea variety, but a pig all the same. A furry, fat, pig.

I can feel tears sting in my eyes. I can feel my mood slip from the euphoria of looking forward to my night out with Aidan, I can feel my inner voice mentally thinking about the outfit I've picked out to wear tonight and realising I'm pathetic to think it could look nice on me, a big, stupid (guinea) pig.

"I'll think about it," I respond to Louise, because I know if I said no she would ask why and this conversation would go on longer. I honestly don't know if I can say another word without breaking into an ugly cry complete with watery snotters.

I turn my head, lift my phone and punch in an imaginary number just so Louise gets the message that the conversation has ended for now. When she leaves, sashaying across the room, head held high, skinny arse waggling, I get up, walk calmly to the toilets and cry as if my heart would break.

My only saving grace is that I remember to do the 'work cry', which is to hold a hanky (okay, some toilet roll) under my eyes so that my mascara doesn't run and my foundation remains unblemished.

* * *

"She's a skinny-arsed, stupid-faced, silly-minded fecker!" Daisy says, topping up my cup of tea and proffering me another Rocky Caramel biscuit (Daisy's current *biscuit du jour* – she takes notions, you see).

I have escaped the office on the premise of 'working on a feature' and I'm sitting in Daisy's office, watching the gorgeous little mites run rings around their care workers in the toddler room.

"We don't like Louise," Daisy reminds me. "We never did and now we never will. Just you remember that. Remember that the people we like, and who like us back would never say such things. I can't believe the fecking cheek of her!" She sighs, plopping herself down in her comfy chair and pushing a box of tissues in my direction.

It has taken me half an hour to get to the punch line of this delightful episode in my life because even though I know Daisy will know exactly what to say to make it all better, I'm still mortally embarrassed to reveal what has been said about me behind my back.

"This is worse than the time that girl asked when the baby was due and I had to tell her five months ago," I sniff, referring to a horrible incident on a bus when Jack was a baby.

"Fecker," Daisy responds, shaking her head. "It's not right. They can't go round talking about people and then trying to change their lives. Who's to say you want your life changed? Your life is pretty damn okay, if you ask me."

I nod, enjoying the sympathy, enjoying the reassurance that I'm not some freakish creature with no life and even fewer prospects.

"Sure, she has no life herself. She should feed herself up a bit, drink a little less and stop tarting herself round half of Derry. Stupid lollipopped-head, bow-legged, slapper fecker!" Daisy continues and I smile because her way with words always raises a grin. Daisy grins too, passes the biscuit tin and gives my hand a reassuring rub. "Right, missus, tonight you will look fab. You will look stunning. Aidan won't know what has hit him and you two will have passionate nooky the like of which has never been seen in Holy Catholic Ireland. You will not think about Lollipop Louise all night and I order you, and I mean this because I'm going to phone the restaurant and check, to have Death By Chocolate for dessert, and when you come to pick Jack up in the morning we will talk about all this again and think of the best way to plot our revenge."

I smile, finish my biscuit and hug Daisy goodbye, promising to drop Jack around after work.

Sighing as I start the engine in the car, I realise Daisy is right. I shouldn't let some narrow-minded bimbo annoy me in this way. But then, catching a glimpse of my reflection in the mirror, I do start to wonder if Louise has a point.

No, I mustn't think this way. I must not let this defeat me, not tonight when I'm under orders to eat a guilt-free Death By Chocolate.

By six thirty I'm home and running my shower, setting out

my perfumes and body lotions. Aidan has just phoned to say he will meet me at the restaurant at eight thirty. It makes it feel more like a proper date now – so secretive, us meeting up like this! I wish we were going to be on our own, but I'll settle for whatever I can get. Turning my Anastacia CD up full volume I start to sing, or more accurately, squeak along. What I lack in talent, I more than make up in enthusiasm. The shower is just the right temperature and I enjoy feeling it wash over me. This is what life should feel like, just nothing to worry about but me and getting ready to see the man I love, assured that within twelve hours I'll be seeing my little boy again. Scraping the razor up my legs, under my armpits and even along my bikini-line, I realise I'm having a pre-sex shower where I make sure everything is just so, just in case tonight is the night. I set aside my comfy yet reliable underwear, and pull out something lacy and uncomfortable – something which will not humiliate me entirely should I get to the stage where my husband and I sleep together. Dressed to impress, I phone a taxi and head to the restaurant. Amazingly, I've not thought about Louise's jibes for a full five minutes which actually shows remarkable strength of character on my part.

And he is there. Groomed, sexy, looking a little tired, but all the more handsome for it, and he sees me and smiles. The smile looks genuine and he reaches his arm out to me, kisses my cheek and introduces me to Matt, his boss. Unlike so many of Aidan's previous work colleagues, Matt actually makes an effort to talk to me and listen to my replies. He orders garlic bread, and offers me some which I take because it would be rude to refuse. He then goes on to tell me how great Aidan is and how he thinks there might be a promotion in the pipeline. Aidan has that smug look of 'I'm the man' about him and boasts about our house, our car, our child. Funnily enough he doesn't talk much about me. By the end of the meal I realise that I have actually enjoyed myself much more than I thought was possible, but my heart really leaps when Matt makes his excuses and leaves myself and Aidan to share the Death By Chocolate and the remainder of the wine bottle.

"That went well," I say enthusiastically, grabbing Aidan's hand.

"I think so," he replies, spooning much too much of the gooey dessert into his gob for my liking.

I try not to be too obvious about my longing to have it all to myself.

"Matt's a cool guy. I really think this could be my big break," Aidan continues.

"Let's hope so, eh?" I respond, knowing that Aidan has been all this time biding his time hoping someone will realise his potential. I know he has it there somewhere. He may have worked a multitude of jobs since we first met, but he has given his heart and soul to all of them – albeit in short and enthusiastic bursts.

"So how was your day?" he asks and I launch into it, telling him about Jack's antics on the way to the childminder's, the heavy traffic on the Culmore Road that morning, then my abridged version of Louise's barbed comments. My tongue is loosened with wine, you see, and I'm making a joke of it now, making it funny – trying to make Aidan laugh with me and assure me, just as Daisy did, that I'm being totally absurd about the whole thing.

He doesn't laugh.

I heard a song on the radio once – I think it was U2 – which said something about disappointing your other half. When I look at Aidan, 90% of the time I am asking myself that question. He would never tell me that I did. He knows it would break me, but sometimes, clichéd and all as it sounds, actions do speak louder than words.

I can see the dreams he had for us have not quite panned out. I'm not the vibrant, funky woman he met. I'm mumsy. Cuddly. Fat. While I have a job that pays the bills, I'm not exactly the Washington DC correspondent for *The Sunday Times* which I'd promised to be by the time I reached thirty. I write about nappies and vomit and Calpol.

I know he wonders what has become of me. Just as sure as I know he loves Jack with every fibre of his heart, I can't help but believe that he is with me simply because we are married – tied together by a mortgage, a child, a hope that tomorrow will be that wee bit brighter.

I've never told anyone that before, not even Daisy because she would tell me I'm gorgeous and talented and a fab mum and she just wouldn't understand that I'm none of those things.

She didn't know me back when I was full of enthusiasm. She doesn't know the dreams Aidan and I used to share, as we talked into the wee small hours. Most of all she doesn't know that what makes his disappointment so painful is that it is only mirroring the disappointment I feel in myself. I had it all, the world at my feet and yet here I am, tied to this humdrum existence. Why pretend to be something I'm not? Louise was right. There I've said it, the one sentence I swore would never pass my lips in my entire life, but I realise that I do need a change. I do need to make something of myself, to shed this (blubbery) skin. I need to make Aidan look at me with love again, not with friendship, not with affection but with full, burning, passionate take-me-to-bed-or-lose-me-forever love.

Because, looking at him, ignoring his indifference to me and that surging hurt I feel because of it, I see the man I do still love. I see the man who, despite his failings, I want to be with. And I know that somewhere, deep down, he has to feel something for me too.

I realise, as I start to cry into the remains of the Death By Chocolate, that I may be drunk.

"Daisy will bust my arse for wasting a good dessert," I mumble before paying the bill and we both head home to sleep. The morals of Holy Catholic Ireland are safe for another night.

\* \* \*

It's funny how my mind likes to rationalise things so that they won't hurt so much any more. Thinking about it, Aidan never actually said I was ugly, or fat, or a (guinea) pig.

I lie awake, and think about everything that has happened. No matter how tired or drunk I feel, I just can't fall asleep. If I *was* happy and confident in what I was doing and how I was looking, then I would not have hesitated in telling Louise to fuck off. The fact that my reaction was to sob like a lunatic in the toilets before dashing across town for a Caramel Rocky with Daisy speaks volumes. Likewise I wouldn't have looked to Aidan for reassurance and been devastated when none was forthcoming.

I don't want to change. Or, to be more accurate, I'm too

scared to change. I just want to be good enough as I am. I want God to realise my intentions are good and let me wake up gorgeous and confident and looking more than a little like Jennifer Aniston.

I'm scared to face the truth. I broke into a cold sweat when they weighed me at the antenatal clinic when I was expecting Jack and at least then I had an excuse for my rounded belly and swollen breasts. I had to fight a very strong urge to stick my fingers in my ears and shout "La la la la, I can't hear you!" every time a doctor or well-meaning midwife tried to mention it. So to reveal it to Louise, of all people, would be hell on earth.

That's not to say I've ignored what I've become. I've maybe not acted on it in the way I should or could have done, but I've not ignored it. It has been there whispering in my mind every time I've moved up a dress size or noticed a foundation tidemark on my chin or realised I really should have washed my hair the night before.

But I don't need Louise and her interfering little ways to sort this out. I'm a strong confident woman. I can do this. I can make myself into the person I want to be, by hook or by crook. I can be stunning. I can be confident again. I can be a wanton sex goddess that makes my husband drool with lust every time he sees me. I can be a fantastic mammy – heck, better than that, I can be a yummy mummy!

Finally, as the sky starts to brighten, I fall asleep and it's another joyous dream where I'm shaking my skinny ass at Louise and giving Aidan the finger as Dermot and I (I feel we are close enough to be on first-name terms) ride off into the sunset.

# 3

It's strange waking up in a house without Jack. I'm so used to the alarm clock that is his singing at seven fifteen that I wake automatically even though the house is silent. You could set your watch by that child – in fact I don't think our battered old alarm clock has had a look-in since he was born.

Aidan is still fast asleep beside me when I stir. His breathing is threatening to turn into a loud rumbling snore until I dig him gently on the arm and he rolls from his back, quietening down almost immediately.

The sun is streaming through our blinds, casting shadows against the wall, warming the room. The traffic is just starting to move and I can hear birds singing in the distance. I stretch sleepily before getting up, getting showered and making my way across town to collect Jack.

Saturday is such a busy day for Aidan, I normally let him sleep it off while I designate the weekend as time solely for me and Jack. It's when I forget about being a working mammy and we head out to town, or to 'soft play', before ending the day with a huge, sticky ice cream or chocolate bar shared sneakily in the car on the way home.

There will be no ice cream for me today though – this is my new regime. My that'll-show-'em attitude whereby I'll knock their proverbial socks off.

I feel fresher today, despite my lack of sleep, as if the worry of the last twenty-four hours has been lifted off my shoulders. I know if I think about it all too much I'll start to wallow again so I make a firm resolution to think as little as humanly possible for as long as possible.

Dressing in my comfiest tracksuit bottoms and oldest T-shirt, I scrape my hair back and rub a damp facecloth over my face, commending myself all the while that it isn't a baby wipe. Already I feel the New Me emerge. She who has perfect skin and follows a proper skincare regime.

Drinking my morning coffee and shunning the buttery toast that usually goes with it, I breathe in, out and relax. I know I have to make a plan to get this to work. I'll show 'em! In the words of Maria in *The Sound of Music*, I have confidence in me.

Striding out the door towards the car, I throw Jack's buggy in the boot and vow we will go for a walk and get some much-needed exercise in. We will become an *über*-fit family who go on adventure holidays and are permanently weather-beaten from all our strenuous activities. Mentally I'm already planning how to write my slimming success story for *Northern People* and dreaming about wearing a slinky and kinky outfit for the photo shoot.

My body will be a temple at which all lay people shall

come and worship. There will be No Excuses, with a capital N and capital E this time. Failure is not an option. Of course, it's not long until the first wobble comes along. There is a square of Galaxy sitting on the dashboard. It has started to melt in the sun and looks deliciously gooey. The balmy July morning air means I can almost smell its chocolatey goodness and my stomach does a little flip-flop, reminding me that Grace cannot live on coffee and affirmations alone.

A battle has started, between that wee angel on one shoulder and the dirty fecker with the horns on the other. The wee devil tells me one square won't hurt, as long as I count it into my calories for the day, while the angel gives me that I'm-very-disappointed-in-you look usually bestowed only by Mammy. The guilt inspires me to eat the chocolate and on I drive, vowing to start again on this quest to find the New Me. I'm almost at Daisy's when my phone rings and herself, with a fractious child in the background, declares loudly I'm to bring milk as she is all out and why hadn't I warned her that Jack turns into the Tasmanian Devil if he doesn't get Weetabix for breakfast?

I pull in at a nearby shop, grab my purse and run straight through the door and straight into the path of Louise, who, you've guessed it, looks as fresh as the proverbial daisy. She is wearing gorgeous figure-hugging jeans, the kind I can only dream about wearing, some bejewelled flip-flops and a breast-hugging white T-shirt. Her hair is scooped back off her face with a pair of designer sunglasses and her shopping basket contains a pineapple, a copy of *Hello* magazine and a fruit smoothie.

She looks at me, casting her eyes on my messiness with that

dreadful up-and-down stare you normally reserve for criminals or fat people wearing Lycra. It is too much to hope that God will suddenly clothe me in an invisibility cloak and let me escape unnoticed from herself.

In fairness, I should have known that if I had the audacity to step out of the house without my make-up, and wearing these oh-so-comfy tracksuit bottoms, I would bump into someone I know. It was just an extra celestial bonus for whoever enjoys getting a laugh on high that today that someone happened to be Louise.

"Grace," she smiles, "how are you? No wee man with you today? Goodness, you look tired!"

I smile back, clasping my purse to my stomach in the vain hope it will hide my bulgy post-baby rolls and reply that I am fine, just on my way to get Jack and, with a laugh and a roll of the eyes for effect, that tired.

"I was out clubbing last night. It was mental. I'm wrecked," I reply, hoping she doesn't ask me where I was supposed to have gone because I really can't remember what they changed the name of Squires to.

Of course, I could just tell the truth – that I was awake half the night mulling over her rudeness, her assumption that I would be willing to humiliate myself in the pages of our magazine for all to read – but I don't want to give her that upper hand once again. She needs to realise that, just because I'm hurtling towards the wrong side of thirty and weigh slightly more than I should, that doesn't mean I can't shake my funky-groove thang on the dance floor.

"Good for you," Louise replies. "You should have given me a call. Me and Briege went out too. It was mental. I didn't get to bed till four – the bags under my eyes must be dreadful!"

I look at her shiny skin and I know I should compliment her obviously very expensive skincare regime and her youthful good looks, but I can't bring myself to say the words. "Cold teaspoons will sort those out, or haemorrhoid cream," I answer, fighting the urge to bash her over the head with a two-litre carton of milk and a packet of Caramel Rockies.

"I'll give it a go," she smiles before waving goodbye and heading to the front of the queue to pay for her goodies. I take up a safe position beside the vegetables and wait for her to leave before I feel safe enough to move myself.

It only takes ten minutes to get to Daisy's house in the quiet morning traffic and it seems that I'm about the only person in her street up and about. The air is still, the only sound I can hear is the distant humming of a lawnmower and I take a minute to allow the peacefulness to wash over me before heading to her front door.

Daisy's house feels like home. Sometimes I swear it feels more like home than my own house. She lives in the kind of house I used to draw pictures of when I was a little girl, flicking through Mammy's catalogue picking the kind of furniture I'd love to have when I grew up. In fact, when I was small Daddy would drive me down this very same street, nestled close to the university, and tell me one day he would love to live here. I can see why it appealed to him so much. When you drive into Daisy's street it feels as though you are leaving behind all the worries of the world and stepping back in time.

The house has a red door, and for some reason that calms me. I like red doors; they feel welcoming and homely. On each side of the door stands a stained-glass window, in hues of reds and greens. Daisy swears she hates them. She thinks they are old-fashioned – but I think they add character and when the light shines through them at just the right angle her hallway lights up and it feels as comforting as church.

As I open her garden gate (yes, a proper white picket garden gate) and walk up the path, I hear a giggle coming from inside. It is a laugh I swear I would recognise from the other side of the world – that infectious giggle of my son.

Daisy is singing to him and as I put my head around the door I see him dancing merrily alongside Daisy's four-year-old Lily, who stops just at that moment to tickle him and make him scream even louder.

This is what parenthood should be like, this effortless joy – this sitting on the floor as the sun streams in the windows, singing 'The Wheels on the Bus' – this contentment. Lily looks up from her singing, sees me standing in the doorway and an amazing smile sweeps across her face, making her cheeks look rosier than ever. Her dark curls hang loosely over her forehead, damp from the exertion of running around all morning and I grin and wave as she hurtles towards me like a mini-hurricane shrieking "Auntie Grace, Auntie Grace!" Her chubby arms envelop me in what we like to call a Big Squishy – that most lovely of hugs that only a child can give.

"Hey, Schmoo-face!" I giggle, squeezing her back.

Witnessing this commotion Jack looks towards me, joins in the screaming and toddles over at the speed of light, using my body as a braking system to stop him flying out the door. I pick him up.

"My mammy," he soothes, stroking my cheek, and I grin, enjoying every second of this delicious contact.

"I'll put the kettle on!" says Daisy, pulling herself up from the floor. She grabs the Weetabix from my carry-bag as she walks past to get to the kitchen.

If I'm jealous of Daisy's front door and picket fence, I'm even more insanely jealous of her kitchen which always has the smell of fresh-baked cookies and fresh-cut flowers. A stunning pink Aga, something I have coveted for many months, stands at one end while, at the other, two large and impressive French doors open onto a gorgeous expanse of lawn where a slide-and-swing set sit alongside a sandpit.

The children run outside to play while I take up my favourite position on the comfy chair beside the doors. There are pictures everywhere that Lily has drawn – tacked up, framed alongside the family pictures of generations of smiles. It's the kind of room you can feel the love in as soon as you enter it. No, it won't win any design awards but it feels like the safest place in the world.

The table beside me is scattered with paints and assorted art-work from Lily and Jack's morning efforts and I find myself amazed that Daisy could be bothered to be so creative with the children when she does this every day at work. I think I would be more tempted to go down the *Barney* DVD route myself.

After carrying two bowls of cereal out to the child-size picnic table in the garden, Daisy comes back in and takes her usual position on the worktop looking out the kitchen window.

She throws me a biscuit, sips her coffee and asks me: "How the feck are you anyway?"

I have the good grace to reply that I'm okay and I'm halfway through the biscuit when I realise I'm supposed to be trying to be good and I'm already on my way to writing today off as a bad effort. I put the biscuit down on the table and throw it a dirty look. The angel on my shoulder would be proud of me.

"Would you believe I bumped into Louise in the shop?" I grimace. "Talk about Sod's Law. I swear she looked amazing and there was me looking like something a cat dragged in, threw up on and dragged back out again."

"You're too hard on yourself," Daisy says, biting into her biscuit and letting out a gentle holler at Lily not to feed the sand to Jack. "I'm sure there aren't many people out there who look amazing first thing on a Saturday morning, but you don't do too bad for yourself."

I look at my tracksuit bottoms and battered trainers and want to hug Daisy just for saying something nice – but I fear she might panic that I'm losing it altogether to be displaying such affection on a Saturday morning.

"Have you thought any more about Louise's offer?" she asks.

"Well, I did, almost all night," I reply, "and I don't think I can do it, Daisy. I don't think I want to be so public about being a lard-arse – I mean everyone would read it and I would be under so much pressure to be successful. You know me – not one to deal with pressure at the best of times." (Again a trait I really should have warned my employer about when applying to be a journalist.)

"Do you want to change?" Daisy asks, staring out the window and avoiding my gaze. I know she is going into serious-conversation mode. She must have been thinking about yesterday's events too. Sensing my silence, my awkwardness, she continues, "Not that I think you need to, but sometimes you seem unhappy in yourself. Do you think this could be a positive way to improve your life?"

Another of my illusions is shattered. I've always thought I've seemed perfectly happy when talking to Daisy. Sure I've barged the bit out about wanting to put Aidan's manly bits through a mangle for his unhelpful attitude at home, and yes, if I think about it, I've given out about Louise on one or more occasions – but generally we've always had a laugh . . . haven't we?

"Ach, shite," she mutters, "I've said the wrong thing, haven't I? I've upset you. Grace – look, I didn't mean to upset you. I'm just trying to find out how you feel about things. If you tell me you're happy, if you tell me you're okay the way things are – and I do love you the way things are," she adds, hastily, "then I will leave you alone and we'll talk no more about the day that is forever to be known as Black Friday."

I put my cup of coffee down, and put on my best I'm-always-happy smile and say, with a degree of confidence I'm not sure I'm feeling: "Daisy, I'm as happy as the next person. Of course I want to change my appearance, but I want that to be on my terms. I want to be a foxy, sexy chick who turns heads. I want to be the yummy mummy at the school gates. But what I don't want, and I mean this, is for the readers of *Northern People* to see me standing in my bra and knickers with my weight blazoned across my tummy in bold print. For Christ's sake, Daisy, my old maths teacher could read it! The wee woman who does the ironing for me could see it! I would be mortified beyond words. I would be a social pariah. I would have to leave town before someone called Greenpeace in to rescue me. Not a fecking chance!" I finish with a flourish, not telling her, and as such breaking the bonds of our friendship, that the person I don't want to see this most disgusting of sights most of all is me.

* * *

I have never been skinny in my entire life and my 5' 9" of height gave me the impression of being what is most commonly known as a 'grand big girl' around these parts. It helped not one jot that most of my childhood classmates had the audacity to be that perfect 5' 2" with eyes of blue (and eeny, teeny arses).

For the most part, my teenage years saw me as a Size 14. The clothes which my peers wore, and which made them look young, trendy and with-it, just looked dreadful on me. It wasn't that they didn't fit – it was just that I didn't fit them. I felt awkward and uncomfortable and the name given to me by my parents became a cruel joke. Instead of Amazing Grace, the crueller bullies at school nicknamed me 'Grazing Grace' – after all, I must have had to do some eating to be such a bloater. No one could understand it, because looking at my gene pool – my slim and gorgeous mammy, my handsome daddy – I was the odd one out. Occasionally in my adult years I have wondered fleetingly if the milkman was a lard-arse. I had a love for exercise back then, especially dance. I loved to lock myself away in my bedroom, my sanctuary from the world, where I was a backing dancer for Bros. I was a maniac, maniac on the dance-floor.

And I grew confident. I felt, for the first time, graceful and I braved the stage at the auditions for a local dance school. This was me, getting ready to make it, getting ready to shake my booty, getting ready to be the person I was destined to be. I thought I did well. I thought I made the right moves. I felt confident. I felt happy. I felt sure of success – until, that is, I walked into my classroom the next morning and heard Lizzie O'Dowd tell the class that Grazing Grace made a complete show of herself at the dance school the day before.

The letter came in a few days later and I tore it up, unopened, threw it in the bin and never danced again.

I watched. I tapped my toes occasionally. I even allowed Aidan to whirl me around the floor when we married but I never danced – I never lost myself in music again.

Sometime in my early twenties I decided, in a wilful act of teenage rebellion a few years too late, that I would be fashionable. So I set about talking to the fashion editor of *Northern People*. I even bought *Vogue* and *In Style* and followed celebs in the fashion stakes. I surrounded myself with fine things – tailored suits for work, boho fashion for weekends and enough shoes that it could take a good ten minutes to find a desired pair while searching through the bottom of my wardrobe. I had my hair cut into a sleek bob and survived on a diet of salads and soups and dropped weight like you wouldn't believe.

I managed, and I am eternally proud of this fact, to fit into a Size 12 pair of trousers from Next. They hang still in my wardrobe – a trophy from my glory days.

It was then I met Aidan and we fell into that thing known as 'domestic bliss' which, basically, meant we stuffed ourselves stupid and drank until we near exploded. Yes, we had plenty of exercise (nudge-nudge, wink-wink) to keep the weight from creeping back on and, when he proposed, my starvation diet kicked up a further notch so that I looked and felt magnificent on the big day in my dream dress – a creation in handmade lace with a slinky fishtail train gliding behind me.

Once again Sod's Law ruled supreme in that the only people who could be my bridesmaids were drawn from the same old 5' 2", eyes-of-blue crowd. So despite my success at fitting into the dress without the need for industrial-strength underwear, I still felt like Dorothy among the Munchkins.

# 4

Springing me back into the present day, Jack and Lily run in through the doors, beaming ear to ear and shouting that they "wanna go to the beach!".

Daisy and I look at each other, roll our eyes to heaven and agree to the demand because we know there is no point arguing with Lily and Jack on a Saturday – there will be enough of that to do during the week when they are dumped into childcare and school and we head off to our respective jobs. Mammy-guilt, we have long realised, buys our kids an awful lot of treats.

"I'll pack a picnic," Daisy says.

The children are dancing around our feet in hyperactive circles. Jack squeals: "Beach, beach, beach!" on repeat until I fear my ears may burst, while Lily has started listing all the things the average trendy four-year-old needs to make a day at the beach worthwhile. She is running from room to room, collecting towels, swimsuits, sunglasses, beach hats and sun cream.

"Mammmmeee!" she squeals from her bedroom. "I can't find my pink sandals!"

"Wear your silver ones then," Daisy replies.

"Don't want to," Lily counters. "I want to match my swimming suit."

Daisy grins and rolls her eyes to heaven once again. It's hard to believe a four-year-old could be so fashion-conscious.

I'll have to introduce her to Louise.

Jack has started jumping up and down to accompany his screaming and he runs to the garden to fetch his ball, bucket and spade from the sandpit. It's a good thing the hangover I was worried about has failed to materialise.

"Have we everything we need?" Daisy asks, closing the picnic hamper and grabbing a blanket for the ground.

"Yes!" Lily responds, having now located her pink sandals and looking like a movie starlet ready for her close-up. Somewhere she has found some lip-gloss and slicked it on – not quite worrying whether or not she has managed to get it inside her lip-line.

Loading the kids in the car, we jump in and set off on the thirty-minute drive.

You see, today isn't a waste after all. We will run and jump and play until we are utterly exhausted and I will have burned off at least 5000 calories by the time we get home.

We pull up at Buncrana and savour the salty air while trying to keep the children in check long enough to unload the car. Luckily for us, there is a gorgeous play-park on the shorefront – filled with colourful swings, slides, roundabouts and climbing frames – and all complete with comfy benches for mammies to rest while their children run riot.

After slapping on the requisite amount of sun cream so that Jack and Lily both look as if they have been whitewashed, we let them free to explore the huge climbing frame just inside the gates and we sit down and allow the warmth of the sun to wash over us.

"This is bliss," Daisy sighs, her head tilted back to catch the full rays of the sun as they beat down.

Already I'm too relaxed to offer a proper reply and make a vague moaning sound to show I'm in total agreement. I can feel the sun seep through my skin, warming my bones, bringing a shine to my hair, recharging my batteries and while, admittedly, I'd prefer to be doing all this away from the screams of over-excited youngsters, it is pretty damn good all the same.

Glancing up occasionally, I see that Jack's little chubby legs are making short shrift of the climbing frame while Lily is playing a mammy's role perfectly in directing the other children away from her charge.

"Do you think we could get them to play this nicely all the time?" Daisy asks, arching one eyebrow and smiling at me.

"Makes a great change from battering the life out of each other over who gets to play Fifi and who gets to play Bumble," I laugh.

"Nothing like a bit of fresh air and exercise to make life easier," Daisy laughs.

I have the good grace to feel guilty that I'm not exactly feeling the burn and busting my buns with effort. I consider strapping Jack in his buggy and heading for a brisk coastal walk, but it would be cruel to take him away from this fun so I reluctantly, or so I tell myself, move just enough to make myself extra comfy before letting the sun's rays wash over me again.

I jump awake to the sound of a snore, which I'm pretty sure emanated from my throat, and sit up to see Daisy in a fit of giggles with the children, who have also heard my snorting. I try my best not to look embarrassed and to laugh along with them, but if I'm honest I'm once again praying for the ground to open up.

Gathering up our hamper and the comfy blanket, we make our way down onto the golden sand where Daisy sets about doling out the sandwiches and drinks while I try and convince Jack that, honestly, sand isn't so good for your digestive system. I lift an egg-and-onion sandwich which has warmed with the heat of the sun and take a swig of ice-cold Diet Coke bought from the chip van which is sending out its sweet, tempting scent and distracting my attention from matters at hand. Oh for fish and chips, soaked in vinegar, eaten from the paper at the beach . . . but I have to remind myself that such pleasures are a thing of the past. It's onwards, upwards and skinnywards for me.

It's easy to get inspiration from visiting the beach. It seems that everyone around us is skinny and wearing one of those tiny T-shirts that show off perfectly honed stomachs with sparkly belly-button piercings. They are walking along the water's edge, looking as if they should be in advertisements for some pro-biotic yoghurt or cholesterol-reducing butter or herbal tea.

Glancing over at Daisy, sipping her fruit juice and nibbling on an apple, I realise she is one of them. Her hair is long and, unlike mine, shining with health and vitality. I would almost think she lives on a diet of Pedrigee Chum, her hair is so glossy. Her skimpy T-shirt and bejewelled flip-flops are not unlike the pair Louise wore earlier. Funny though, I don't get the same urge to slap Daisy round the head with a pineapple, despite her almost-flat stomach.

Of course she gave birth years ago. I'm a relative newbie. I console myself with the thought that in two years' time I too could get away with a trendy piercing or tattoo (as long as no one looks too closely at the map of stretch-marks painted across my belly).

I make a mental note to ask Daisy to give me advice on her diet and fitness regime, figuring that anything which includes a daily dose of caramel and biscuit can't be too hard to follow. And then I climb up on the sand and set about running after my son who has just realised that there is water to be played with and has plonked himself and his egg-and-onion sandwich unceremoniously in the sea, his nappy visibly expanding amid the strain of the copious amounts of salt water.

Lily comes racing towards us, her pink sunhat resting on top of her curls which are equally as shiny as her mother's, and we splash in the water until it starts to turn cold and Jack is too weighed down by his nappy to walk any further.

"This is fun, fun, fun!" Lily squeals, dousing me with a bucket of seawater and screeching with laughter and I find myself, wet and cold admittedly, grinning with her. Daisy's laughter only dries up momentarily when Lily and I gang up on her, there being a great deal of joy in our recklessness. When we are all wet and tired we climb back to the car, dry ourselves off with the array of brightly coloured towels we had packed and set off home.

"This has been so much fun," Daisy says as the kids drift off to sleep during the drive.

"Just what the doctor ordered," I reply.

"You know, I think that doctor has another prescription in the offing," Daisy says.

"And what might that be?" I ask.

"A bottle of wine and a sleepover for the kids? I take it Aidan is working and we could have a nice gossip in your garden while the kids sleep."

I agree it sounds like a great plan, even if I am more than a little amused that Daisy has referred to our plot of concrete as a garden. We are not blessed with the gorgeous lawns and French doors that Ms Daisy Cassidy has. Having opted for character when buying our house (i.e. old and cheap), we sacrificed a garden for a decent-sized kitchen and instead have a yard which houses a couple of wheelie bins, some beat-up toys and two plastic garden chairs. Admittedly we get the sun in the evenings so it can be quite pleasant if you just sit there, close your eyes and drink yourself into such a stupor you can ignore the decay and destruction round you.

But I like the thought of getting in a proper girly adult chat with Daisy. All too often she has a team of children running round her ankles at the Little Tikes nursery, or we have Lily and Jack and their dastardly deeds to contend with. The nearest we usually get to a proper drink is playing Russian Roulette with milk which has been left out a little too long in the heat.

Besides, when it comes to alternatives, I don't have anything you could conceivably describe as interesting in the offing. Funnily enough Dermot Murnaghan is busy of a Saturday evening and with Aidan at work, it's usually just me, my wine and *Casualty* for company. Generally I'll be in bed by ten thirty, or if I'm not I can be found mopping and hoovering into the wee small hours.

I'm tending to think a bottle of wine with Daisy could just be preferable to that.

So we stop at Daisy's, throw Lily's Ready Bed and pink pyjamas (with matching slippers, of course) into the boot of the car and make our way home. I know Aidan will have already left for work, so it's nice for once to come home with a bit of company. We push the door open, bath the kids and put them to bed and I uncork a bottle of Sauvignon Blanc and pour out two large glasses.

I stick the CD player out of the kitchen window and play some chilled-out Michael Buble to help us relax, before announcing that I'm going upstairs to change into something more comfortable and less filled with sand.

I'm singing to myself with contentment when I open the bedroom door and notice an envelope sitting on my pillow. Instantly I recognise Aidan's writing and my heart lurches. Sitting down I hold the crisp envelope in my hands and start to shake. I know what this says without even having to look at it. This is like the dance-school rejection all over again. I've made an eejit of myself, crying into my chocolate dessert and harping on about what a baggage Louise is. This has been inevitable since that moment.

I know he has had enough and is leaving us. The bastard! How can he do this? To me and to Jack? Most of all to Jack, I kid myself, but I know I'm feeling the personal rejection most of all because he is tied to me by choice, not by blood, and how dare he reject me?

I toy with the notion of ripping the letter up, saving myself the humiliation of seeing the words, but then I know I have to see them to believe them for myself. I want to see how the bastard coward has betrayed me. I want to know if he, and his usually shocking use of the English language, has managed to make sense.

Taking a swig of my wine, hearing Michael Buble sing about 'The Way You Look Tonight' in the background, I crumble a little. But slowly I tear at the envelope. Removing the single page, I sigh. One page – one page to destroy four years of marriage, eight years of love.

I'm only worth one page.

How could I have thought I could be worth any more? Stupid, silly, gullible, trusting Grace! What are we going to do? I hope he doesn't think we are moving out because I love this house and I'm sure as hell not selling it.

What will I tell Jack? Will there be a custody battle, because I'm sure I'll win. I've written enough features about parenting to know the courts always side with the mammies – not the loser dads who walk out.

I unfold the page. I'm drawn to it as your eye is drawn to an accident. I can barely see the words for my tears, but I read them anyway, slowly.

*Grace*, (No 'dear', I note – this has to be bad news.) *You know I'm not one to write very often but I just don't know how to get through to you any other way.* (You could have just talked to me, arsehole!)

*But I'm worried about you and about us.* (Here it comes . . .) *I didn't mean to upset you last night by ignoring your concerns about Louise.* (Nope, you were saving it all up for now, weren't you?) *I just feel tired of listening to you giving out about how unhappy you are* (here comes the punch line . . .) *and you not doing anything about it. I want this to work* (You could have fooled me, Mister!) *and I'll help you any way I can, but I can't make you happy if you aren't willing to help yourself.*

*Please let me know what I can do to help* (Erm . . . he wants to help?) *and I promise I will try because I do love you so much and I want you to believe that for once in your life.* (Feck . . . I was not expecting that!)

*Love,*

*Aidan*


I am speechless. Still crying, but speechless. I'm not sure what to think, or even how to feel. In some ways I guess it is good news. He wants to make this work, but then again he is fed up. But, he wants to help me but he is not sure he can make me happy. I lift my wineglass to my lips and take a large gulp – big enough to make me splutter. I'm conscious that Michael Buble is still singing downstairs and Daisy is waiting for me, but I don't know how to deal with this now. I don't know what to say or even if I should say anything. You see, it's okay for me to say bad things about Aidan. It's okay for Daisy to know that he never picks his clothes up off the floor or that he always leaves the back door unlocked inviting burglars in or even that he changes jobs as often as he changes his crusty socks – but I don't know if I can really let her know he is unhappy with me. That is a whole other kettle of fish – a way of admitting I'm not perfect and that other people are well aware of my faults – people who are supposed to love me, faults and all.

And yet, he loves me. He wants to make this work. He wants to make me happy and this should make me jump for joy. I should be mentally pushing those doubts aside and rejoicing that eight years, one marriage, one mortgage and one baby later, he still loves me.

45

He loves me even though I'm fatter, older, poorer and grumpier than those first hazy days when we would lie about all day making love, drinking cheap wine and sharing our dreams for the future.

He loves me even though I live in baggy pyjamas and am always snoring by the time he makes it through the door in the evening – but then again if I don't get happy, perhaps he won't love me any more. And that, that single thought, for all his faults, is too scary to contemplate.

Downstairs Michael Buble is inviting me to save the last dance for him. I can hear Daisy singing tipsily along and I decide, for once, to keep this part of my life to myself until I can make some sense of it.

I wash my face, slap myself a little round the cheeks to even up the colour and hold a cold flannel to my eyes to reduce the puffiness. I hide the letter in my bedside table and go back downstairs to the garden – painting on my happiest ever smile – and top up Daisy's glass, turn the music up and make a total fecking eejit of myself crooning along to 'It Had To Be You'.

I go to bed, slightly drunk, just after midnight. The sea air has left me exhausted. Daisy and Lily are tucked up in the spare room and I lie down and fall immediately into a deep sleep. My dreams are weird. They basically involve me and Aidan in a host of weird and wonderful situations, each one with him walking away from me at the end.

After a while I wake and am aware that he has got into the bed and has snaked his arm around my waist. I know he is still awake because he isn't snoring or farting or generally taking up three-quarters of the bed. I don't know how to react. I think I have forgotten how to tell him thank you and yet I'm not even sure I want to say thank you. I mean, he is supposed to love me. Why am I being so grateful about it? And yet he went to the effort of telling me about it, in writing – using a pen and everything. And he didn't even phone me first to ask where the pens were kept!

I decide the best plan is to pretend to be asleep. I let out a snore and hear him sigh and turn over in the bed to face away from me. I wonder if I'm pushing him away already but I'm too tired, and too drunk, to think straight. I fall back asleep and strangely dream that I'm Floella Benjamin and he is Humpty.

# 5

When I wake up the bed is empty beside me. I gaze at the clock and see it has gone eight-thirty. In the distance I hear the sound of Aidan and Jack playing downstairs. Lily and Daisy are chattering to themselves and I wonder how I've managed to sleep through all the commotion. I must have been much more tired, or more drunk, than I thought.

I stay in bed, stretching out and allowing myself to wake up slowly, allowing my brain the rare opportunity to engage before I get up. I remember yesterday, that fabulous day at the beach, the warm sandwiches, the water, the glass of wine and then the letter.

I remember Aidan putting his arm around me and then turning away and I try to make sense of what I'm feeling but it's not happening. I say a silent prayer, thanking the Big Man upstairs for Daisy and Lily being downstairs as I know Aidan and I can't get into any deep and meaningful conversations over the bacon baps that always make up our Sunday morning breakfast.

Slipping out from under the covers I walk to the mirror and take a good look at myself. My hair is wild mass of frizz – a combination of tossing and turning all night and the sand-and-salt combination of our day at the beach. My skin has that sallow quality about it, born of too many glasses of wine. My pyjamas are a wrinkled mess and I look fatter than usual. Sighing to myself, I start to run the shower, shouting downstairs that I'll be down in ten minutes. I let the water rush over me, waking me up and quelling the uneasiness that is rising in me, which I'm not entirely sure isn't just the product of the over-indulgence the day before. Lathering on the luxurious shower gel from Lush, I take a deep breath and start to realise that Aidan and I are going to have to talk today. I wash my hair, climb out of the shower and set about finding the perfect outfit in which to discuss my failings and the current unhappy state of my marriage. I get into my jeans and I pull a T-shirt over my head. Towel-drying my hair, so that my curls sit loosely and shiny, I pull the worst of the offenders back in a scarf. Slipping on some mules and emptying the contents of a trial pack of Beauty Flash Balm onto my sallow face, I start to feel human again. If it wasn't for the clawing sense of anxiety so clearly visible in my eyes I would look, for all intents and purposes, distinctly happy.

Going downstairs, I stop in the doorway and pause for a moment at the sight of my two boys playing together, smiling and laughing. At the end of the kitchen, where the big squishy sofa sits, Daisy is supping a bottle of Lucozade while Lily smooths her hair. It looks like a lovely role reversal. Surveying the scene, you would almost think Daisy and Aidan were together and Jack and Lily were their perfect 2.4 children. I'm sure it's not wise to imagine your best friend and your husband together in a romantic clinch however, so I shake the thought from my head and say hello. I find it strange making eye contact with Aidan. It's bizarre – we know each other inside and out. We have shared every moment of the last eight years together and yet, with this revelation that he is tired of trying to make me happy, I wonder if we know each other at all. He glances up at me and instinctively pours me a cup of coffee – milk, no sugar – the way I always take it. He presents me with a bacon bap – the bacon crispy and smothered in red sauce the way I always take it and he mumbles something about me looking nice. I glance up, and realise the emotion I'm feeling most of all with my husband at the moment is shyness. I smile at him, nervously, sure I'm feeling a slight nervous twitch in my eye and then I turn to give Jack a huge kiss as he sits in his high chair munching at grapes.

It's an hour before Daisy leaves. Just before she leaves she hugs me and whispers that I should call if I need anything. I wonder if she senses something is up and I half-expect that my phone will beep to life with 101 text messages throughout the day, demanding to know just what is going on. Then the door is closed and we are alone, except for the ever-increasing demands of our toddler.

"My mum is going to take care of Jack this afternoon," Aidan announces. "I thought we could go for a drive and maybe stop for lunch somewhere."

I nod. It's so totally unlike him to make plans of any description that I know he is pretty serious about this.

"We'll leave in about an hour," he says, before lifting a giggling Jack and taking him into the nursery to get dressed. Sitting on the sofa, I listen to the slow ticking of the clock and wonder how the day will pan out. I wonder if we can manage to talk things through. I wonder if he will listen to me.

\* \* \*

There is a gorgeous place in Donegal known as Mamore Gap. To give directions is fairly simple. You drive into the middle of nowhere, take a turn left, go up the biggest, scariest hill you have ever seen and hey presto – instant picture-postcard scenery! I love it there. It feels like a million miles from nowhere. I could never drive there on my own – the roads are too steep and the potential for a Grace Adams special, i.e. a fecking disaster, is much too great. But inevitably, any time I find myself there, staring out over the North Atlantic, I feel a mixture of exhilaration and perfect peace.

For some bizarre reason known only unto God the weather remains lovely. We have driven almost in silence, listening to the radio, and then, when we lose the signal as you inevitably do halfway up a mountain in the back of beyond, we put on a CD. I'm impressed with Aidan's awareness that I love this place but when he pulls the car over at one of those specially designated vantage points, I start to feel the butterflies kick in.

"So . . ." I say.

"So . . ." he replies.

We sit in silence for a bit longer.

"I suppose you want to talk about things," I push on, desperately trying to break the ice.

"I thought it might help," he answers.

"I'm not sure what you want me to say or do."

"Just tell me what's wrong with you."

"I didn't actually realise there was all that wrong with me till quite recently."

He does one of those sarcastic snort things that really, really annoy me.

"Well, I didn't," I answer, feeling myself slipping over to the very dangerous defensive zone.

"You can't tell me you're happy," he says, turning his head and staring at me full in the eyes.

For a moment I wonder if it is a question or a statement.

"I'm happy enough," I respond.

"You used to laugh more," he says, turning his gaze away, staring out to sea. I'm about to answer when he interrupts, "You used to be, oh I don't know, just more confident. More self-aware, more settled. I don't know what's changed in you, Grace, but I feel as if you're walking under a big dark cloud and I can't for the life of me figure out what the fuck is making you so unhappy."

"I still laugh. I still smile. I'm great with Jack."

"But what about me? Why aren't you great with me? Or with work? What happened to your ambition?"

So my job isn't good enough now. Is that what we're getting at?

"I can't be ambitious any more. I have a baby to consider."

"Bollocks!" comes the reply. "You lost this confidence before you had Jack. You lost this confidence a long time ago, Grace. First I blamed myself. I thought, well, it's because she wants a baby. And then we had a baby. But were you happy? Like fuck you were!"

I bristle at his use of the word 'fuck', because I know that means he is really annoyed. If he wasn't totally pissed off, if this was just a regular chat between husband and wife, he would have used the word 'feck' instead.

He is on a roll now though. "I'm not saying you don't love Jack but you treat each day as a chore. You wake up tired, you go to bed tired. You never want us to do anything together."

"You're never there," I counter. "You work every evening – when are we supposed to find time together?"

"So it's my fault now, is it? Grace is unhappy because Aidan is a *shit* husband."

"I didn't say that. Stop putting words in my mouth."

"Well, tell me then. Tell me what is making you so sad, so angry, so fucking unbearable these days?"

Tears spring to my eyes. He is shouting at me. Aidan never shouts. He is as gentle as a church mouse and I'm trying to find the words to tell him what he needs to hear, what he has to hear and I'm trying to reach out and beg him to stick with me through this but all the time I'm fighting this rage that is building up inside of me. I turn to him, trying to hold in my sobs and blurt out: "I don't know, Aidan! I don't know!"

He sighs, switches on the engine and we drive home in silence.

Pulling up outside the house, he tells me he is going to get Jack and orders me to pull myself together by the time he comes back.

When I was in labour, when I thought I was literally going to be torn apart, when I was begging for death or, at least, an epidural that worked, my midwife told me it was time to get angry. She told me I was to get angry with the pain and use that anger to get through this trial and succeed in having my baby. By Christ, did I get angry! Only problem was, for a long time after, I forgot to get un-angry again.

And when that anger did subside, when it faded to nothingness, it was replaced by an overwhelming sadness. I felt, and I don't know why, a grief – the loss of me, Grace. The loss of what motherhood should be like, the loss of that dream that I'd always had that being a mammy would be perfect and wonderful and I would never have to question my feelings for that little bundle of love I called my child. I felt empty, like I could do what I needed to do but I couldn't feel any of that love and joy it was my right to feel. Surely my months of pregnancy, my hours of labour, my bringing this gorgeous boy into this world entitled me to be happy?

I couldn't look myself in the face. I couldn't say I felt like a mother. I couldn't accept the compliments heaped on my child because I was a fraud. I was a failure. I didn't swan through my pregnancy enjoying this most natural of states. I didn't even bloom. Well, I did for three hours one day before the heartburn hit again and I threw up.

And when I was giving birth to my much-wanted, much-needed child, I begged for someone else to take care of that birthing process for me – to cut my child from me, to suck him out, to beam him up – whatever the fuck it took to make the pain stop.

But the pain is still here. I can feel it now, pushing through, and maybe, just maybe, it is time for me to get angry again. To get angry with that pain, to push it aside, to tell it to piss off and leave me alone and let me be me. Let me be a mammy.

And I'm angry now. Angry for all the times I've cried when I should be laughing. Angry for all the times I felt lonely in a crowded room. Angry for the Size 20 trousers in the wardrobe when I used to be a 14. Angry for not standing up for myself when I knew I was right. Angry for all the chocolate bars I ate to try and make me happy again. Angry for not demanding to be listened to. Angry for pushing Aidan and Jack away when the thing I wanted most in this entire world was to pull them as close as humanly possible and never let go.

And I'm throwing things. I can hear my shouting and grunting and I can see plates smash on the floor – those fecking ugly plates I've kept using just to keep my mother-in-law happy. And I'm tearing up those stupid books the so-called parenting experts sent me. I'm going through the photo albums and tearing out any picture where I'm with Jack and I don't look happy, because how dare I not smile in the presence of such innocence?

And then the tears come. I run upstairs, spurred on by some force I'm not quite sure of and I throw some clothes in an overnight bag. I leave my mobile sitting on the hall table. Scribble a note saying that I love Jack and I'll be back tomorrow and I jump in the car – my body heaving with sobs, my ribs sore from the exertion of all the squealing I'm doing – and I start to drive.

Two hours later I find myself in a hotel room somewhere that is two hours away from Derry. I'm seated on the edge of the bed, gulping down wine straight from one of those eeny bottles from the over-priced mini-bar. It's still light, but the clouds have rolled in a bit and I sense it could start to pour down with rain soon. I hope it does. I want to climb under the duvet, drink all the alcohol in the mini-bar and play raindrop races (a Daisy Cassidy special) with myself. I want to watch the rain stream down the windowpane, washing away all this hurt.

I realise that Aidan is not going to be all that happy when he comes in with Jack and finds our best, though admittedly ugliest, crockery smashed over the floor. I realise it might look more than a little bit loony that I've left my phone behind and scribbled a quick note. Chances are he is thinking I've topped myself and for a brief moment I start to think it would be quite wonderful to fake my death, move somewhere exotic – like a Caribbean Island – and start again with a whole new identity. I would call myself Lola and sell cocktails from a hut on the beach and have a faraway look in my eyes. The locals would love me and some tall, strapping man by the name of Carlos or Jesus (pronounced Hayzuss) would seek to make Messeeez Lola smile again.

But I couldn't do it. I couldn't leave Jack, my little munchkin. I couldn't walk away from him. (Well, obviously I could – I just did, didn't I? I just left him with a note that he can't even fecking read because he is only two. What kind of a shitey mammy am I?). And I couldn't leave Mammy and Daddy. They would hunt me down and kick my arse from one end of the exotic white sand beach to the other. They tried hard enough to have me in the first place – they wouldn't tolerate me faking a walk into the Foyle.

I'm aware I've fucked up. I'm aware my histrionics are neither big nor clever and that Aidan will not be impressed – but I can't deal with this right now. I just need time to clear my head, time to work out what is going on without seeing that disappointed look in Aidan's eyes, without Jack clinging to me, without my mam phoning to give advice, without Daisy wondering if I'm okay.

It has started to rain, so I climb under the covers – still fully clothed – and stare at the windowpanes. I'm watching the raindrops run down the glass, seeing them pool together and gather strength in their unity, running faster down to the windowsill. I once heard my mammy tell Lily that is what family and friends are like. We come together in friendship, get stronger and run ahead with ourselves. I thought it was a lovely analogy. Lily just said that the bigger raindrop was hers and that she won the race.

I'm not sure how long I lie there, just watching, but I know that every ten minutes or so I tell myself I really should just phone home and tell Aidan I'm fine, but I can't bring myself to do it. I feel too tired, too tired to lift the phone, punch out the numbers and describe how I feel. Too tired to think. So I lie a little longer and see the light fade in the sky. Slowly I drift off to sleep – waking to a dark room, a sore head and a heavy heart.

I reach for the light and see it has gone midnight and I start to feel guilty about what I've done once again. I don't know how to make amends. I'm not sure where to start, but I realise I'm a grown-up and I have to do something. So I do what any self-respecting twenty-nine-year-old would do: I pick up the phone and dial that all too familiar number.

"Hello," I manage to say.

"Hello, Grace?" an anxious voice answers.

I take a deep breath. "Mammy," I answer, before breaking down.

"Where are you, Grace?"

"I'm not sure. A hotel, somewhere past Letterkenny."

"Find out, ring me back and I'll come to you," she says,

before hanging up.

Thank God for mammies. I know Mammy is going to make it all right.

Once we have ascertained where I am and how to get there, Mammy assures me Aidan is more worried than angry and she says she will phone both him and Daisy to let them know I'm alive. She says my daddy has been saying the rosary for me and sends his love and she tells me she will see me soon. I lie down and close my eyes again, and fall asleep quickly, sleeping soundly until the ring of my phone lets me know the mammy person has arrived.

I have a strange relationship with the woman who gave me life. She is my best friend in so many ways, but she doesn't take any shite. She isn't like Daisy, who tells the truth but at least tries to sugar-coat it. Mammy tells it like it is and if I don't like it then, as she would say, I can lump it.

But even with her quirky and often questionable advice, her brash way of getting the message across, she loves me and would, I know, in a heartbeat lay down her life for me. She almost got arrested when I was getting bullied at school. I remember the day vividly when she marched screaming into the playground and threatened to 'bust the arse of any wee shite who hurts Gracie!'.

Of course, well-intentioned as her threats were, they made the bullying worse. I became a laughing-stock – but I never told Mammy. It would have crushed her and even at that stupidly young age I knew she had been crushed enough in her life.

I can't remember the first time I really became aware of the fact that I was the only one of my friends who didn't have a brother or sister, but I do remember Mammy excitedly telling me she was pregnant and letting my pudgy four-year-old hands pat her tummy and say hello to my little brother or sister. At the time Mammy and Daddy used to hug a lot and I remember Daddy saying more rosaries than normal, praying for a miracle.

Mammy blossomed. She was never sick. She just had this radiance about her, this maternal glow and I loved the feel of her, the smell of her, the warm cuddles, the smiles that rained down on me. I wanted to call my little sister Hamble or Jemima after the characters on *Playschool* and I was determined I didn't want a brother – boys were smelly.

Then one day I came home and Mammy was crying. She was sitting on the bathroom floor, her face pale as the white porcelain behind her. She was crying, "Not again, please, not again!" and Daddy was rubbing her hand comfortingly, crying too.

I didn't understand it at the time. I ran to my room, hid and spent a good hour trying to figure out what had happened. It was then that Daddy came in, gave me a hug and told me Mammy had gone to see the doctor. An ambulance had been called and I was going to have to be a brave girl.

There was no mention of a baby after that, no patting of tummies, no maternal glow, just a sadness that lasted for what seemed like an eternity until one day, dusting herself off, Mammy turned to me and told me that from now it was just us Three Amigos and that was how it was going to stay. Sometimes I wondered if she'd had the baby and he had been a little boy and she was so keen to keep me happy that she sent him away.

When I saw the sadness in her eyes, I planned that upon my sixteenth birthday I would hunt him down and reunite us all and tell him that I was sorry for being such a dreadful sister. And once I said this to her and wondered why she looked so hurt. I think I was twenty, and Mammy was slightly pissed, when she finally told me the dreadful truth that after I was born she had suffered four miscarriages – finally being told by a doctor that she would be better to save herself the heartache and accept that her family was complete.

If anyone understands sadness, it is Mammy, and when she walks into my hotel room I know I don't need to explain anything. I just need to curl up in her arms, laying my head on her shoulders, feeling her soft arms around me, and sob until I can sob no more.

We cry together, she tells me to let it all out and when the crying is done we fall asleep on the great big king-size bed. I'm struck by the fact that, even though I'm twenty-nine, I'm comforted beyond words to be there beside my mother, feeling secure in her presence. Perhaps there is a feature for *Northern People* in that, I think wryly before falling off to sleep yet again.

# 6

I have a mad love for hotel breakfasts. I get giddily excited at the sight of the buffet table, laden with all its tasty treats. From the warmed croissants, begging for a good battering with the butter knife, to the sautéed mushrooms peeking out beside the juicy sausages, I am in Overeater's Heaven.

The greatest joy of our relationship is that Aidan has the same, if not more, affection for hotel breakfasts that I do and any time we are together we spend a good hour and a half stuffing ourselves stupid with fifteen courses of cornflakes and yoghurts and fried stuff before heading back to bed again to sleep it off. Therefore I know something is wrong when I realise today I don't want the company of a hotel dining-room, the clatter of breakfast dishes, the jolly chat of the young waiting staff. Mammy, being the super-efficient woman that she is, orders us some room service and busies herself getting that wee table in the corner ready for our repast.

I have reverted somewhat to the mental age of a thirteen-year-old, nodding in reply to any questions my mother throws at me, and bursting into snottery tears when she suggests I phone Sinéad and let her know I won't be in today.

"Go'n, you do it!" I splutter, perfecting my best puppy-dog-eyes look that I know has always worked a treat.

"Okay then, you rest there," Mammy replies, patting my head and lifting the phone.

I like that she is taking care of me. I like that she is in control, and I'm almost expecting the famous blue blanket of my childhood to come out of her Mary-Poppins-style bag of tricks so that I can wrap it around myself. She phones Sinéad and I mentally cringe while I hear her say that I'm not well. I hope that if I cringe enough my ears will pop inside my body and I won't be able to hear her make the excuses. I know Sinéad won't be happy, you see, not with five days to go until deadline but I know I can't face it today – not least because I'm in the back-hole of nowhere and it has gone ten o'clock.

She hangs up and a knock comes to the door, with perfect timing to save me having to ask what Sinéad said. Mammy opens the door, takes our food off the scruffy-looking waiter and tells me to sit down. I'm not in the form to argue. She serves breakfast while I nod and shake my head at the appropriate moments, my teenage-style sulk remaining. As I start to try and eat my bacon-and-egg combo, the food sticks in my throat and I start to cry again.

"Oh, darling – you really are having a crisis, aren't you?" Mammy says, putting her knife and fork down.

I nod, sobbing.

"What's wrong, Grace?"

There is that fecking question again – What's wrong,

Grace? – looming over me, forcing me to think about things.

You see, on paper, nothing is wrong. Everything is tickety-boo in the personal and professional life of yours truly. My career is going great guns. I'm even asked on the radio from time to time to talk about vaccinations, nits and schools and other such child-related issues. With the exception of Louise, I get along with my colleagues. We even have a laugh from time to time. Even though I can't go to the pub for the post-publication piss-up any more, I think they still regard me as one of their own. Aidan is lovely, if a little irritated by me most of the time, and I have a gorgeous healthy son. We own our own house, have two cars between us and I am blessed with fabulous parents and a surrogate sister in Daisy.

So why then am I unhappy? Why do I always wake up wishing for an hour more (or several) in bed? Why do I question myself day in and day out? Why have I, in Aidan's words, become so fucking (not fecking) unbearable? And so you see, the only answer I can give my mother is that I don't know.

But my mother is a tenacious old baggage and she isn't about to give up that easily.

"Grace, it's perfectly obvious to all and sundry that something is wrong and, if you've got yourself into such an unholy state about it, then I'm pretty sure you have a wee notion as to what it is."

"I'm tired," I sob, making for the bed, clambering under the duvet and pulling it over my head petulantly.

"So am I," she replies, pulling the duvet back down, "but I'm not flouncing about making a holy show of myself about it."

She has a point. Strike One to Mammy.

"I'm – I'm – I'm fed up with everything," I stutter.

"Like what?"

"Like life, the universe and everything," I reply.

"Grace Anna Adams, you do not get away with it that easy!" Mammy says, her tone stern. "What do you mean by life, the universe and everything? Because, believe me, young lady, you don't know everything about life."

I see the old glint of pain in her eye and I realise she has a point.

Strike Two to Mammy.

"Like being me, like being fat and useless, and being angry at myself for being angry all the time!" I shout. "And being scared and not being good enough for anyone or anything!"

"You are good enough for me," she replies.

Strike Three to Mammy.

After I've stopped blubbing, I'm informed we will be driving back to Derry and we will be going to see the doctor – where we will talk about my unresolved issues and see what help we can get. Then Mammy is going to sit down with myself and Aidan and we are going to talk like proper adults and, when all that is done, I'm going to brush myself off, prepare myself to face the world again and go back to work. I have no part in formulating these plans – I just know better than to argue with them. So I pack my bag, pay my bill and drive up the road – Mammy all the while just behind me in case I look like doing a runner again.

I'm embarrassed talking to my doctor, not least because he looks younger than I am, but also because he looks as if he wouldn't be out of place as one of the leads in *ER*. I would have preferred an appointment with the nice lady doctor, but as Mammy had a hard enough time convincing the po-faced receptionist that this was in fact urgent and we were not, repeat *not*, going to leave the surgery until we were seen, I realised that I would have to endure this – if only to stop her humiliating me further.

I sit on the edge of the seat in his stark room, trying to avoid his gaze, and feeling exceptionally self-conscious. Perhaps all I needed all this time was a talking-to and a hug, because somewhere on the drive to the doctor's I've realised I just may have been overreacting over the last couple of days and I may, if you pardon my crude use of language, have made a complete tit of myself.

"Grace isn't very happy," Mammy splutters and the doctor has the good grace not to laugh.

"How long have you been feeling like this?" he asks.

"Months now, but it has been really bad the last few days. I think she may have had a wee breakdown," my mother answers and I shoot her a death stare which shuts her up.

"Grace, can you tell me about how you're feeling?" he asks.

I take a deep breath. Here goes nothing.

"I'm not too bad, honest," I say, "but sometimes I feel like nothing I do matters."

"In what way?"

"I'm tired all the time, and I can't seem to shift weight and I just feel lonely and inadequate and all I want to do is crawl under a table and hide."

I can't believe I've just said that. I'm not sure where it came from. But I force myself to shut up because I don't want to get committed to the local loony-bin, so I resume my slightly manic staring at the floors and walls.

"How long have you been feeling this way?" Dr Dishy asks, shooting my mother that same death stare I just used in a bid to keep her quiet.

"I don't know," I reply.

"She says that a lot," Mammy interjects before we both glare at her.

"I guess I've felt like this a few times before, but not as bad as now. Well, I felt bad after Jack, my son, was born but I put that down to the baby blues – but I feel worse now and I'm pretty sure there is no such thing as toddler blues." I give a lame smile and he has the decency to smile back.

"Let's see what we can do to help you."

I feel at once euphoric and exhausted. In my hand rests a bluey-greeny slip of paper emblazoned with the name of a tablet which will, it is alleged, help me feel better, but more than that I have the reassurances of Dr Dishy that I'm not going insane and there's lots that can be done to make me feel human and normal again.

I am Charlie Bucket and this, I hope, is my Golden Ticket. Things are going to be better from now on. Apparently, according to Dr Dishy, I am suffering from depression and anxiety. You would, wouldn't you, have thought that as the former Health and Beauty Editor of *Northern People* I would be kind of well up on the symptoms of depression? But, you see, I didn't feel depressed. I didn't have the urge to curl up in a corner (under a table, yes, but not in a corner) and phone the Samaritans.

I never contemplated killing myself. I didn't cry at the drop of a hat (with the exception of the last three days obviously). I didn't mope around in black (except for the RBTs which were more an effort to hide the girth of my arse than anything else) and I washed my hair whenever time would allow which admittedly wasn't as often as it should have been. I felt down, but my down-ness, my sadness has, I realise, become so much of a normality that I didn't even notice it had got worse.

I'm sitting in my car, outside our house, and I know Aidan and Jack are inside because Aidan's car is parked in front of my own and through the window I can see *Bob the Builder* playing on the TV. I wonder to myself when did it get so bad that I had to feel nervous faced with the prospect of going into my own house and talking to my own husband and my own son?

Mammy squeezes my hand and I know it is time, so holding on to my Golden Ticket tightly, I get out of the car and walk through the door, Mammy in my wake.

Jack squeals with excitement and runs to cling to my legs, while Aidan just looks at me with a mixture of affection, worry and anger. I want to run to him, to hug him and have him comfort me, but I'm unsure of myself now.

"The doctor has some ideas to help," Mammy says, breaking the silence, which for once I am grateful for.

"He's given me tablets," I say, offering my prescription to Aidan for inspection.

"And we are going to look into a few therapies," Mammy adds, before scooping Jack up in her arms and whisking him into the living-room to see what crazy japes Scoop and Dizzy are up to now.

"I was worried," Aidan says, looking at me with genuine concern. "I didn't mean to push you away – I just didn't know what else to do."

"You did nothing wrong," I answer, stepping that little bit closer. "If anyone needs to apologise it's me. I don't know what has happened to me, Aidan. I'm scared and I just couldn't listen to it any more."

"Listen to what?"

"Listen to people telling me I'm not good enough."

"I never said that."

"I know that now," I said. "I just couldn't hear anything else before." And I walk towards him, stretching my arms open to him, inviting him to hold me. For the first time in a long time I'm allowing him in, allowing him to see my vulnerability, welcoming his touch instead of pushing him away and when he holds me in his strong arms, I breathe out. His skin, warm from the afternoon sun, feels so good against mine. His lips, brushing against the top of my head, feel so tender – despite the stubble which shows he hasn't shaved today. I realise I've been missing out on so much. I've been so afraid to allow him to love me that I almost lost him.

"I can't pretend I understand," he says, "but I'll try."

And that about sums it up, because I don't really understand it either, but I'm going to try and from now on things are going to be different – but, more than that, they are going to be better.

# 7

Aidan and I hold each other through the night. We don't leap on each other's bones and make mad passionate love – we just allow ourselves to be together, to talk a little, but to cuddle more, remembering what it is like to be a couple – not just parents, or overworked professionals – and it feels so nice.

I sleep so peacefully, smiling for the first time in a long time when I wake up. Yes, I'm still tired and I'm still unsure of myself but I realise that a little part of me, somewhere deep inside, is feeling just that little bit hopeful.

Of course, the glow can't last forever. I know I have to face Sinéad, who by now will be at high risk from cardiac arrest as deadline approaches. I know I should have had the proofs for the Messy Play feature on her desk by now, and that problem page is still not finished. I'm also painfully aware I wasn't there to supervise the 'Mummy and Me' photo shoot the day before where famous mums and daughters were going to celebrate their friendship for the benefit of Liam and his trusty camera.

I pull up into the carpark and take a swig of cold Diet Coke to settle myself, before lifting my bag and walking into the office. I consider just sitting here at my desk, with Dermot for company, and saying nothing – but I've known Sinéad long enough by now to know she appreciates a quick "Hi there and hello" if someone has been off sick. In cases such as these, when someone (aka me) has been off sick five days before deadline, she appreciates a "Hi there, hello" and a grovelling apology before the day begins.

"Wish me luck, big man," I whisper to Dermot before making my way into the lion's den.

Sinéad's office is a strange place. It has a soft leather sofa which you sit on if you are feeling relaxed, discussing up-and-coming features for the month and sharing a bit of gossip about the other staff members.

There are also stiff, proper office chairs, moulded plastic and cold steel, which you most certainly sit on if you have taken a day off on the sick and need to let your boss know you are still serious about continuing your employment at *Northern People*.

I sit on the hard seats, while Sinéad finishes a phone call, and I look around me.

On the walls there are past covers of our bestselling issues and a smattering of awards, one of which is rightfully mine for a feature on being a 'Have-It-All Mummy'– how ironic that seems now!

On the right-hand wall there is a whiteboard, carefully marked out with page numbers and ad plans. I see a big question-mark in gaudy red ink beside the page reserved for my Messy Play feature and I start to feel uneasy.

Sinéad hangs up the phone, sits back and looks me up and down and I know she is waiting for me to start talking as she lights up a cigarette and inhales deeply.

"I'm really sorry, Sinéad, I just couldn't come to work yesterday," I start, waiting for her to voice concern.

But she sits there in stony silence.

"I was feeling really out of sorts," I continue, realising I am making myself sound like perhaps the biggest tit in the history of the world. Who the feck uses the expression 'out of sorts' any more, apart from old women who wear cardigans and live on tinned prunes?

Sinéad is still silent, apart from the ever-so-subtle sucking sound that comes with each inhalation of her cigarette followed by the slow exhalation. I watch the smoke curl and rise above her, heading in the direction of the window. I realise I am actually jealous of it and its escape route.

"Seriously, I'm sorry," I continue. "You know me – I never take time off unless I really need it."

Silence.

"The thing is, you see, I had to see the doctor because I kind of had a bad weekend."

She speaks at last. "Aye, Louise was telling me you were out clubbing till all hours on Friday night."

Fuck. I forgot Louise spreads gossip like rats spread the plague, and now if I admit I was lying to Louise then I'll look like an unholy arse for pretending to have a life when I so clearly am lacking in the life department. I pause, glancing around the room in the vain hope that the shovel I can use to dig myself out of this particular hole is waiting for me to grasp on to it for dear life.

Sinéad speaks again. "So I knew there must be something up because, God love you, Grace, it wasn't today nor yesterday you saw the inside of a club. Are you having some kind of wee breakdown or something?"

I'm shocked by her perceptiveness – but then I suppose she didn't get to where she is in the world without being able to read people.

She grins and exhales. "For fuck sake, why in Christ would you tell Louise you were out clubbing? You should know she would tell everyone else in the office and while she's too dim to realise it's pure-bred bullshit, some of the rest of us have a bit of savvy."

I'm embarrassed now. I can feel my face flush, the red heat rising to my cheeks. "Ach, I just wasn't quite awake when I saw her and it was the first thing that came into my head," I say, rolling my eyes as if I'm joining in the Grace-is-a-stupid-big-eejit joke.

"Grace, I've never known you to be concerned about what other people think," Sinéad says and suddenly I wonder is she really that perceptive after all. "Now, do you want to cut through the bullshit and tell me what exactly is wrong because we have a magazine to put out and if I'm not mistaken there are several fucking huge holes in pages where all the parenting shite should be."

(When she puts her mind to it my esteemed editor is quite the wordsmith – but she does like to use the odd expletive or two – I'm almost immune to it now.)

So how do you tell someone, in five minutes or under, that you are kind of having a not-quite-midlife crisis and you are now officially a member of the loony brigade complete with tablets which may make you drowsy?

I opt for the Sinéad-Flynn, no-bullshit approach.

"Well, the thing is," I say, taking a deep breath and then allowing the words to tumble out, "I kind of did have one of those wee breakdown things – just a wee one, mind – not enough to affect my work or anything – with the exception of yesterday, which I'm sorry about. But I'm getting help now, honest, and I'm on tablets and the copy will be done by five this evening."

She lights another cigarette, looking kind of amused and shocked at the same time by what I have told her. "Holy fuck, Grace, why didn't you let me know?"

"Well, I didn't actually know myself. It kind of crept up on me. One minute I was eating egg-and-onion sarnies on Buncrana beach, the next I was sobbing under a blanket. Kind of funny in hindsight . . ." I trail off.

"Do you need more time off?" She actually looks concerned. "I can fill the space and you can rest."

The offer is tempting. I could just turn on my heels now, say goodbye to Dermot and go home and crawl into bed for a little while. Or maybe a long while. And then, when I wasn't feeling so dog-tired any more, I could go and get Jack from Susan's and we could spend some quality time together. I could start to make it up to him – prove to him I'm a good mammy after all.

But strange as it sounds, I don't want time away just now. I need my routine – my daily dose of Dermot – a demand on me to get out of my pit in the morning because I know if I don't have that then I will become one of those big fat ladies who actually stays in bed so much my body will merge with the mattress in some freaky biological phenomenon.

It also dawns on me that I actually enjoy my job – the

writing part anyway. Okay, I'm not the best in the world at answering the phones and I don't really enjoy all that networking and other such bullshit but I like the writing – the drafting of words, the designing of a page, the meeting people who want to talk to me about themselves and allow me into their lives.

"I'm fine, Sinéad," I say. "Trust me, if I need time off I'll tell you about it, but for now I'd rather just keep going and see what happens."

"You sure?" she asks, stubbing out her cigarette and throwing her office window open wider. "Because I'm sure we could manage if you needed it."

The wee niggly voice in my head is wondering if she's trying to get rid of me, and I find myself unsure of my own thoughts. I try to find my determination, and affirm that yes, I'm sure. I want to go to work. (Who'da thunk it? – as my dear old daddy would say.)

"Thank fuck for that!" she laughs. "I thought we were hammered there. Jesus, Grace, don't ever do that to me again. I mean, get sick if you want, and I'm saying this with my best Human Resources head on me – if you need time off, take it – but taking that HR head off and speaking as your boss, thank Holy Christ and the wee donkey you will still be here."

I laugh, realising that even though I've just been sworn at profusely, my boss actually values my contribution.

"You should have seen that fecking photo shoot yesterday," she adds, rolling her eyes as she offers me some chewing gum. "There was no one to supervise but John, and he didn't know where to look. I swear he hasn't seen so many women in the one room in his whole life."

I grin at the thought of grumpy John, our cantankerous

sports columnist, soothing the egos of ten famous mums and their children.

"That," I say, "I would pay to see."

I stand up to leave, aware that a deadline has to be met, but as I turn to reach for the door Sinéad stops me, adding: "Look, Grace, don't be afraid to talk about what you're going through. You'd be surprised how many of us have been there before."

I nod and walk back to my desk, astounded that someone as level-headed as Sinéad could ever have experienced any kind of difficulties. She seems so calm, so in control. Just goes to show, I realise, you don't know what goes on in anyone's life.

I'm up to my eyes proofing the photo-shoot page while simultaneously trying to deal with a worried parent whose two-year-old refuses to have his nails cut when Louise sashays over to my desk and takes up her usual position, perched on the edge.

She lifts the proofs from where I'm looking at them, studies them, sighs and puts them down again. Craning her neck round she looks at the copy on my screen and tries to show a genuine interest in parenting problems and all the while I'm just getting on with it, waiting for her to speak.

"Gra – ace!" she trills, somehow finding an extra syllable in my name.

"Yep?" I answer.

"Have you thought any more about 'Changing Your Life for *Northern People*'?"

I wish I could tell her just how much I've thought about it. How it's taken up almost every minute and hour and my thoughts for the last four days, but instead I take a deep breath and answer, "Yes, I have."

"And?" she answers, drumming her perfectly manicured fingers on my desk.

"Okay then," I answer. "As long as you don't, and I mean this, ever ask me to wear my underwear for a photo shoot or ask me to reveal my weight."

Louise looks almost speechless. I can see her fight the urge to jump up and down and do one of those stupidly annoying girly squealing thingies. "Oh Grace, that's amazing! Thank you, thank you, thank you!"

So I guess it's official. I'm a (guinea) pig – but it doesn't really scare me any more. You see, yesterday, as Dr Dishy and I talked things out – after he had shunted Mammy out of the office so we could talk honestly, I told him about Louise's experiment and he asked me what I had to lose from taking part. Of course, I had answered that my dignity was the obvious answer, but he countered that crying in a hotel in the middle of Donegal was hardly awe-inspiring behaviour.

I had been shocked by his honesty. I was expecting him, given his obvious youth and good looks, to merely hand me my prescription and send me out to the face the world. I was not bargaining on the good talking-to that came with it.

He said he believed that if I wanted to change, really wanted to change, I would have to face some of my demons. Of course, he hadn't forced me to agree to the life change – but he had given me enough food for thought to know that signing up for this was going to either kill me or cure me and I was hoping, as indeed was Aidan, that it would do the latter. As Aidan and I had cuddled last night, talking through our fears as best we could (given that I still don't have much of a fecking notion why my brain has hit meltdown) he said that this experiment of Louise's could be the perfect chance for me to take control of my life – a life I have for a long time only felt like an observer of.

Dr Dishy had reminded me that, even though Louise had come up with the idea initially, he could see no reason why I, an intelligent woman (yes, he did think I was intelligent despite my obviously manic condition in his office) couldn't pull a few strings to make things work in my favour. And this was exactly what I was about to do.

Once Louise had started breathing normally again (about two seconds before I was going to slap her across the face to calm her hysteria, more's the pity), I added my killer conditions.

"This is going to be on my terms," I said. "There will be no, and I mean *no*, colonic irrigations or other nasty invasive procedures. This will be a holistic approach to improving my sense of self-worth as well as my physical appearance. You will not talk about my weight to any one in the office. You will not gossip and you will give me full copy approval on everything you write."

Louise looks stunned. She has the appearance of a bunny caught in the headlights, her eyes darting a little wildly, searching for an escape route. She isn't used to Assertive Grace – well, how could she be when I'm not even used to her myself? With every sentence, every word, I'm pushing my own boundaries faster and farther than I ever thought possible. I'm actually shocking myself for the first time in a long time and it feels amazing.

Louise's mouth is flapping open and shut a little, trying to find the right words to assert her authority but as far as I'm concerned she can go and scratch.

"But I'm Health and Beauty Editor, Grace," she says. "I'm

the one who approves copy here."

"But I was Health and Beauty Editor for a long time," I smile sweetly. "I think this little project will be safe in my hands, don't you?"

At that I pick up the phone and dial that old pretend number again, making it very clear the conversation is over. When she slopes back to her desk, looking dejected, I give Dermot a little smile and whisper: "Me and you, kid, on top of the world!"

I know I have a week to get used to the idea of changing my life – a week to think about what and how I want to change and I intend to savour every moment. I'm not saying I'm not going to want to chicken out, because I know more than most how the path to hell is paved with good intentions.

I have tried to get my life in order before. My starvation diet before my wedding proves I can find willpower if I really need it, but this is about more – much more – than looking good in a lace gown. You see, this time I want to capture that magical feeling but I don't want it to be just for one all-too-short day. I want it to last.

Dr Dishy has ordered that I come and visit him at least once a week in this initial period, more often if need be. He wants to make sure my mental status is stable, that I'm not about to go running off to wee hotels in Donegal at the drop of a hat. He also wants to make sure that I carry through on my promises to find out what is making me so damn miserable and work to change those negative little thoughts into positives.

Now I've made those first moves I feel proud of myself. I feel ready to take on the world and, if Louise would just stop sulking at the other end of the room, I could be completely

80

relaxed and happy.

The phone rings, interrupting my thoughts. It's Aidan, showing an uncharacteristic concern for my morning in the office.

"How did it go?"

"Surprisingly well. I'll tell you all about it later."

"Did you tell Louise you would do the whole 'Change Your Life' thing?"

"Yup, I sure did."

"And how did she take it?" he asks, and I can almost hear the mischievous little grin in his voice.

"Not the best," I say, feeling the smile creep across my face too. "I told her I'm calling the shots on it and it won't be some namby-pamby colonic-irrigation Botox-fest."

"Good for you, but do you have to talk about those colonic thingies? Jesus, I'm having my breakfast!"

"Sorry," I grin.

"So," he adds, and I wonder what he is getting at.

"Yes?" I reply.

"Grace, now that's one down and one to go."

"What do you mean?"

"You need to phone Daisy. She's spitting fecking chips that you went away and didn't call her."

Feck. Daisy. I hadn't really thought about her up until now, but Aidan is right. She will be going bananas by now and much as I love Daisy down to her wee tartan knickers, the last thing any sane person in this world would want to do is get on the wrong side of her.

# 8

We've only had one major falling out before, Daisy and me – but, trust me, the Troubles, Hiroshima, and the Easter Rising combined were calmer and altogether more civilised affairs in comparison. At the time The Great Falling Out, as it has come to be known, seriously threatened the future of our friendship and it had taken a good few weeks and virtual banging of our heads together by Mammy for us to see sense. It had taken a month or two longer for that bond of friendship to re-establish itself because some things said in that horrible heat of the moment were not so easy to forget in the cold light of day – on both sides. The worst of it was, it had all been over a man. A stupid feckless man. And it had all been a terrible misunderstanding. But, as I have said, the road to hell is paved with good intentions.

I can feel my heart sink at the thought of calling Daisy now, but I know the longer I leave it the worse it will be and, as it stands, things are going to be pretty damn shocking anyway. I couldn't bear a screaming match down the office phone however, and if I dare nip out Sinéad will have me hung, drawn and quartered so I opt for the coward's way out instead: a text message.

I decide the simpler the better, so I send the very basic message of **"Dais, mst tlk. Pls can we mt after work. Finish @ 6?"**

The phone silently mocks me, as I try and lose myself in my problem column, perilously aware of the impending deadline. A half hour passes, then an hour, then two. My stomach is grumbling with a mixture of hunger and nerves but just as I make to get up and walk to the shop for a quick bite to eat, my phone beeps into life, playing the theme from *Sex and the City*, aka Daisy's Theme.

It is a text message. **"Pssd off with u. Y didn't u tell me?"**

Oh dear, she really isn't one bit happy at all, is she? My heart beats a little faster.

Sitting back down I text back. **"Soz. Head fecked. Pls can we mt? 6 @ urs?"**

A few moments later, I get my reply: **"Buzy 2nite. Washing hair. Call u ltr"**

This is bad, very, very bad. A sick feeling washes over me. I want to fix this, but I'm not sure how.

* * *

Somehow I muddle my way through the rest of the day. My emotions soar from being really excited about the changes I'm going to make to plummeting at the mess I have made of the only friendship that has ever really mattered to me. Of course Daisy is pissed off. I would bust her arse if she ever pulled a stunt like that on me, but then I wasn't thinking rationally at the time. Christ, I don't even think I was thinking full stop.

Shortly before five, Aidan phones for a progress report. (Wow! Two phone calls in one day and none of them asking me to locate anything!) I tell him of my worries, of Daisy's reaction, and he orders me to take a bottle of wine and a king-size Galaxy round to her house straight after work and that I'm not to leave until it is all ironed out. I try to tell him I'm too much of a coward but he will have none of it.

"It's an order, Gracie," he says. "Get a taxi home when you are suitably sloshed and the pair of you have fallen in love again."

Aidan gets my need for a friendship with Daisy. He has always been one of those blokes who could talk to anyone and charm the birds from the trees. He has never really understood how I, as a journalist, could be so painfully shy when I'm away from the comfort and armour of my desk.

He knows about the bullying I suffered at school. In the early days of our relationship he even offered to track the offenders down and break their legs. (Jokingly, I hasten to add.) But what he never could understand, whether it was because he has always been surrounded by friends or because he is a man, is the loneliness I have felt at not having a best friend.

Not having had sisters, or indeed a friend to talk to at school, made for a very lonely childhood. I think that is why I immersed myself in books and writing – finding fictional friends for myself when I couldn't find the real ones. While Aidan could never understand why I didn't have friends hidden in every corner, he knew that once I met Daisy something in me shifted. I became aware I was somebody who was worth something. The healing process from all those years of bullying began, and that is why, even armed with a bottle of wine and a king-size Galaxy, my heart is thumping like crazy as I walk that pathway to that familiar red door with the stained-glass panelling on either side.

I knock on the door and can hear the sound of Lily coming haring towards me at lightning speed, the click-clacking of her dress-up heels rattling loudly against the period tiling. She opens the door and looks me up and down, her perfect little nose slightly upturned.

"Hey, Schmoo-face," I grin, belying the fear that is bubbling up inside of me. "Is your mammy in?"

Lily darts a look behind her in the direction of the kitchen and then gestures at me to come closer so that she can whisper in my ear. I get close to her, breathing in the freshly laundered smell of her gorgeous Cinderella pyjamas and feeling her soft curls brush against my cheek.

"My mummy is very cross with you, Auntie Grace. I'm not supposed to tell you she is in."

I'm struck by her honesty, and whisper back, "I know, sweetie. I was a bold girl. But I need to talk to your mammy anyway."

At this Daisy sticks her head around the kitchen door to see who is chatting to her little one. She looks distinctly unimpressed to see me – in fact she has a face on her that would curdle milk.

"Actually, Grace, we were just about to go out. This is a bad time," she says, not quite looking me in the eye.

"No, we weren't, Mummy. I was getting ready for bed,"

Lily interjects, garnering a deathly glare from her mum which prompts her to burst into tears and run into the living-room.

I want to run to her and give her a Big Squishy but I'm sensing that Daisy doesn't want me over the threshold of her house.

"I really don't think this is a good time," Daisy says.

"But we need to talk," I answer, waving my bag of goodies at her, hoping the sight of wine and chocolate will bribe her into forgiving me. It's a time-honoured tradition for us, to show up with a bag of treats when something needs to be talked over, or mended. It has never been known to fail – not until now anyway.

"I really think I'm too angry to talk," she adds, while the squealing moves up a pitch in the living room as Lily demands the attention of a grown-up to comfort her.

"I'm sorry you feel that way," I say, feeling tears prick in my eyes. "I think you'd better go and see to Lily."

I turn and start to walk down the path. I'm waiting for Daisy to call me back, tell me I'm a big stupid fecker and get the long-stemmed wineglasses out, but she doesn't. Instead I hear a closing of a door and my tears start to fall.

I climb into my car, throwing my peace offering in the back seat, and try to compose myself. I feel as if I need to get away again, but I know I can't. I don't think it would help this time. Instead, I switch on the engine and drive home to seek comfort in the arms of my husband and son but feeling, all the time, that something has gone dreadfully wrong.

Once Jack has gone to bed, after I have comforted myself by cuddling him and enjoying some slobbery toddler kisses, I open the wine and pour myself a glass. Aidan comes in, he knows he doesn't have to speak, so he just gives me a cuddle and lets me have a little cry. Despite everything I'm remarkably impressed that I don't get myself into an hysterical mess this time.

"I'm going to run you a bath," he says, kissing the top of my head, "and you are going to sit in it until you have turned all wrinkly and you have eaten at least half of that chocolate."

I breathe him in, enjoying this closeness and I get ready for my bath.

Once immersed in the bubbles, candles softly glowing around me, I pick up the phone and ring my mother. I relate what has happened, barely pausing for breath, and she makes the appropriate soothing noises.

"You know I love Daisy as if she were my own daughter," she begins.

"Thanks, Mammy," I say, rolling my eyes.

"You know what I mean, dear. But we all know she can be a fiery one. She has been hurt before and she doesn't like secrets. I can see why she feels aggrieved."

"But I didn't know what was going on myself!" I say, in a somewhat exasperated tone of voice.

"I know that," Mammy answers, "but you know Daisy's defences can fly up quicker than a rat up a drainpipe."

"But how do I make it better?" I ask, sinking my teeth in the Galaxy Caramel.

"I don't know, darling. Give her a little time to breathe and see what happens."

Damn. You see, mammies are supposed to know what to do. They are supposed to have magic sticking-plasters for almost every situation.

"Grace," she says, "I love you. Take care, my darling. Tomorrow will be better."

"I love you too, Mammy," I say and hang up, realising I'm absolutely exhausted and just too tired to think about this any longer.

Sinking into my bed I feel the cool, fresh sheets envelop me (fair play to Aidan – running a bath *and* changing sheets!) and I drift off to sleep. I don't know if it's the exhaustion of the day, the glass of Merlot or the 'happy pills' that have done the trick, but I sleep soundly, putting all worries and stresses to the back of my head. Occasionally I'm aware of Aidan beside me, his soft touch, his occasional hug and even though I'm only half-conscious I hope this means things are on the up for us.

*　*　*

When I wake up he is lying beside me, staring at me as I sleep.

"We are going to be okay, aren't we, babe?" I ask.

"I hope so," he answers.

Given the last few days I don't think I can ask for fairer than that.

# 9

I am quite shocked at how fast the last three days have passed. I'm sitting outside now, on the fire escape at work, taking a breather and lapping up some of the late evening sunshine.

The September edition has just been put to bed. The rest of the staff are standing around smoking their lungs out and talking about going to the pub. I'm just planning on going home. Aidan is working and Jack and I will have the whole night to ourselves. I've promised the wee man that we will go for a drive to Buncrana, to drink in that summer evening air. He doesn't really understand – he is only two – but it is more important to me than ever that we do these things together, whether I'm tired or stressed or just wanting to lie on the sofa and feel a little sorry for myself.

The atmosphere in the office is buoyant to say the least. Louise has got over her almighty huff, largely due to a verbal arse-kicking from Sinéad who reminded her I was in fact quite damn fecking good at health and beauty stuff. Of course, being Friday, Louise is also already planning a night on the town drinking until she passes out and her friends have to carry her home. Even grumpy John has a smile on his face. He confided in me earlier he was really proud of how the photos turned out at the shoot – and to his credit they weren't the worst we've ever had – even if the subjects all had a certain look of fear about them.

I find myself smiling along, even though I've been fighting a wave of nausea all day which is an apparently recognised side effect of said happy pills, which I'm starting to think should be renamed bokey-feeling-in-the-pit-of-your-stomach tablets. So I'm guessing, even if I was footloose and fancy-free, I wouldn't be up for a drinking session tonight anyway. But I do feel good inside because I've managed four days at work, calm, collected and together. Aidan and I have talked this week, a lot. I'm not saying we have found a magic cure to all our problems, nor am I saying he doesn't still find me 'fucking unbearable', but we are making progress. We did have an 'incident' last night where I broke down in floods of tears over some soppy documentary on adopted children and I couldn't stop crying long after it was over. Aidan had warned me not to watch it, but, of course, I figured I was now a stronger person. He tried to be sympathetic to my sobs but, to be fair to him, there is only so much bawling any man can take in a week from an over-emotional woman. He threw a box of tissues in my direction and stormed off upstairs, leaving me to cry that little bit more.

Usually in circumstances such as these, when upsetting programmes involving children are on the telly, I would phone

Daisy and we would cry together, speaking in some hybrid language of our own making, gulping between sobs and blowing our noses in unison. We would put the world to rights and hang up a bit more settled, but Daisy and I are still not speaking.

I am taking the advice of Mammy and giving Daisy room to breathe and think things over. I am reminding myself on an hourly basis that Daisy can be a stubborn one from time to time. I know enough about the grudges she can hold against those whom she has perceived to have wronged her to know that this could be a long wait. I can't say it is easy. I miss her terribly. I find myself picking up the phone to text or call several times a day and I have to use every inch of willpower not to.

Aidan says I should be angry with Daisy – after all, I've been going through a shit time – but, while part of me wishes she would see things from my perspective, I know that being angry won't help. I'm also aware that in her eyes I have committed two of the most horrendous sins of all time. First of all, I didn't tell her I was feeling as if one or two sandwiches were falling out of my picnic basket leaving me a couple short – which was simply because I didn't have a fecking clue myself it was happening until it had happened. The second, and this dawned on me when I woke on Wednesday morning, rested and feeling brighter, was the more serious of the offences and I knew this was the reason for the callousness and door slamming. I had, in her eyes, abandoned my child. Admittedly, as I see it, I had abandoned him with his granny and his daddy and had been gone a mere twenty-four hours, but this would not cut the mustard with Daisy Cassidy. Daisy has a thing about absent parents, arising from the dreadful

TMF (The Mighty Fuckwit) incident which we are not allowed to speak of ever again.

TMF is Daisy's ex and Lily's dad. Even though I've known her for two and half years I am yet to discover what his real name is. While I don't know if he is a Billy, a Bob or an Elton, I know that he hurt Daisy more than anyone has ever hurt her. His cardinal sin was not so much that he fell in love with someone else (known in these circles as The Slut) and left Daisy when Lily was eeny, it was that he failed to see his gorgeous elfin-faced daughter as the precious, gorgeous little woman she was and fecked off out of her life. When Daisy upped sticks and moved to Derry, TMF didn't make any efforts to stop her. He didn't plead with her at the airport not to take his gorgeous girl away. And when he did decide he wanted her, he just set about breaking both their hearts again.

Daisy says she is glad he is gone, but should the topic ever come up of parents who abandon their children a hard, stony glare sets on her face as she launches into a one-woman attack on "dirty feckers who leave their wains". Usually I nod and agree with her – of course, I say, I could never leave Jack, not even overnight . . .

Therefore I have realised my leaving of Jack, overnight, with only a stupid wee note to tell him I wasn't leaping off the bridge, will put me in the same category as "those dirty feckers" and, if I know Daisy like I think I know Daisy, she will be not be thinking about making friends with me right now – she will be planning my demise by firing squad.

I want this to settle, to pass and for us to be friends again. I feel all at sea, and much as Jack listens he isn't much for answering back with witty one-liners and support. When the dark moods come, as they do, at least once a day, I wonder if

Daisy will ever forgive me. I wonder if I will ever see Lily again. I imagine seeing them in town and their crossing the road to avoid me and our becoming ships that pass in the night. The thought of that, and the loneliness that would accompany it, is unbearable. I had already made the decision that should Aidan and I ever have another child I was going to ask Daisy to be godmother even though she is an unholy heathen. The fact that she wouldn't be there to do that hurts me more than anything. Besides, we have no one else to ask. Aidan's only sister, Máiréad, did the duty last time around along with Himself's best friend Jamesie. The rest of Aidan's friends are drunken ne'er-do-wells and as for mine, well, there isn't exactly a queue.

Shaking these negative thoughts from my head, in the manner which Dr Dishy has ordered me to do, I say goodbye to my work colleagues and jump in the car to head to Susie's to pick Jack up. This is not the first time this week I've thanked my lucky stars that Daisy had not had a place for Jack in Little Tikes when he was tiny.

The sun is beating down and the inside of my Focus (a sensible, family car, more's the pity) is like an oven. I open the windows as far as I can and switch on the engine, the radio simultaneously springing to life.

There is an old Harry Belafonte classic playing. I recognise it from the film *Beetlejuice*, and as I drive I sing at the top of my lungs about shaking my body and jumping in the line, even though I have absolutely no idea what that means. I realise I may be getting strange looks (not least because my windows are down and everyone can hear my not-so-melodic tones), but I don't give a damn. I imagine myself dancing, shimmying and shaking, wearing nice shoes and a skirt that has loads of movement and makes me look super-sexy and I feel that old longing re-emerge – that dance fever which I've hidden for so long. Instead of burying it, however, like I normally do, I allow it to wash over me.

When I pick Jack up, strap him in his car seat and head straight towards Buncrana, I keep the music up loud and I sing, much to his amusement. I guess I figure if I sing loud enough I'll drown out the bad feelings and concentrate on what is actually working in my life – which right now is my relationship with my gorgeous boy.

Jack was born in the early hours of a Tuesday morning after twenty-eight hours of labour in which I wanted to die. He had been planned for, prayed for and worshipped before he was conceived. (There was fair bit of praying – well, taking the Lord's name in vain – during the whole birthing process as well.)

If I'm honest, when he arrived, contrary to all my expectations my primary feeling was exhaustion, seconded by a need to do everything the proper way for him. But my feelings were not of overwhelming love. I loved him, yes, I can't deny that – but this was not the most-amazing-feeling-in-the-world experience I had been told about since the moment I held my first Tiny Tears doll as a young child. Motherhood is tough and the induction period is a real baptism of fire. My personal experience was that I was exhausted and sore and very unsure of what to do best for my child. I didn't know if I was feeding him enough, or too little, or not winding him properly, not bathing him enough, cuddling him too much or cuddling him too little. I became obsessed with baby books offering miracle routines and spent so much time trying to be the 'perfect' mammy that I actually became the perfect basket-case instead. Aidan of course just saw that I did everything I should. He was exhausted between working late shifts and helping with his son and it never occurred to him that I might have been floundering. I remember feeling as if I simply could not manage another feed or another nappy change and, while I did everything the wee man needed, I did it mechanically. Even hugging came down to doing so because whatever daft routine we were on that week dictated it was hugging time. I ignored whatever maternal instincts I did have if they didn't match the Baby Whisperer's EASY Routine and the result is I never allowed myself to get to know my own baby's personality. And if you don't know someone, how can you fall in love with them?

I don't know when I realised I was falling in love with Jack, but when it started – as it was a gradual process – I felt that strange mixture of elation and fear normally reserved for falling in love with Mr Right.

Every day brought, and continues to bring, a new joy. The passion I feel for him scares me though. I wonder how on earth would I ever manage if something happened to him and my fear is that, because I didn't want him with all my heart in those early days and weeks, justice will be meted out to me in the form of having that which I hold most dear stolen from me.

I glance in the rear-view mirror and see him sitting there, his curly fair hair sticky with sweat, his cheeks rosy red, his tiny new teeth a glorious white in his smile and I feel my heart swell. I have to stop myself from crying, from breaking down with the sheer emotion of this love. So I sing louder, and he joins in and when we arrive at the beach, the sun still blazing, I lift him from his seat and pull him to me, breathing his toddler smell (a mixture of Quavers, lavender bubble-bath and crayons) before we run hand in hand to the park.

He whoops with joy in the swings, shouting at me to push him higher and higher, and when he is bored with that we walk to the beach and collect shells and stones in his tiny blue bucket. He runs in and out of the water, not giving a damn about getting wet or standing on stones and for a moment I'm envious of the way he embraces life without a care in the world.

Looking at my watch I realise his bed time is long past, but I don't care. We are having too much fun so we play until he comes and cuddles into me and we watch the sun start to set over Lough Swilly. I wrap him inside my huge cardigan and carry him back to the car, his sleepy eyes staring at me, and as I strap him into his seat and plug his sweet mouth with a dummy he pipes up that he loves me.

Driving home I feel tired, but contented. I don't care that I'm going to be home alone and, for tonight anyway, I don't care about Daisy and our falling-out. I go home, put Jack in his cot and climb into a bath myself – not feeling the need for a glass of wine or a bar of chocolate.

I decide I'm going to treat myself tonight, so when I eventually climb out of the bath I light some candles in the bedroom and scent the oil burner with jasmine. I slather myself in body cream and take my favourite, expensive, perfume from its exalted position at the back of the shelf and spray it on generously. It's the same bottle of Chanel No 5 that Mammy bought me for my wedding day. There isn't much left now and the thought of the bottle being finished upsets me so I dole it out on special occasions only. Deep-conditioning my hair and slipping into my fluffy robe, I lie back and switch on the stereo, allowing the music to wash over me.

Between the sad songs and the happy songs I find myself singing along at the top of my voice until I fall into yet another peaceful slumber. When Aidan comes home, reeking of beer and cigarettes, he cuddles up close to me and for once I don't move away. When he strokes my arm, I let him. When he caresses my thigh, I let him. When he turns me towards him and kisses me, softly yet deeply, I let him and then I let him make love to me.

When we are finished, and he tells me he loves me, I let him – but more than that I let myself believe him.

# 10

I wake in the morning to Jack's usual medley of songs. Today we are being treated to the *CBeebies* overture – shouted and not sung at the top of his lungs. Looking at the clock I see it has gone nine and I can hardly believe it. Aidan stirs beside me, turning and putting his arm around me, pulling me back into bed as I'm just about to go and rescue the wee munchkin from his cot.

"He's grand for the moment," Aidan says, "So stay here, give me a cuddle and tell me you love me."

"I love you," I say grinning.

"Enough for a second performance?" he laughs, moving closer as I wriggle away from him.

"Not with Jack awake next door," I answer, shocking myself by feeling remarkably in the mood for the suggested encore.

"I'll try and get home early tonight," he says, stretching out in the bed.

"Won't it be really busy?"

"Well, it will be, but there are certain perks in being manager, aren't there?" he grins.

"Manager!?" I squeal.

"Yep, Matt was true to his word. I've got my promotion and he says if this works out I could get the lead job in the new place."

I lean over and kiss my husband full on the lips, ignoring his stinking morning breath. "I'm so proud of you," I grin, and then I go and get Jack just to boast to him about how clever his daddy is.

When we are dressed I phone my parents to tell them the good news. They are delighted, and actually quite relieved. They've always worried slightly about the fact the financial burden in our house has fallen on my shoulders for the majority of our married life. Daddy in particular is old school – a man should be the provider – and I know he was secretly disappointed I went back to work after Jack was born. No amount of protestation on my part that I actually *wanted* to return to work cut it with Daddy who just rolled his eyes a lot and offered up a few more prayers.

"We'll have to go down there some night for a few drinks," Mammy said.

"As long as you don't bring Himself," I laugh, immediately knowing that my kind, lovely daddy would hate to spend more than two seconds inside Jackson's, a bar famed for its cocktails, dancing on top of the bar and loud music. It was our answer to Coyote Ugly – known locally as Buck Ugly – and not the place for a good Catholic like my dad.

Mammy on the other hand would have a ball. After a few

vodkas I would be fighting to keep her off the bar and that was what I loved about her – she knew just how to enjoy herself. Sometimes when she was lost in singing, dancing and woohooing with her friends I would see that same innocence in her that I saw in Jack at the beach. She simply didn't give a damn. Perhaps that was the product of the hurt of her past, or the privilege of age but whatever it was I hoped it was one trait I would inherit when I hit my late fifties.

"Meet me here later," she said. "We'll go and get him a wee present to say congratulations."

"Sounds like a plan, Mammy," I say, before hanging up and getting myself ready.

I strap Jack into his buggy and we walk the short distance to my parents' house. Aidan sometimes gets frustrated that we live so close to the in-laws, but then I remind him that if we didn't I would just annoy him all the more instead of clearing round there for a cuppa.

As the day is so nice Mammy and I decide to walk into town. I know the two-mile walk will most likely kill me so before we leave I jokingly remind Daddy where my will is kept. He rolls his eyes to heaven and gives me a hug, offering to hang on to Jack while we do our shopping. I decline – mostly because if the exertion of the walk does get too much I like the fact I could use the buggy to hold me up. I might even turf Jack out and climb in myself.

"How are you feeling anyway, love?" Mammy asks as we set out.

"Jeez, you don't waste any time, do you?" I laugh.

"At my age you can't be wasting time," she retorts, and I dig her in the arm.

"By the way you're talking you'd think you were a hundred

and two! You're barely out of nappies!" I laugh.

"You've got that all wrong, love. It won't be that long until I'm back in them again, but enough of changing the subject – how are you?"

I try to think about things. "Physically I feel pretty yucky. I'm tired and nauseous and no, before you get any notions, I'm not pregnant."

Mammy rolls her eyes.

"Mentally, I'm okay. I'm up and down – that is probably the best way to put it."

I don't want to talk about this now. I think in the last week I'm all talked out – well, at least until Monday when I have my check-up with Dr Dishy. I know he will expect me to do some more chatting then.

"Look, I know you are probably getting fed up talking about this now," she says (what is it about mothers that they can read your mind?), "but promise me if you do need to talk you will come to me – and don't be fecking running away with yourself again."

"I promise," I say and we walk on, stopping only to comment on the lorries, buses, cars and diggers for Jack.

By the time we have reached the Craigavon Bridge my legs are starting to ache and my excess weight is leading to a certain puddle of sweat forming between my gargantuan bazookas. I know it's only a five-minute walk until we reach Foyleside so I take a deep breath and push the buggy onwards. Jack is in a frenzy of excitement because he can see a boat and I'm trying to talk with him while concentrating on breathing the best I can.

"So how are things with Daisy?" Mammy asks.

"Not now, Mother," I say, my face growing redder with exertion.

"Well, I just wondered. Do you need me to knock your two heads together again?"

"Seriously, Mammy, not now!" I puff. "Let's just get into town – get a cold drink – and get something nice for Aidan. I saw some cufflinks – in Debenhams – which would be perfect."

"Don't change the subject, Grace," Mammy says in her stern voice.

"I'm not changing the subject," I puff, "I'm avoiding it. I'm hot, I'm bothered and I need to pee – this is not the time to talk."

"You two are like big children!" Mammy says, taking the buggy from me and hurtling on at the speed of light, leaving me to feel like a big, fat useless lump of a thing trailing behind.

"Would you ever just stop?" I shout, stopping her in her tracks.

She turns and looks at me with the face of a wounded animal.

"I just don't want to talk about it because she still isn't speaking to me. She has no intention of speaking to me and I doubt any amount of head-knocking will change that and I just don't want to think about it for today, okay?"

"Grace, you can't just bury your head in the sand and pretend it isn't happening!"

"That's the point though, Mammy, isn't it? I'm not pretending it isn't happening. I'm right slap-bang in the fecking middle of it – all too aware that it is happening and I don't see how talking about it right now is going to help."

"Don't get snippy with me, young lady," Mammy says.

"I'm not," I say, almost crying now. "Can we not just have

a nice day without thinking about these things?"

Mammy makes a noise that is somewhere between a sniff and a grunt (a snunt, perhaps?) and we walk on in silence. The tears are pricking in my eyes and I feel like a chastised schoolgirl, not the twenty-nine-year-old sensible mum of one with a good job and a nice line in prescription drugs.

We are almost at Brooke Perk, our favourite coffee spot, when Mammy turns to me and says: "I saw Daisy yesterday. She called round for tea and, you know what, I didn't think I could ever meet a more pigheaded person than you – but, lordy, she is a right one!"

I'm dying to ask her why Daisy visited. I'm dying to ask what was said and a part of me, the same part that was made to feel like the child back on the bridge, is internally rehearsing my 'She's my mammy not yours, Daisy, so you can't be coming over for tea any more' speech.

I realise for the first time I'm a wee bit pissed off. How dare Daisy go and see *my* parents when she doesn't even have the decency to open the door to me? What makes her think it can all go on as normal when she is effectively cutting me out of her life?

Why, and this is the clincher, has she not realised that I need a friend now and not some judgemental old baggage who holds all my faults up to my face and makes me accept them whether or not I'm ready to?

I suppose that is the thing with Daisy. She knows me – she knows every thought that goes through my head and she isn't afraid to give me a good arse-kicking when I need it – but this time, this time the arse-kicking is uncalled for. I didn't need my arse kicked this time – I needed a hug.

"I'll be back in a minute," I say, rushing to the toilet. I

expect to cry, but instead I'm bloody angry, more angry than I have ever been in my life.

How dare she? When I helped her out when she was down and lonely and welcomed her into my family? How dare she close the door on me? How dare she stop me from seeing Lily? I didn't wrong Daisy – I made a choice – a stupid one admittedly, but it was mine to make, and how dare she stand in judgement of me over it? I storm out of the loos, scaring the holy bejaysus out of a wee woman just heading in for a pee, and head towards my mother.

"Phone Daisy," I say. "Tell her you are taking care of Lily. We are going to talk whether madam likes it or not."

"Okay," she replies, knowing better than to answer me back when I'm in one of these moods.

I'm showing the same resilience now that I did when I ordered her never to go near that school again to deal with the bullies and a thought flashes across my mind that in this instance Daisy has been a bully too.

We finish our tea, barely speaking except to chastise Jack for playing his latest game of crush-the-bickie-into-the-floor and then Herself makes the phone call and, thankfully, Daisy knows better than to answer back to Mammy. The scene is set, arrangements made, and we are ready for the showdown. Batten down the hatches, people. This could be interesting.

As I've already explained, Daisy sauntered into my office one day looking for a feature to be done on Little Tikes. I was still Health and Beauty Editor but, given my increasing girth and obvious impending mummyhood, Sinéad was foisting some of the parenting features onto me. Good research, she called it.

On the day Daisy arrived I was feeling a little sorry for

myself. The baby had been kicking like a good 'un all night, necessitating at least a million trips to the loo, and I had dreadful heartburn. I always got grouchy on the days I had to drink any of those vile antacid medicines – they are indeed the devil's pish.

Swigging some back and grimacing to try and stop myself throwing up, I looked up and saw this wee Scottish whirlwind standing in front of me.

"Daisy Cassidy," she said, stretching out her hand and shaking mine. "Vile, stinking stuff, isn't it? I would nearly rather throw up and drink that back down instead."

I had the good grace to laugh.

Daisy started to explain to me about Little Tikes and how she wanted to up its profile, and in doing that she also started spilling out details of her life and what had brought her to Derry. I was a little taken aback to say the least. I wasn't used to such honesty – more to having to pull teeth to get a story. It soon dawned on me that this bubbly, confident woman was really a wee bag of nerves and uncertainties underneath, so I decided I liked her. I liked that she was vulnerable. I couldn't be dealing with people who had no chinks in their armour – they tended not to like me and to make it their mission to hunt out my chinks and attack them.

While we worked on the feature we met for lunch and I discovered that we had quite a lot in common actually. We had the same taste in books, shoes and bags but more than that we shared the same sense of gallows humour. As the weeks passed, and we kept talking even though the feature was long put to bed, I realised I could be myself with Daisy and she wasn't repulsed or disgusted.

So she, and Lily, became part of our family. Mammy and

Daddy welcomed her like the second child they had never been blessed with and Aidan quite liked the person I was when she was around. (He swears it wasn't just her impressive cleavage that attracted him.)

When Jack was born, and Daisy was the first person to rush to my bedside, champagne smuggled in her fake Prada bag, I knew I had finally found a friend. In the two and half years since we met we have only had one falling out: the aforementioned TMF incident. At that time I was gracious enough to fully understand why Daisy was doing her mentalist routine because of it, and I spent a good fortnight scraping and bowing before we were back on track. While it hadn't been my fault, I had been caught up in the whirlwind as much as Daisy.

But not now. Now I'm angry, and determined that if anyone is going to do any scraping and bowing it isn't going to be me. No, sirree. My arse-kissing days are over.

Once Jack and Lily are safely ensconced in my parents' backyard (the paddling pool brought out as a special treat), I make my way to Daisy's house. I won't be knocking at the door this time and giving her the chance to ignore me. I have a key and I'll be using it. The garden is as lovely as always, but the big red door doesn't look quite so welcoming any more – in fact it looks downright scary. I take a deep breath and a couple of drops of the Bach's Rescue Remedy I now keep in my bag. Putting my key in the door, I turn the lock and walk in. The house is deathly silent, bar the ticking of a big grandfather clock which stands at the bottom of the stairs. I walk through to the kitchen and see that the French doors are open and Daisy is sitting at her wrought-iron garden table, glass of wine in one hand and cigarette in the other. (Daisy

109

only ever smokes if she is really, really drunk or really, really stressed. I start to wonder which one she is today.)

"Grab a glass," she says curtly and I follow her instructions, all the while cursing myself for not being a grown-up and telling her to feck off. I pour the cool Sauvignon Blanc out and take a sip. It tastes bitter, suiting the mood, so I put it down and stare out across the garden to the trees and planters at the far end.

"You've no right to be angry with me, Daisy," I start. "I didn't do anything to you. This for once is not about you so I don't know why the feck you are getting so high and mighty about it."

"You could have told me," she says.

"I would have, if I'd known myself, but it's not really something you pencil into the diary. Friday, get eyebrows waxed – Saturday, take Jack swimming – Sunday, flip your lid."

"Very fucking funny!" she snarls.

"I'm not trying to be funny. I'm trying to make you see that this is about me and how I feel and I can't always be thinking of other people all the time."

"Well, you certainly weren't thinking of anyone but yourself last Sunday!"

"I know that, but excuse me for having a day to myself. We can't all be perfect. We can't all keep going no matter what happens."

"But what *has* happened, Grace?" she says, raising her voice just that little bit too much. "What is so shit about your life? You have a job, a husband, a home, a baby. You have everything you ever wanted, so what exactly do you have to be so bloody miserable about?"

"I'm sorry," I say, "that my husband hasn't run off on me and left me to fend for me and my child alone. I'm sorry that I have a house and a job and I'm sorry if despite that I still feel crap. Perhaps this is exactly why I didn't tell you, Dais, because if I did you would have reminded me I've no right to be pissed off. Jack's dad isn't some wanker who fucked up our lives but that doesn't mean my life is bloody perfect, does it? *You* are not the only one ever to feel down or get hurt."

I realise almost as soon as the words come out that I've gone too far. I see the hurt in Daisy's eyes. Immediately I want to unsay all those things, to wind back to the clock and not say those things I knew would cut Daisy to the bone. I don't like confrontation, even when I'm only defending myself.

I feel sick. I run to the bathroom and throw up, until my eyes are streaming and my stomach hurts.

I rest my head against the cool white tiles and try to regain my breath. Looking up, I see Daisy standing at the door, holding a glass of water in her hand. She pushes it towards me and sits down on the ground beside the bath.

"I'm sorry," I say meekly. "I went too far."

"Have you stopped chundering now, do you think?" Daisy asks.

"I think so. It's these tablets – they don't half make me queasy."

"Tablets?" She raises an eyebrow.

"The ones the doctor gave me – antidepressants."

"I didn't know you were on tablets."

"You didn't ask, Dais," I say wearily. "You just shut the door." And I feel tears prick in my eyes. "Did you think I was making it up? Did you think I ran away that day just because I fancied getting the mini-bar all to myself?"

She shrugs her shoulders.

"I'm sorry," I say. "I don't know what is going on with me. I've not felt great for a long time but I've realised I was hiding it away and then I went home at night and sat alone in the house. I was letting it all eat away at me and I was becoming a bitter, horrible person." I've started to cry. "And I know, believe me, that I have so much more to be grateful about than most. I have my house, my husband, my baby, my family and you, but for some reason that has stopped being enough and I wish that it was. I wish that I could be content and happy to be who I am but I'm not. When I look in the mirror I see everything I hate and I hear these wee voices telling me over and over again that I'm useless. I'm fat, I'm ugly, I have no style, no sense of fashion and I'm not even a good mother."

"Pish!" Daisy interjects.

"No, it's not pish, Dais. There are days when I get home from work that it's all I can do to count down to bedtime and then when Jack does go to sleep I lie there, just waiting for him to wake up again – not relaxing. And I dread that, because I'm so fecking tired all the time and all I want is a good night's sleep. What kind of mother gets pissed off with her own child over wanting some sleep?"

"Every kind of a mother," Daisy says. "We've all done it, Gracie. It doesn't make you a bad person. It makes you human."

"Then why do I feel so useless? Why do I feel so out of control?" I'm sobbing now, doing my ugly snotters and all.

And Daisy moves towards me, reaches out and pulls me into a huge bear hug. She strokes my hair like she would one of her charges at Little Tikes and she makes all the right soothing noises. It takes a time for me to realise she is crying too.

"I didn't know, Gracie," she says over and over, "I just didn't know."

* * *

It's funny how a bathroom floor can become the most comfortable seat in the house. I'm not sure how long Daisy and I sat there, but I know we talked and talked. We also apologised and apologised to each other over and over again. A bit like Aidan, Daisy says she doesn't really understand what is going on but she will try to be supportive anyway.

I told her all about Dr Dishy, all about agreeing to Louise's plan to get my life back on track and how I'm pretty determined to stop playing a victim and to get on with my life. I even told her about my trip to the beach with Jack, our sleepy cuddles and my singing. She looked kind of impressed, and also a little horrified.

It was gone seven before I lifted myself up off the floor and phoned Mammy to tell her it was okay to bring Jack and Lily around. With Aidan working, Daisy and I decided it would be best if I stayed over at hers. I just didn't want to be alone, and I wanted to make sure everything really was okay again with me and my best friend.

And so here I am, lying in the spare room, staring at the eggshell walls, the subtle gold-coloured frames of stones, seashells and flowers, and feeling Jack cuddled on the bed beside me. Tomorrow we'll go together to Mammy's for Sunday lunch and then on Monday Daisy will hold my hand when I go back to see the delightful Dr Dishy. She has already been on Amazon, buying up books on depression and says she is determined we will get through this.

I still feel guilty, though. I should not have said those things. I know Daisy doesn't love TMF any more. Things have gone so far that she doesn't even hate him any more – she holds him in total non-regard. But I know, while forgiveness has been achieved, she will never forget those horrible months of betrayal and hurt and, looking at Lily, her innocence so apparent, I can understand why.

I kiss my boy's forehead and he sucks that little harder on his dummy, his face looking  babyish and far removed from the wee toddler boy he has become. I kiss him and thank my lucky stars that he has never been hurt by anyone who loves him and I thank those same stars for Aidan and his ability to be a great daddy, even when his husband skills are lacking.

"Mammy's here," I whisper in the dark, "and I'm not going anywhere, baby. I'm going to get through this, for you."

In the morning we are woken by a four-year-old bundle of mischief jumping on the bed, her dark curls looking almost as mad as my own. "My mummy says we are all friends now, Aunty Grace," Lily chirps, as Jack rubs the sleep from his eyes.

"We are, darling, and we're not going to fall out ever again."

"I really, really, really didn't like it when you were cross with each other," Lily says. "Mummy was very grumpy and wouldn't let me phone to speak to Jack."

"Mummy and Aunty Grace have just been very silly, darling, but it's okay now," I say, tickling her precious little tummy. "Now, Schmoo-face, go and tell your mummy I want a full cooked breakfast!"

Lily bounds off the bed, closely followed by Jack who is yelping with excitement and shouting "Sausages!" over and over again. I smile, stretch and slip on the robe hanging on the back of the bedroom door, grateful that Daisy keeps an old one in my size and I'm not trying to squeeze into one of her hand-me-downs. I shuffle down the stairs and see the children have run, pyjamas and all, into the back garden while Daisy is cooking up a storm.

"Cooked breakfast indeed," she laughs. "You really are pushing your fecking luck! It's a good thing you have an excuse for needing pampering or you'd have got those eggs smashed on your head."

"Dinnae get yer knickers in a twist, lassie," I counter in my best Scottish accent – which is actually absolutely dreadful – and Daisy bursts out laughing.

"Blummin' cheek!" she says.

I sit down in the armchair, curling my feet under me.

"Daisy," I say.

"What now? Eggs Benedict, perhaps? Bucks Fizz? Two slices of potato bread?"

"Love you," I say.

"I know, doll, and I love you too. Even if you are a crackpot."

# II

Today is going to be an interesting day. I'm not sure if it will be good, bad or indifferent but for once I find myself awake long before Jack – just staring out the kitchen window and thinking of what is to come.

I like the first day of a new issue. When we meet in work we get together with coffee and doughnuts and brainstorm until we have a packed features list. Sinéad tends to get a bit manic and over-excited about the whole thing – which I'm pretty sure is down to the sugar rush of the doughnut she eats before we all arrive. I have a packed schedule myself this month with features on Controlled Crying, preparing for Christmas (I know, it's only the tail end of July – but this is October's edition we are talking about) and Halloween.

And, of course, I can't forget, this is the start of the great guinea-pig experiment. This time we are serious.

"Look who I found!" Aidan grins, carrying a sleepy-headed

Jack into the room.

"Morning Stinkers," I say, kissing him on the cheek and then turning to kiss my husband.

"You nervous?" Aidan asks as I set out the breakfast bowls and reboil the kettle.

"Kind of," I say, "but I'm a little excited too. I'm not sure what way this is going to go and it feels good for once to do something different."

"Are you seeing the doctor today?"

"Yep – four thirty. Daisy is going to come with me and do the whole hand-holding thing."

"God, I'm glad you two have made things up," he says, putting two slices of toast in the toaster. "There is only so much a man can listen to about bags and make-up."

I throw a tea towel at him and Jack screams, "Again, again!" and I wonder has it really only been eight days since we were on the verge of meltdown.

Aidan reaches into a cupboard and pulls out a pink lunch box, with darker pink hearts on it. "I got you this," he says, "for your new start. I've packed it for you already but you are not, repeat *not*, allowed to look in it until you get to work. Scout's honour?"

"Yes, boss," I say.

"Do the salute," he teases, and I do before giving him a hug and setting about getting the troublesome toddler fed and dressed.

I arrive at the office, my funky new lunch box under my arm, and congratulate myself that I've not had a sneaky peek yet. Sitting down at my desk I say my usual greeting to the lovely Dermot (those eyes still get me in a frenzy) and prepare my features list for the big meeting. I'm just about to open the lunch box when Louise breezes over, dressed in a brand-new designer suit with her hair obviously highlighted since Friday.

"Lovely day, isn't it?" she quips but doesn't bother to wait for my reply. "Just wait until you find out what I have lined up for this feature, Grace! You will be a new woman. Just you wait and see! That Adam of yours won't be able to keep his hands off you."

"Actually it's Aidan and don't you forget this has to have my say-so, Louise. I'm not doing this to make an arse of myself."

"Of course, of course," she mutters. "It's nothing I wouldn't do myself – well, not much anyway."

I am about to interrogate further when Sinéad walks into the office and makes her traditional rallying-of-the-troops announcement.

"All right, you eejits, my office now!"

I lift my notepad, walk past Louise and bag myself a comfortable seat on the sofa.

"Right, folks, let's get down to business. September was a blinder – well done, all – I hope to see increased sales when we hit the stands on Thursday. But you know the business, we can't rest on our laurels, so what've you got for me?"

One by one we list our features, either getting the yea or the nay from She Who Must Be Obeyed and then it comes to Louise, who by this stage is almost peeing her designer knickers with excitement.

"Well, we all know Grace has kindly volunteered herself for a life makeover," she starts and my colleagues nod and wave. "So I've lined a few things up. I mean, first of all, she needs to lose some weight. Seriously, that baby is two now, Grace, no excuses. You'll be off to see Charlotte at Weightloss Wonders tomorrow night. She is keeping you a seat in the front row.

Second of all: well, those clothes – I mean it's more slummy mummy than yummy mummy. I mean it's just *so* not the image we want to put across for our Parenting Editor, now is it, Sinéad?"

I look to my boss, hoping for a modicum of support and receiving none.

She merely shrugs her shoulders and says: "Well, everyone loves free clothes, don't they?"

Green light for Louise.

"So in two weeks' time you have an appointment with Lesley at City Couture for an image overhaul, Grace. We tried to get those Trinny and Susannah ladies but even they admitted some cases are hopeless."

Annoyingly she is laughing at her own jokes while everyone else looks on a little embarrassed.

"Leah at Natural Nails will do the whole manicure-pedicure thing and I have a friend who does that Reiki stuff for the holistic approach. It will be fab. You won't look back, Grace, honest. Imagine how good it will feel to get rid of those saddlebags and your dowdy clothes and feel like a real woman again!"

Now, I am fully aware that if Daisy or my mam had offered free clothes and a makeover to me in the confines of a private conversation I would have been jumping up and down and doing an American-style whooping thing. But this is not in the confines of a private conversation – this is in an office – in front of my colleagues and so-called friends – and the red mist is starting to descend again.

The thing is, though, the red mist is now my friend. It helps me confront those who need confronting, it helps me take control. It is no longer a force to be turned inwards against myself, it is a force to be reckoned with and the Day of Reckoning has just arrived.

I do my best fake laugh, cross my legs and sit upright in my seat so as to look as though I mean business.

"Very good," I say, adding caustically, "for a first attempt. But let's see how I envisage this. Sure I'll go along to Weightloss Wonders and City Couture because, yes, I wouldn't mind shedding a few pounds and getting some free clothes, but I also thought it would be more in the interest of our readers to credit them with just that little bit of intelligence. There's a wealth of complementary therapies out there designed to help women like me – you know, busy professionals juggling home and work. I thought it might be good to investigate which are worth their weight in salt and which are a load of bollocks. We also know depression is the modern woman's epidemic so how about we look at that? Because you can't change someone's life just by changing how they look. You need to change the inside also – *that* is what good health is all about, Louise."

"Brilliant, Grace, brilliant," Sinéad smiles. "This is just the kind of stuff we need – keep it coming!"

Louise uncrosses her legs, sits with her mouth gaping open, all picture and no sound and I start talking about my ideas about proper issues affecting real women.

"You know what would be fan-bloody-tastic?" Sinéad says, biting into a strawberry doughnut. "If we could get a medical expert on board – someone to talk about it from a professional point of view."

"You know," I say, "I might just know the very man."

The others slowly flood out of the office while Sinéad and I keep talking. Louise is sitting in the corner chewing petulantly on her lip and looking if a wasp has just crawled up her arse. I feel fired up and excited about this now, and I feel as if part of the old me – the me I left behind in the labour ward – has come back.

Walking back to my desk an hour later, I open the lunchbox and find it packed with a variety of healthy snacks. There is an apple, a yoghurt, a banana and a treat-size Mars Bar. (He knows me well enough to know I can't go cold turkey on chocolate.)

Hidden at the bottom is an envelope which I open to find a locket I had long forgotten about. Made in silver, with a gold Celtic knot on the front, my parents gave it to me when I graduated from college but now I see it has been cleaned up and, turning it around, I see a new message engraved on the back. *"We believe in you."* I open it and it contains two pictures – one of Aidan and one of Jack – and I start to think I believe in myself a little too.

My phone rings and I pick it up, smiling as I trill my usual introduction down the line for once.

"So I was wondering," a wee Scottish voice asks, "just how dishy is Dr Dishy? Are we talking Dr Hilary Jones off the telly or are we talking George Clooney-Lay-Me-Down-And-Give-Me-Mouth-To-Mouth?"

"I'd say he's a bit like that foreign one in *ER* actually."

"And is he single?"

"I don't really know. I didn't much have the chance to ask him between threatening to slit my wrists and begging him not to give me a one-way ticket to the local insane asylum."

"Tsk!" Daisy tuts. "Call yourself a friend, pah!"

"I know, I know," I grin. "Can you ever forgive me?"

"Not sure I can, Gracie my dear, not sure I can, unless of

course you make it your mission to find out for me."

"I thought you were sworn off men for life?"

"No harm in knowing all about the man treating my best friend for her raving loonyness, now is there?"

"Suppose not," I say, glad to hear Daisy laughing and joking with me.

"Meet you are there at 4.15?"

"It's a date."

"How sad is it that the dates in my life revolve around the local health centre?" she laughs before hanging up.

Lord only knows what Dr Dishy will make of Daisy when she walks into his office this afternoon – he will start to think I only hang around with crazies and crackpots.

By four o'clock my stomach is growling a little so I give in to temptation and eat my Mars bar. I don't follow my usual pattern of inhaling it in two bites – instead I savour its chocolatey goodness, slowly letting the caramel melt on my tongue and I lose myself in the moment.

I open my eyes and see John looking at me rather strangely.

"Are you quite all right, Grace?"

"Just perfect," I say before grabbing my bag and heading to the door for my threesome with Daisy and Dishy.

Arriving at the health centre I see my friend has brushed and tousled her hair and has just applied her best new shiny lip-gloss.

"This is serious, Daisy," I scold. "You can't be going in and flirting with him. Remember you are here to hold my hand and not his."

"I know hon, I'm sorry. I just wanted to make a bit of an impression."

"Daisy, you are beside *me*. I have been sitting in a baking hot office all day, I'm pretty sure that stain on my trousers is an organic life form of its own making and my foundation has slipped off my face to somewhere near my kneecaps – you are doing pretty damn okay in comparison if you ask me."

We walk into the building and I start to feel a little nervous. I realise these people, these staff, will have seen me a week ago looking like I'd just escaped from the loony-bin, tearstained and shaking. I think they will be judging me now, making up wee stories about my life, looking up my records and pitying the poor child and poor husband I live with.

"Breathe, Grace! Come on chick, you can do this," Daisy says, sensing my unease and taking my hand as we move towards the front of the reception queue. I squeeze her hand tightly and she turns to the young girl behind the glass and says: "Grace Adams, an appointment with Dr Di – shit, Grace, what is his name again?"

I realise I don't know and my face turns red. "Erm, I'm not sure."

"She told me he looks a bit like yer man from *ER*," Daisy adds with a wink and the receptionist laughs.

"That will be Doctor Stevenson, Shaun Stevenson," she says and directs us down the corridor to the waiting area with a wry smile on her face which lets us know we are far from the only people in Derry to have fallen under his spell.

I sit down and lift one of those tatty old magazines they leave there to amuse you while you mull over your aches and pains. Today's choice consists of a *Woman's Weekly* circa 2004 and *Golfer's Monthly*. No sign of a *Northern People* anywhere. Daisy opts for *Golfer's Monthly* – to laugh at the pictures of the jumpers if nothing else, and I settle down to read a feature on a woman whose nipple fell off in the bath after plastic surgery went drastically wrong.

In the background the radio is playing some insanely cheerful song about sex on the beach or some other such nonsense and all I think about is getting sand up the crack of your arse.

Occasionally the lights beep above us, calling all the sick people in Derry in for their five minutes of pampering with the doctor. Daisy is talking to herself now, flicking the pages and stifling giggles as the fashion goes from bad to worse.

"Fecking covers for golf clubs, in case the wee dears get cold, would you believe it?"

Mentally I see Daisy, aged about eighty. She will be one of those wee grannies who dress in suitably grannified dresses (you know the floral patterned ones with the wee thin belt across the middle) but with a massive bobble hat she has knitted herself and a pair of the latest Nike trainers. She will strike up conversations with anyone at bus stops, the queue at the Post Office, wherever, and offer boiled sweets to random strangers and she will continue to do just what she is doing now and swear at stupid inventions we don't really need.

The health centre has air conditioning but you wouldn't really notice it, not today anyway. My palms are sweating and I'm leaving greasy marks on my *Woman's Weekly*. And then the light beeps which lets me know that Dr Dishy will see me now.

"C'mon, Daisy," I say and stand up, and she follows suit, stuffing the magazine into her bag as she goes.

The room seems bigger than last week, the chairs more comfortable. We say our hellos and sit down.

"You are looking better already, Grace," Dr Dishy says.

"Well, I haven't spent all morning crying and I've managed

to put some make-up on so that is always a start," I reply, trying to lighten the mood.

Daisy coughs as if to remind me I haven't introduced her so I do the necessary. "This is my friend Daisy. She is here for a little moral support."

He looks at her, his dark brown eyes twinkling, and he smiles, stretching out his (strong, manly) hand and shaking hers. "Hi, Daisy who is here for moral support, perhaps you can tell me how you think Grace is doing?"

I'm a little stunned he isn't asking me outright, but I figure there has to be a method to his madness.

"Erm, I think she isn't doing too badly. She is taking control of her life a little but she is still prone to occasional hysterical outbursts," Daisy answers, batting her eyelids in Dishy's direction.

"What sets them off?" he asks and it takes a few seconds before I realise he is talking to me. I wonder should I tell him my last emotional outburst was over Daisy not speaking to me – or would that make us both look like a pair of prize plonkers. I decide to save our blushes – for now anyway.

"Not much," I answer. "I'm quite tearful, but I'm trying to get better. Silly things can get me going though. I feel quite edgy and defensive a lot of the time. That said you should have seen me kick some butt in work this morning over the 'Change Your Life' feature."

"Yes, I meant to ask what you had decided about that one?" he asks, raising an eyebrow in a Dermot Murnaghan style.

"I'm doing it," I answer, "but on my terms. I want it to be about more than what I weigh or what I wear."

"Good for you," he answers and I feel strangely pleased that I seem to be in the good doctor's good books. "I actually have a couple of things you could try if you're serious about taking an holistic approach?"

"I am, doctor," I say.

And he turns to me as if in slow motion and says, "Please," (oh, how I love how he says 'please'!) "call me Shaun."

I nod and sigh and I swear Daisy squeaks beside me in pleasure.

We set about discussing our options, including a very bizarre 'Movement and Mood' workshop he would like me to attend and we discuss whether or not to alter my medications, before I'm packed off to the real world again with orders to come back in a week.

I'm just about to close the door to his office when I remember my promise to Sinéad. "Doctor, I mean Shaun," I say, "have you ever written for a magazine?"

* * *

"Oh. My. God! How dreamy is he?" Daisy asks as we walk towards Brooke Perk for a cup of coffee and a healthy wholegrain sandwich (see, I'm sticking with this healthy eating malarkey).

"Daisy," I grin, "you're a grown woman, not some sixteen-year-old. You can't be using words like 'dreamy'."

"But he is dreamy, Gracie, pure fecking dreamy, isn't he?"

"Yes, he is. He really is," I say, linking arms with her and pushing through the door to find our favourite seat in the corner, giggling like schoolgirls.

As we eat our sandwiches a short time later Daisy looks at me and says, rather sorrowfully: "It's not really the same without a Caramel Rocky, is it?"

I nod and agree but I can't let myself be swayed, not when I need all the willpower in the world to get me through the next couple of months.

"Get thee behind me, Satan," I tease. "I have that Charlotte one at Weightloss Wonders to face tomorrow night and I'm dreading the weigh-in."

"I'll go with you and hold your hand if you want," Daisy offers, pulling a piece of soggy tomato from her bread and examining it as if it was a piece of dog dirt.

"What, and do our Little and Large routine? They'd laugh you out of the place, Dais. You would get pelted with low-fat marg and that spray stuff they expect you to use for frying."

"Don't be daft. I need to lose about a stone."

"From which finger?" I scold, surveying my skinny friend in her figure-hugging jeans.

"Seriously, all these soda farls aren't doing me any good. I'm fighting to stay in these things," she says, gesturing to the aforementioned jeans. "C'mon, it will be fun! It will be like a night out on the piss, without the piss."

She winks and I know there is no saying no to her. As long as she doesn't expect me to tell her my weight. No, that will be between me, Charlotte and Our Father in Heaven.

When I get home I hear squeals of laughter coming from the backyard. I walk through to the kitchen and just watch the scene from the window for a while, enjoying seeing my two boys play together. Jack has his sand-and-water tray out and has discovered that his daddy squeals like a girl when doused in cold water. He has his small blue bucket and is filling it with water, a look of glee mixed with pure devilment on his face as he tosses it in Aidan's direction. I dare not let them know I'm here in case I get a bucket of water in the face too.

Besides, I'm enjoying this too much. I love just standing here, twiddling my locket between my fingers, and observing them together.

Aidan's nights off are precious for so many reasons, but not least because they allow him to spend time with his son.

I stand for as long as I can before the urge to run and hug a soggy and cold Jack becomes too much and I shout a quick hello through the window. "Hey, there," I grin and am rewarded with two huge smiles.

"Maaammmeeeeee!" Jack shouts before tearing towards me at the speed of light, dropping his bucket and enveloping me in a huge squishy hug which threatens to squeeze the life from me.

"I'd say someone is happy to see you," Aidan laughs, pushing by us to get a towel from the kitchen.

"Well, I'm quite happy to see this little man too – and you look quite good as well," I grin.

"My God, Grace, is this you actually coming home from work and not spending fifteen minutes giving out about how crap it was and how you hate Louise?" Aidan smiles.

"Well, I do still hate Louise. You should have seen the stunt she pulled today in the meeting, but this is the new positive me, remember? The one who doesn't give out about everything."

"Well, I like the new you. She kicks some ass."

"Quit your being smart, or I'll kick yours too."

A few hours later, I am sitting on the floor of the nursery as the sun sets outside. Jack is asleep in his cot. He is lying in that way only babies can, on his tummy, his bum in the air, his fair curls splayed out on the pillow and I'm happy. I don't want for anything else in this moment, just for my son to sleep peacefully and for the sun to set and for life to stay like this.

I walk downstairs and Aidan is back outside, sitting on the plastic seats – a glass of wine poured for each of us and some citronella candles burning softly.

"Is he sleeping?" he says. "You were gone ages."

I sit down and sip the wine, enjoying how it makes me feel sleepy and relaxed.

"This is the life," I sigh, staring out over the wheelie bins and towards the hills.

"So how did it go at the doctor's?" Aidan asks.

"Not so bad. Daisy was more than impressed. I think she may have a wee notion on the good doctor."

"But how did you get on? Has he said you're better?"

"It's only been a week, Aidan. It's not like the flu. You don't pop a couple of pills and feel better all of a sudden."

"But you seem better," he says. "I mean, I've not seen you cry since Friday."

"I do seem better and I'll admit it, I'm feeling better but I'm having to work at it. I still get really scared sometimes that I'll lose it again."

He looks down at his drink and sits silently for a moment or two, as if trying to find the courage to say something he just can't.

"Was it something I did, Grace?" he asks at last, his dark eyes searching for mine in the candlelight.

"What do you mean?" I ask.

"Well, the reason for you feeling like this? Did I do something wrong?"

I'm stunned by his question but more because I don't really know how to answer. No, I suppose he did nothing wrong but his feelings of disappointment that I was not the wife he wanted me to be have, I guess, played their part. As I gained weight, first of all with pregnancy and then in the aftermath when the only things I had the energy to eat were chocolate biscuits washed down with lashings of milky tea, as I became this zombified version of his previously vibrant wife, as I spent my days in tracksuit bottoms and pyjama tops, baby-sick encrusted on my dressing-gown, hair not washed, he pulled away from me.

When he cuddled me, he did so in the manner normally reserved for at best an old acquaintance and at worst your granny. Passion was a non-starter and we became ships that passed in the night. When I returned to work, taking on the Parenting Role, he lost any interest in my work entirely. He cared for his son, yes. He loved being a parent, yes – but he did not have a great interest in nipple-creams and playgroups. And I know, you see, that it's partly my fault – that I allowed him to lose interest in me. I was just too tired to make that effort to find out what passed for intelligent conversation in those days. I was too tired to make the first move in the bedroom so a quick hug and a peaceful night's sleep were fine by me. Oh, yes, it suited me and my expanding body down to the very ground I left cracks in as I walked along. I should have challenged him then. I should have reminded him I was a woman. I was his wife, his partner, his lover, his friend – not just this creature who survived on McVitie's Digestives and who he had witnessed push a 7lb baby out of her delicate lady area.

But I couldn't challenge myself then. I would try, intermittently, to do so. I would buy loads of fruit to replace the biscuits. I would buy an occasional pair of jeans or nice hair-clips and I would cook a meal and make the pair of us sit down together to enjoy that old familiar feeling of just being a couple.

But all it would take would be for Jack to wake or for the phone to ring and the spell would be broken and we would both, with a certain sense of relief, go about doing our own things. I would head to bed to grab a few hours' sleep and he would sit up – working on rotas, playing the computer, anything that would mean he didn't have to have a conversation with me.

Sleeping suited me just fine too, because I didn't have to have a conversation with myself or challenge myself on my general pathetic-ness of late.

So who really is to blame here? And who will it benefit to hear this? So I do what I've been doing for the last two days and bury the negative down.

This is the New Me, remember? The one who stays positive.

"No, Aidan, you didn't do anything wrong," I say and sip my wine.

# 12

I went on my first diet when I was eleven years old. I remember the day well because it was the last day I had sugar in my tea.

Until then I had a cup of milky sugary tea every morning. Mammy would make tea for breakfast and serve it with two sugars and a healthy dollop of milk. Along with my sweet, milky tea I would have two slices of toast with real butter – none of your fancy margarine nonsense for us. The toast would always be piping hot in the way it can be only after being grilled – not cooked in one of your Fancy-Dan toasters. The butter be melting slowly over it and it would taste delicious. Forget chocolate and cake – toast with real butter and sweet tea were the ultimate in comfort foods.

At eleven years old, tall for my age at about 5'2", and heavier than your average eleven-year-old (I was, I seem to remember, seven stone and I thought this was ginormous!), I decided it was time to take some drastic measures. I'll never forget the look on Mammy's face that morning when I told her I didn't take sugar any more, that I was 'sweet enough'. Equally I can remember the look on my own when I tasted my bland, vile tea devoid of sweetness. I have never really enjoyed a cup of tea the same way since.

I can't remember now if I managed to lose weight back then, but I know it was only the start of a lifetime of trying, and trying, to lose weight and then to keep it off. I seemed to find a dress size to match my age, being a frumpy Size 16 at the age of sixteen and skating perilously close to an 18 by the time my adult years came into view. By this stage I was long established as Grazing Grace. I didn't even attempt to engage in any of the conversations about fashion and make-up with my classmates – there was no point. They shopped in Top Shop, I ferreted around the Plus-size section of Dorothy Perkins buying what fitted as opposed to what looked good.

Of course, I had varying degrees of success from time to time. I did look stunning on my wedding day. I had shunned proper food for measly salads and meal replacement drinks and on several occasions when I had overindulged, I'm ashamed to admit this, I put my fingers down my throat to get rid of the evidence.

I did look amazing. I still look at the pictures now, all that antique lace, that fishtail sweeping around my feet, the subtly plunging neckline and I feel as if I'm looking at a different person. She, Mrs Adams, is the person I want to be. She looks so damn happy and just a little bit smug and I want to be her. Of course, it wasn't perfect in that dress. When they brought our meals out, I dared not eat much in case the seams went!

Once the wedding was over and we were sailing around the

Caribbean on honeymoon, I let myself go a little. I ate, drank, was merry and gained half a stone. From then on I battled to keep control of my weight until, falling pregnant with Jack, I found the perfect excuse to eat as much as I could fit in my big fat mouth. By the time he was born I had gained three stone, and by the time he was three months old, and I should have been back in my pre-pregnancy jeans, I was still two and half stone up on my previous weight.

When I looked in the mirror I no longer saw Mrs Adams Smug Married – I saw Grazing Grace stare back at me. I saw puffy cheeks, a double chin, bingo wings, spare tyres enough to open my own branch of QuikFit and eyes that were just resigned to never being noticed for the right reasons again. I looked as tired and fed up as I truly felt in the very pit of my stomach.

And now there is another feeling in the pit of my stomach – raw, fluttering, boke-making nerves. I am standing outside Weightloss Wonders and Liam our photographer is with me. Daisy is running a little late, so it is the two of us, each not sure what to say to the other. He's not sure if there is anything he can say in this instance not to make me feel like a big fat blob and I'm not sure I can say anything without bursting into tears.

I know in a moment Charlotte will arrive and I will have to don my best professional journalist face as I talk to her about how I'm going to change my life. I'm going to stand on the scales and Liam is going to take a picture (without looking at the result!) and my humiliation will be done and dusted for another day. The thing is, though, that I feel sick to the pit of my stomach. I have barely eaten a bite all day as if hoping my good intentions would be enough to shift an excess couple of stone off my body before stepping on the scales.

I'm wearing light cotton trousers and a T-shirt. I have flip-flops on, and I have even declined to wear an underwired bra just in case it adds to my weight. I am more hungry than I have ever been in my life, my treat-size Mars Bar going untouched in my lunch box today.

When Daisy phoned to say she would be late I'm sure I grunted something indecipherable down the phone to her in return. Seems one of her charge's parents was running late and she couldn't exactly leave little Katie to wait outside Little Tikes on her own, now could she? In my pre-weigh-in rage and panic I thought Daisy was being entirely unreasonable to put the needs of a four-year-old above those of her oldest, dearest, fattest pal.

Now my panic has switched to the silent variety, whereby I am in danger of chewing my nails, complete with fingers and most of my hands, off with nerves and I have broken out in a rather unattractive sweat – which is doing absolutely nothing for the make-up I have caked on for my photo shoot. I seriously contemplate getting up and walking out, but then I would be falling at the first hurdle – letting Lollipop Louise, who had never needed to diet in her whole entire life, get one over on me. Oh no, I must be strong – I'm in this for the long haul.

The door opens and I know Charlotte has arrived. I have heard much about Charlotte in recent years. I have even interviewed her over the phone in my Health and Beauty Editor days but I have never met her. She has a certain celebrity status in Derry. She is the woman who will help you lose weight, who will stick with you through thick and thin (literally) and who knows everything there could ever be to know about dropping dress sizes.

I've often wondered what she looked like – imagining some Derry version of mad Lizzie from *TV-am* (showing my age there!) but instead I'm intrigued when I see a young, fairly normal woman in front of me. Yes, she is thin, but she isn't gaunt. She looks, dare I say it, healthy and she doesn't – much to my shock – look me up and down in a way which makes me think I am akin to something she has dragged in on the bottom of her shoe.

"You must be Grace," she trills, shaking my hand firmly. "Louise has told me all about you. Are you ready to change your life?"

In the words of Lofty, the blue digger thing in *Bob the Builder*, I reply: "Yeah, I think so."

"C'mon then," she says. "Let's get you weighed and this picture thingy done before the rest of the class arrive. We don't want to alert them to your secret mission, do we?"

"I guess not," I mutter, mentally visualising myself as Undercover Elephant – ready to set out on a new mission to find the leaner, slimmer, happier Mrs Adams – last seen circa 2001.

Liam follows and starts working out lighting and focus and other such things. Charlotte takes her scales out, writes down my personal details on a little purple form, then asks me to stand on the scales and assess the damage.

I think about this for a moment. I can't remember the last time I weighed myself. I've been in denial about my size for so long it's really not worth depressing myself by forcing bad news on me. I guess, given the comfort of my waistbands, the extra room I now feel in my tops, that I'm going to come in about the 14 stone mark. Taking a deep breath, I step on, my nerves jangling, as Liam snaps contentedly from the corner. I can't look down. I cannot bear to see those numbers glaring up at me, so I step off the scales again and take my seat beside Charlotte.

"Well done for making the first move," she says, congratulating me on getting (or did she say fitting?) through the door to tonight's meeting. "Right," she says, "here is the deal. You weigh 15 stone and 5 lbs."

"What the fuck?" The words jump out of my mouth as quickly as I can think them and my hand flies up to my mouth as if in some desperate attempt to push them back in.

"Don't get annoyed, Grace. That is that last time you see that number again. It's downwards from here on in. I promise."

At that stage, my face crimson, I sense Liam is still snapping away and I want the ground to open up and swallow me whole – only I'm willing to bet even the ground would get full up before I was properly consumed.

"Do you want to set a goal?" she asks.

I think about what I would like. I remember being 11 stone just before the wedding and feeling fabulous, so I tell her to put that down on my card – ignoring the fact that I would need to lose four stone and five pounds to reach that goal (61lbs if you want to think of it that way – 122 packets of sausages).

The doors start to open and one by one the Weightloss Wonders traipse in for class. Some are so skinny it's hard to understand what they are doing here and others are clearly in the same boat as myself. I leave Charlotte behind and find myself an inconspicuous seat at the back of the class.

Daisy bounds in just as the last people are taking their turns on the scales. She steps on, blushes profusely in the manner which I also did, and sits down beside me with a face like thunder.

"Eight fecking stone and four fecking pounds!" she says. "I can't believe I've let myself get so bloody fat! No more soda farls for me, not a one. Nope!"

I try to smile and look encouraging but the fact is her starting weight is less than my goal and secretly I want to slap her silly. Thankfully Charlotte starts speaking then and my violent urges are swept away in a sea of nutritional advice and hints on exercise.

I leave, feeling marginally okay about what the scales have told me. As Charlotte has said, this can be the last time I see those frightening figures jump out at me. Next week the number will be lower, and the week after it will be lower again. All I have to do is survive a week without cheese, chocolate, alcohol or Caramel Rockies. Can it really be that hard?

"Right, my lovely! This time next week you will be a right skinny minny!" says Daisy. "Are you for taking the kids out on Saturday?"

"Hang on a minute, missy," I say. "Aren't you going to do this Movement and Mood thingummy with me that Dr Dishy recommended?"

"Shit, I forgot about that. Do you think he will actually be there himself?"

"Not sure," I say, "but there is only one way to find out."

"Right, you're on. Friday night, is it? Mammy doesn't mind taking care of the two little ones, does she?"

"Are you kidding? She loves it! She is already talking about putting a tent up in the kitchen and having an indoor picnic."

"Forget the class. I wanna do the picnic!" Daisy laughs,

before kissing me on the cheek and running off. "Call you tomorrow, Gracie Pops!" she shouts back and like a whirlwind she is gone.

I get in my car and start the engine – suddenly ravenous but not sure what exactly I can eat. Usually if I wait until after seven for my dinner I'll stop at the chipper on the way home for a sausage supper, but I know that is so out-of-the-window now. So I stop in at Tesco, pick up a bag of salad and some lean chicken breasts and make my way home, excited about the new skinny me.

"I'll show you, Mrs Adams!" I say, cranking the radio up and singing along to Barry White crooning about his lady being his first, his last and his everything. I'm already imagining the new, slim, sexy me walking into Jackson's one evening and Aidan grabbing the mike from behind the bar and serenading me with that very song as I shimmy and shake my way towards him à la Olivia Newton John in *Grease*.

I'm just sitting down to my new healthy tea when Aidan walks into the room, fresh from his shower and ready for work.

He says, "You look surprisingly chipper for a woman who has just shared her weight with someone else. Are you sure you are my wife? Are you sure you're not a robot or an alien replacement?"

"Very bloody funny!" I laugh, adding, "I suppose you have eaten?"

Aidan looks at what I have prepared and turns his nose up in disgust. "Me man," he says in a fake caveman voice. "Me eat meat. Big steaks. Not rabbit food. Me no like rabbit food."

"You'll be lucky," I reply. "There will be none of your fancy steak and chips here for a while."

"I think I may just eat at work more then," he says, kissing me on the nose and heading out the door.

The night is so calm that I decide to eat my dinner outside, balancing my plate on my knees as I stare over the concrete yard into the sunset. It feels strange not to reach for a glass of wine, or to contemplate a sticky dessert for afters but I'm feeling calm about this now. When I'm finished eating – and when the sun has set and it has started to get cold outside – I walk into our living room and stare at the picture of me on our wedding day and promise that I will be that happy again.

Arriving for work the following morning, I'm amazed I'm still feeling positive about things. The rush to get ready was as manic as always, with Jack demanding peas for breakfast and me getting myself in a whole bloody panic while trying to find a clean blouse to wear. I'm sure my hair would be looking better if I had the chance to wash it before getting out this morning but I didn't want to be late for work – not when this was set to be my busiest-ever month.

I switch on my computer, smile at Dermot, and take a swig from my water bottle – which reminds me it is time to take my happy pills. I've realised now I have to balance the intake of my happy pills quite delicately. Yes, they make me feel sick, and if I take them close to bedtime they seem to wake me up to a point where I find myself counting the Artex swirls at four in the morning. Taking them during the day gives me a certain edge and, yes, while a good vomit is never too far away, I'm also better able to concentrate on the job in hand.

"How did it go last night?" Sinéad asks, wandering into the office and slinging her trademark box of doughnuts down on my desk. I eye up the box of treats and try to stay strong. I have a banana with me for my mid-morning snack. I'm pretty sure if I think hard enough and visualise Mrs Adams in her finery long enough, the banana will start to appeal to me almost as much as the doughnuts.

"Fine," I say to Sinéad, "just fine. I'll write a prelim report on it and fire it through on email before lunch."

"Delighted to hear you sounding so upbeat, Grace. Nice that you have a bit of fire about you. Come and see me later and we will discuss how everything else will pan out." She turns on her heel and walks into her office, a puff of cigarette smoke escaping just before she closes the door.

I sit back and sip more water. Two litres is a lot to get through in a day, especially for a coffee fiend like myself. I wonder if my kidneys and post-baby bladder will take the pressure.

"Hey, Gracie, looking good, pet!" Liam cheers, walking in the door waving his camera at me.

"I want to see those," I counter. "Right now." And I'm out from behind my desk in record speed.

Sensing a commotion from the other end of the office, Louise lifts her head and shouts over: "Ooooh, are they the pictures from last night? I'm just dying to see them!" Quick as a flash she is beside me and following me into Liam's room, known in the office as The Den.

Even though there is no longer a need for dark rooms in our profession, thanks to the arrival of digital photography, Liam still maintains he needs a room of his own. On his poncier days he maintains that he is an artist and artists need time to create their masterpieces. Sinéad and I have a sneaking suspicion that Liam actually just likes time on his own to listen to his country music, look on Ebay and download porn onto his company computer.

It's a strange phenomenon to me that, even though the

dark room was retired from business some three years ago, there is still a distinct smell of developing fluid in the air. On warm days such as these it can be quite cloying.

"Give me a few seconds to get her up and running," Liam says, patting the side of his computer as it was a horse, a pet or his latest wife. He sits back, puts his feet up on the table – not caring to offer either me or the Lollipop a seat.

"Right, here we go," he says and onto the screen pop six images of me – each worse than the one before. In the first I look terrified. In the second I have broken out in a cold sweat. In the third I have that 'what the fuck?' look about me and in the rest I look as if I have just been told all near and dear to me have just been wiped out in a freak shark attack.

I stare at them – at the person I have become and my heart sinks. Surely a year's worth of eating bananas and not doughnuts cannot undo this damage?

"Perfect," Louise says, clapping her hands with glee. "You always need the before pictures to look really crap so that the afters look better."

She turns on her heel and I stand in a state of stunned silence.

"Don't fret, petal," Liam says, sensing my unease. "Photoshop is a wonderful tool."

"Don't touch them," I say. "Leave them as they are. In fact, could you email copies over to me too?"

He nods, looking a little confused by my instructions, and I turn and walk back to my desk and wait for the wee email icon on my desk to flash, letting me know the pictures are there for me to see, to keep and to do with what I will. It does, and I look at them. Each one screams 'Grazing Grace!'

at me. Each one reminds me of the bullies, of the pain, of the sense of low self-worth that has enveloped me over the last few years. Each one reminds me I'm a failure.

So I save them to my screen and then, when that is done, I set the worst one – the one where I look as though I might actually throw up – as my desk top. I'm not going to look at Dermot any more. I'm going to look at my big, stupid, gormless face looking back at me until I can face myself in the mirror again.

I'm going to be strong. I'm going to be amazing. I'm not going to look at Dermot again until I would be happy to look at him square in the face in real life. I reach my hand to my locket and remind myself that someone believes in me and then I set about eating my banana – just to see what happens.

It's eleven thirty when the phone rings.

"I'm fecking starving!" a familiar voice squeals down the line at me. "I swear I'm hallucinating from lack of caramel and biscuity goodness!"

"You're not hallucinating, Dais," I laugh. "Come on, you can't be cracking on the first day. I mean, I'm used to eating fifteen times as much as you and I'm not giving in yet, so you can't either."

"I know," she whines. "I'm just *sooooo* hungry!"

"Well, if you had seen the pictures I've seen this morning you would not be contemplating feeling hungry again any time in the next two and a half thousand years," I say.

"They couldn't have been that bad," she soothes.

I ask if she is online and send the pictures to her through the magic of email. I'm waiting for the gasp of shock when she opens them, but she stays remarkably calm.

"Not your most flattering angle, I agree," she says. "Okay,

I promise never to phone you again and talk of caramel and biscuit combinations until we are real sexy ladies."

"Thanks, babe," I say, and hang up – realising the damage is done, and I am now indeed hungry myself.

Thankfully, at just that moment Sinéad calls me into her office to discuss how the feature is going to progress.

To many people Sinéad is quite a scary lady – but not to me. I have known her much too long now to be scared of her, and besides I've seen her drunk. I even helped carry her home on her hen night. I'm pretty sure if Sinéad was not my boss, and not tasked with kicking my arse from time to time, we could actually be really good friends.

The thing with Sinéad is that you have to know how to deal with her. You have to know that come the end of the month she tends to go off her head a little while deadline approaches. I have also figured out that sometime around the middle of the month there is a similar tendency to lose control which is tied in with her monthly cycle. (It's bizarre that I know that, but you tend to work these things out in a office.) Sinéad does not suffer fools, or excuses gladly. She is as straight as they come. She will tell you when she likes your work, but by the same token if you are not quite up to scratch she will come down on you like a ton of bricks.

To some of my colleagues, Sinéad is a bitch. To me, she is a woman working damned hard to get ahead in her profession and, for the most part, I'm happy to take her arse-kickings because I know I will only ever get one if I deserve it.

My biggest debt to her, however, was that she took a risk with me. I was young, just out of college and rather inexperienced, when she took me on board as junior features writer. She pushed me damn hard and within two years I was

Health and Beauty Editor and Sinéad and I were sharing Cosmopolitans once a month at the post-deadline party. Every now and again, when I had a drink in me, I would get all mushy and attempt to tell her how grateful I was for her giving me a chance but she would always cut me off at the pass. "Save your bullshit for the next edition!" she would roar and the conversation would revert to what it was before. It was kind of hard to take, because I wanted to be her friend. I had so few in my life – but the boundary was forever drawn as worker and employee.

"Right, young lady," she said as I sit down on the sofa. "Let's talk about this without the bimbo interfering with her suggestions on Botox and face-lifts."

"She thinks I need Botox and a face-lift?" I ask, taken aback.

"She thinks everyone over the age of twenty-six needs Botox and a face-lift," Sinéad says, taking a slug from her can of Diet Coke. "Seriously, Grace, she might have her finger on the pulse of what the young people are up to these days but she hasn't a notion about writing or putting together a good features list."

I'm almost tempted to ask why, in that case, Sinéad hasn't sacked her yet – but I don't because I don't want to become the office bitch. I spent too much time on the other side of the fence to get caught going down that road. Before I can start though, she is off on a roll.

"Obviously you can't be expected to change everything about your life in the space of one month," she says, "so we have to plan this carefully. What have you got for me?"

I sit back, absorbing the notion that my life – this pickle, for want of a better word, that I have got myself into – is no more to Sinéad than a feature for a magazine.

"The advertising guys are getting really excited," she butts into my thoughts. "They are booking support ads here, there and everywhere."

Please God, do not have them phoning my mother-in-law for a support ad! She would be convinced I had brought shame on her family.

"What kind of support ads?" I ask gingerly.

"Well, obviously Natural Nails, City Couture and Weightloss Wonders are on board. All the trendy-lefty health food shops and therapy centres are jumping on the bandwagon too."

"You don't expect me to try them all?" I ask, suddenly seeing the next month of my life swept away in a wave of energy-healing sessions, yogic flying and colonic irrigation.

"Nope, Grace. I know you by now. I'll trust you to do this properly. I just want to know *what* exactly you intend to do properly."

So I reel off my plans. "First of all there are the shameful pictures from Weightloss Wonders and my ongoing food and mood diary (e.g. ate chocolate, felt good, ate lettuce felt strangely uninspired). The Movement and Mood workshop on Friday should provide a fair insight into the loony-lefty alternative-therapy movement and, along with my image overhaul at City Couture and our ongoing comments from Dr Dishy, sorry, Dr Shaun Stevenson, we should be aiming high for an eight-page spread."

"Sounds amazing, Grace," Sinéad says, lighting a cigarette and inhaling deeply. "Sales should be up with this one. Everyone likes to read of the underdog triumphing."

Oh great – so now I'm not only a (guinea) pig, I'm a dog

(worse still, an under one).

She sits forward, adopting her concerned face, and adds: "You do know, Grace, fabulous sales figures aside, this is about you feeling better about yourself. If there is anything we can do, please let us know. We do have a duty of care to you after all."

It's nice that Sinéad has said that – nice that she cares, but I know her well enough to know she is now in a trance thinking about her end-of-year bonus and the accolades such a feature could win for her.

"I will, Sinéad," I say.

"Do you want to talk about it?" she asks and I know she is saying the words because she thinks she has to. Her heavy make-up and Fancy-Dan power suit cannot hide the fact that she is terrified I will actually start to spill details of my personal life out, here in this little office.

Sinéad and I can have the best of craic. We can talk about music, movies, TV and fashion until the cows come home but we don't do personal. The closest we ever came to it was during my pregnancy when she talked about her own experiences as a mother. Then she showed emotion, and by emotion I mean genuine affection and excitement – the kind normally reserved for the day the magazine hits the stands and the sales figures come in.

"I'm fine," I say, smiling. "I'm sure you'll get to read all about it anyway." I walk out of her office and realise she will probably not actually get to read about it, because I still haven't quite figured out what 'it' is. Perhaps all it takes is for me to lose some weight to be happy, but I have this nagging feeling that it might take a little more than that.

At the moment though, losing weight is my best shot so I

look at the clock and try to get excited about the fact that in approximately ninety-three minutes' time I can have a jacket potato with tuna for lunch.

# 13

I'm not sure what to expect of the Mood and Movement class. Dr Dishy sent me an email telling me to wear loose and comfortable clothing and to bring a water bottle in case I got thirsty.

He explained this was the first workshop of its kind but it was designed to help you feel more comfortable in your body. Initially I took that to mean it would involve weird tree-hugging-type movements and primal growls and would make me feel anything but comfortable, but as I had already booked the event into Liam's busy schedule I could hardly back out now.

Daisy is very excited about the whole thing. I've tried to explain to her that I don't actually think Dr Dishy will be there but she has gone and spent a mini-fortune in Pineapple transforming herself into the kind of dancing queen only seen before now in *Fame* and Geri Halliwell videos. She even spent

£10 on a designer water-bottle, while I'm settling for a 60p bottle of Ballygowan from the corner shop. I have found my least tatty tracksuit bottoms though and a semi-fitted T-shirt which I think already looks better on me than the last time I wore it. I'm starting to wonder if this Weightloss lark could actually be working.

The workshop is taking place in a musty room at the top of an old refurbished building. The windows seem to be fastened shut and the sun is glaring directly through them. Already I'm wondering what exactly I've let myself in for. Eight other people are there – ranging in age from nineteen (automatically Daisy is giving her the Evil Eye and wondering if she knows Dishy too) to eighty. They all look equally nervous, apart from a man in his mid-sixties who, rather worryingly, is wearing a pair of cycle shorts which leave little to the imagination.

He looks as if he might enjoy this, a little too much if possible. Liam is standing at the back of the room – hugging his camera to him as if it is some kind of magic protective armour with a sly grin on his face. I know he is thinking these pictures are going to knock the socks off those he took on Tuesday night. Knowing Liam, and his somewhat warped sense of humour, he is probably planning a 'Grace Adams Wall of Shame' montage to be unveiled at the Christmas do. Funnily enough, after having spent the best part of three days staring at the bloated images of myself, I've become quite used to them. Obviously I miss the pang of lust I used to get when Dermot stared back at me from the computer screen but the new images are the best deterrent in the world when the sweetie machine comes a-calling at four o'clock.

Daisy is doing a weird jumping-from-foot-to-foot thing

which means she is either limbering up for the class or desperate for a pee. I'm not sure which.

"You okay?" I whisper, and immediately wonder why I'm whispering when the class hasn't even begun yet.

"Yes," she replies, craning her neck to the side as the door opens.

I know she is hoping it's himself, but sadly it is a man and woman dressed in weird flowing tops. The man is carrying a stereo and the woman is carrying a bundle of yoga mats and I suddenly start to feel very afraid.

Sensing my unease, Daisy reaches her hand to mine. "We are in this together, hon," she says and gives a tight squeeze. I'm not comfortable moving my body. I would love to be. I would love to be as free as I was when I was a teenager and dancing around my bedroom, but in the absence of a bucket-load of vodka to calm my nerves I sense this could be more rewarding than beneficial.

The man speaks, first of all raising his hands to the sky as if to summon the spirit of some long-forgotten god. "Hushhhh," he says. "Welcome to Movement and Mood. Today we will seek to find your internal energy and channel it with the vibrations and energy of music."

I look at Daisy who I can see is trying to suppress a giggle and I force myself to look away before I join her.

The woman now speaks. "I am Mary and this is Samuel. Channelling into our inner energy has helped us become stronger people, physically and emotionally. It has helped us to learn to slow down and appreciate the world more. It has taught us about the beauty in little things. It has made us better people, better parents, better friends and better lovers."

Daisy snorts and I cough quickly to hide her giggles. I know she has the same image in her head that I do, and that is of Mary and Samuel lifting their flowery kaftans and bumping uglies to the tune of 'I'm Horny, Horny, Horny, Horny!'.

"Now, if we can all find a mat we can get started," Samuel says before noticing Liam standing at the back of the room.

The same look of merriment is dancing across Liam's face.

"Sir, are you not joining in?" Samuel asks, laying an extra mat on the floor and beckoning Liam forward.

Not one for mincing his words, Liam replies curtly: "Are you on the glue?" and snaps a few quick images of me lying on the floor before whispering "Good luck!" and running out the door.

"Right," Mary says, clasping her hands together in the manner of a primary-school teacher. "It's time for the warm up. I want to let yourselves go. Lie down, close your eyes and imagine you are walking through the garden of your soul."

I must, I tell myself, concentrate and get into the spirit of this. So I lie back and close my eyes. Some suitably plinky-plonky music plays in the background while Mary leads us on a meditation where we walk down a garden path to find the bench in our soul where we will reside for the rest of the class. I realise this is quite relaxing and I'm coping without bursting into giggles, even though I'm pretty sure I can hear someone snoring at the other end of the room.

"Now," Samuel says as the plinky-plonky music fades to one solitary pan pipe, "stay lying down, bring your knees upwards and raise your hands to the sky as if to invite healing energy into your body. Listen to these words. Feel their healing power. Sit on your bench and relax. Let the light flow into you!"

The music changes and Louis Armstrong starts to sing about it being a wonderful world. I'm coping now, but only just and when Samuel starts to sing along, loudly and badly, changing all the 'I's' to 'you's' ("You think to yourself, what a wonderful world") I start to shake with laughter and feel actual physical pain trying to hold it in. Please God, let this song end soon, I pray, keeping my eyes tightly shut because I know if I open them I will look at Daisy and she will look at me and we will both we goners.

"It's okay to find this emotional," Mary says. "In this busy world it is all too easy to forget it really can be a wonderful world."

I hear Daisy's telltale squeak of mirth and have to bite my lip to stop myself from joining her and cross my legs to protect my weak pelvic floor.

Thankfully it's a relatively short song and I'm able to regain my composure when asked to sit up. I look around and notice Mr Cycling Shorts is wiping a tear from eye, muttering that was "powerful stuff".

"Okay, everybody, stand up!" Samuel yells. "Are we going to have some fun?" A half-hearted yes comes back from three of the ten participants. The rest of us look at our feet. "C'mon, people, do you want to get better? Do you want to connect with the real you?"

Again I am tempted to answer, à la Lofty from *Bob the Builder*, "Yeah, I think so!" in a squeaky voice, but I mutter a quick yes while still looking at my feet.

Mr Cycling Shorts is shouting "Yes!" at the top of his voice and I'm starting to wonder if he is a plant.

"Let's go, people!" says Mary, changing CDs and once

again adopting her primary-school-teacher pose. "Do you remember when you were a child? When you were innocent and carefree? Do you remember the simple pleasures in life? How happiness was measured by how many daisy-chains you made or how many ice creams you ate?" Samuel interjects at this stage and I wonder if they have actually scripted the whole session. "To get in touch with the 'you' you are now, you must get in touch with your inner child. So please join in, let your inhibitions go, and enjoy!"

I admit I'm feeling nervous. The eighty-year-old in our company looks slightly on the verge of cardiac arrest and Daisy is swigging from her designer water-bottle as if it contained vodka.

The music starts and I can barely believe my ears. Anyone for a rousing rendition of 'If You're Happy and You Know It'? Mr Cycling Shorts is clapping, stamping his feet and shouting "We are!" like a good 'un and when I look at Daisy I see she is joining in too. "If you can't beat 'em, join 'em," she whispers and I try to leave my self-consciousness behind. I'm starting to dread what their next trick will be.

"Well done!" Samuel cheers afterwards. "Do you feel your mood improve?" This time four people reply yes and I have to admit I've not laughed so much in years.

Samuel believes we may now be fully warmed up and so he announces it is time to find the song within our soul. I do not have a song within my soul. Perhaps there is the odd verse of 'Little Peter Rabbit' or the theme tune to *Balamory* in there but I doubt there is actually a song.

We are asked to lie down on our mats, and I do so with that certain sense of trepidation rising again. We are told to breathe in, raising our hands above our heads – looking for all intents and purposes like synchronised swimmers without the water to hold us up – and Samuel instructs us to tune in to our inner beat. I'm not entirely sure how to do that, but in the distance I'm vaguely aware of Mr Cycling Shorts doing his best Patrick Swayze in *Dirty Dancing* impression and saying, "Guh-gunk, guh-gunk!" over and over again. I look over and Daisy is lying, eyes closed, and I wonder has she actually gone to sleep.

"Now," Mary says, "I want you to find a note you are comfortable with. It doesn't have to be in tune, it just has to be a noise. And I want you make that noise as loudly as you can."

I'm not sure I have ever thought about being comfortable with a noise before. Generally I talk and sometimes I warble. When I was in labour I know I made a sound akin to a cow mooing, but without my cervix dilating at an excruciatingly slow rate I doubt very much it is something I can easily repeat. From the general quietness around me, I sense everyone else – apart from Mr Cycling Shorts who is humming – is having the same difficulties.

"I'm sensing you might need some help with this exercise," Samuel says, and so he and Mary stand together and start to sing random notes – encouraging us to copy them and to join in wherever we can.

I manage not to laugh, until that is, they bring the triangle out and start banging on it like it is some primitive drum finding the beating of our collective consciousnesses (or something). And then I'm lost, and Daisy is too and we laugh so hard and garner so many dirty looks from Samuel, Mary and Mr Cycling Shorts that we can do nothing but laugh all the harder.

Sitting in Jackson's afterwards, looking very out of place in our sportswear, I turn to Daisy – having just composed myself – and say: "Do you think Dr Dishy will be really pissed off with us that we got thrown out of that class?"

She snorts and raises an illicit bottle of Bacardi Breezer to her lips, all thoughts of Weightloss Wonders out the window for tonight. "Gracie, if he is the type of person who would have expected us to keep a straight face throughout that travesty then I don't think I like him any more!"

I laugh, feeling brighter in myself tonight than I have done in such a long time. I'm comfortable in my own skin, sitting here without full war-paint on, in my tracksuit bottoms, while Aidan keeps us supplied with a steady stream of drinks and my friend, my mad friend in her Pineapple get-up, is talking about having an interest in a man.

Much as I wouldn't mind Dishy for myself I have to concede I'm an old married lady and perhaps my friend would be in with a much better shot.

Daisy always looks happy, but I know there is a sadness in her, a loneliness that due to my lack of a penis or manly arms I can't fill. I know she looks at myself and Aidan and is sometimes jealous. Of course I do my bit to inform her of his bad points, frequently, but I know that at times – on a Saturday night when she is alone and Lily is in bed – she would just love someone to cuddle up with. And Lord knows she deserves someone to look after her – someone who will heal her pain – who will make her feel cherished. Someone who will give her a damn good seeing-to on a regular basis.

TMF had wanted to be that man, thus explaining our falling-out because I had been taken in by him and even tried to persuade Daisy to let him back in her life. If I hadn't found out shortly afterwards that he had fed me a pile of lies, including a false name – and if he hadn't then walked away from his two girls when life got a little tough again, I would have thought him quite the catch.

In fact, my telling Daisy, prior to finding out that he was indeed The Mighty Feckwit both by name and by nature, that I thought everyone deserved a second chance was the cause of our almighty ruck, She didn't trust men after that, and I knew it would take someone really special to break down her barriers.

I wonder if Dishy could be that man and suddenly I'm having a little fantasy of setting the pair of them up. I smile to myself but then I realise my dabbling will most likely not be welcome after last time. Sipping my cold drink, I vow to keep my promise to stay out of Daisy Cassidy's love life forever.

Besides, I have much bigger fish to fry at the moment. "How the hell am I going to explain this one to Sinéad?" I groan. "She is expecting at least two pages on Movement and Mood."

"Surely Sinéad appreciates honesty more than most, Grace. Tell her you had to leave early to protect your continence *and* your sanity. She's a mother – she'll get what you are talking about."

I nod sagely, with the wisdom that a couple of illegal drinks can offer, and then head off to the toilets. All this talk of weak bladders has made mine wake up and call for attention.

I stumble to the toilets, pushing my way past the glamorous skinny girls in their micro-minis, with their highlighted blonde hair and their Wonderbras and I grin to myself. They are here on the pull, I think, and then there is me, here with the new manager behind the bar pouring me drink after drink and buying me lockets and making love to me on an

159

occasional basis and look at the state of me. I look like shite. I look dreadful, overweight, sweaty, with non-designer trainers on. But I have one up on them. I sit on the toilet, my head nodding in time with the music and I feel deliciously drunk. I will not let them make me feel bad, not tonight. I am better than them. I have found the song in my soul. I have found the movement to match my mood. I'm almost tempted to dance, to climb up on that bar and shake my groove thang, but thankfully sense stops me.

I stumble back to Daisy, who by now is looking the worse for wear, so we say goodbye to Aidan. For just a split second I think I see a look of relief wash over his face, but I'm too drunk to care. We make our way outside, grab a taxi and head back to mine where we make half a loaf of toast before saying our goodnights.

I'm aware of Aidan coming in during the night and, while the room is spinning, I'm aware he doesn't slip his arm around me. The old me would be paranoid – the new me refuses to think about it, so I go to sleep – if for no other purpose than to stop the room spinning around me. In the words of the lovely Scarlett O'Hara, tomorrow is another day.

# 14

The room is still spinning as I wake up and I try to make it stop. I bury my head under the pillow and even though my eyes are now closed I'm pretty sure I've just seen my wardrobe sail by as if on some weird subconscious roundabout. My mouth is dry and my tongue feels distinctly furry. My stomach can't decide if it wants to throw up or be fed and I lie for a few minutes trying to regain my composure.

Food, I decide, is the answer. So I put on my slippers, pull my hair back in a hair-band and make for downstairs and the comfort of my cupboard. As I walk past Daisy's room I hear a vague moaning and I realise her room is swimming too.

"Get up, lazy-bones!" I shout. "I'm going to make some breakfast!"

I make my way downstairs and find Aidan sitting in front of the TV with a face on him like he has been chewing a wasp.

"You okay?" I ask, as I pour myself a large glass of cooling apple juice.

"Fine," he replies curtly and I'm not quite sure what is going on.

I start to fish through the fruit and veg in the fridge for something distinctly un-Weightloss-Wonders-ey – something that will require tomato sauce, real butter and which will ease my hangover. Spotting some bacon, I decide sarnies are in order, so I call in to Aidan – hoping the temptation of a bacon bap will rouse him from his sour mood.

"I'm going to make these baps for me and Dais!" I call. "You want some?"

"No," he replies, equally as curtly and Daisy throws me a confused look as she walks into the kitchen.

"What's up with your little ray of sunshine this morning?" she whispers, tipping the orange-juice carton to her head and heading straight for my medicine cabinet for two paracetamol.

"Dunno," I say. "I suppose he must have had a bad night last night."

But I'm having flashbacks. That little look he gave me as Daisy and I stumbled giggling out of Jackson's, the fact that he didn't put his arm around me when he came to bed – the fact that he is being, to coin his own phrase, an unbearable feckwit now. And I start to feel a little uneasy.

"Are you going to hurl?" Daisy asks, seeing my whiter-than-white pallor.

"Not sure," I reply. "Would you mind sticking that bacon on? I'm going to find out exactly what's wrong with Himself."

"No probs, boss lady," she replies, saluting me and switching the hob on.

I walk into the living-room, closing the door behind me and sit down on the footstool which is lying directly opposite to

King Grumpy Drawers.

"What's the matter, Aidan? Don't try to tell me there isn't anything wrong because A) you have just turned down a bacon bap and B) you look like someone has just asked you to donate your testicles to medical science in return for a can of Tesco Value Cola."

He looks at me, shakes his head in what I can only read as disgust and turns the TV up a bit.

"Aidan," I repeat, "what? Did I do something wrong? Did I forget to pay you for a drink? Or did I snore all night or something? Because I'm baffled here, Aidan, really I am."

"You're *pathetic*!" he snarls, looking at me like I'm worthless and I'm left almost breathless by his words.

I'm trying to defend myself but I don't know how I can because I honestly don't know what I've done to defend myself for. I look at him, stunned into silence, my face awash with confusion and he looks back at me, sighs and looks resigned.

"You say you want to change, Grace. You say you are going to change and I put my faith in you, but you can't last four days."

Is this because I had a drink? Is this because I broke the Weightloss Wonders rules? Is this what merits this outburst? This proclamation that I am pathetic?

"Because I had a drink?" I mutter, shocked.

"You had seven, Grace, and then you came home and ate nearly every slice of bread in the house and now you are making bacon baps and you don't seem to care about your promise to lose weight and get better."

"I never promised to lose weight," I say, tears springing in my eyes because Aidan has never commented on my weight before. From a Size 12 to a Size 20 he has maintained he is happy with me and yet now he is disappointed, bitterly disappointed, that I've had a couple of drinks with a friend. I realise he must have been ashamed of me last night – watching his fat wife in her fat clothes getting fat on drink and, in those immortal words of Lizzie O'Dowd, 'making a show of herself'. I wipe the tears from my eyes, get up and walk out of the room and suddenly I don't want my bacon bap any more and the good mood I was in evaporates, replaced by feelings of disappointment in myself and in Aidan. He believes in me, but only as long as I don't step out of line. I take the locket off, sit it on the side table and paint on a fake smile.

"This isn't enough," I grin to Daisy. "Get dressed. We are going to Kernan's for breakfast."

"Sounds like a plan, lovely lady," she says and makes her way upstairs to get dressed.

I walk into the bathroom, run the shower and cry a torrent of tears. Scrubbing my fat, useless body, wishing I could wash away the pounds, the shame, the sense of being useless – of being Grazing Grace. But I can't, so I dry myself off, dry my tears and get dressed. Breakfast is waiting.

"Are you sure you're safe to drive?" Daisy asks as she straps on her seatbelt and takes a slug of water from her newly refilled designer water-bottle.

"I'm fine," I say. "Besides, the fresh air might just clear my head."

We set off and drive towards Letterkenny in search of the wee diner with the best breakfasts in the North West bar none.

"You're very quiet," Daisy says.

And I'm a little surprised because it feels like I haven't shut up. It feels like I've been chatting nineteen to the dozen with myself trying to erase the hurt of this morning, trying to rationalise Aidan's cruel words, trying to remind myself just how good and how supportive he has been over the last few weeks.

"Sorry," I say. "I'm still tired, I guess."

"Well, you better snap out of it, missy, because you have some amount of eating to do and then we have to go and pick up the terrible twosome from Mammy's and I don't think your beloved son is going to accept the excuse of you being tired."

She laughs and I start to laugh too, and then, to my eternal embarrassment, I start to  cry – big ugly explosive snottery tears.

"Jesus, Gracie, what the hell is wrong with you?"

I try to answer, but all comes out is a random sequence of squeaks and howls and splutters and all the while I'm trying to drive because I know Daisy wants a sausage bap.

"Pull the car over," Daisy says calmly, and I'm aware I'm shaking my head and muttering about sausages and mushrooms. "*Now,*" she says, less calmly – her voice raised in a mixture of concern and pure unadulterated fear.

I respond, pulling into the lay-by, and I take huge gulping breaths trying to regain my composure.

"Listen to me, Grace," Daisy says, turning my face towards hers. "I want you to imagine yourself sitting on the bench in the garden of your soul. Now, along with me, sing 'If You Are Happy and You Know It' . . ."

Daisy had ushered me into the passenger seat, handed me a box of tissues, phoned Mammy, told her we would be late and driven towards Glenveagh National Park – my ultimate sanctuary.

She didn't say much on the drive, just soothed and hushed and promised it would be okay. "You don't have to talk about it now, doll. Just whenever you are ready."

Occasionally I tried to speak, to explain my hurt, but it wouldn't come out because I felt ashamed – like a big, fat freak. Could my husband really be so shallow as to be annoyed about a couple of slices of toast and a few Bacardi Breezers? I would laugh about it, if I wasn't so angry and hurt. Now we were sitting on a bench in the gardens, overlooking the lough and breathing in the fresh country air – the August sunshine warming us. Daisy had purchased a few sandwiches from the small tea room and we were eating our make-shift picnic, supping Diet Coke and making small talk.

"Do you want to tell me what that was about, Gracie?" Daisy asks, through a mouthful of ham-and-tomato sandwich.

I stare out to the lough, take a deep breath and say, "Aidan is ashamed of me."

"What?" she asks, incredulously. "He has been a wee dream!"

I start to cry again and I'm annoyed at myself for showing my weakness like this – when I'm supposed to be on the road to recovery. "He is annoyed that I drank and ate last night and didn't stick to my diet. He says I'm 'pathetic' and that I don't really want to change. But I do want to change," I say petulantly. "It's just so hard."

"Jesus, Grace," Daisy says, anger building in her voice, "is he serious? You had a drink and he goes off on one? Fecker, how dare he? My God, you have turned yourself inside out over the last two weeks and you have one slip-up, one night off and he makes you feel like this. Bastard!" Daisy's accent always gets stronger when she is angry. She becomes a feisty wee Scottish fighting machine and her face screws up in anger. She looks both terribly frightening and exceptionally cute when she is like this – the cute factor coming from just how much she reminds me of Lily – all bluster and drama.

"He's right though, Daisy," I sigh. "Four days of a determined effort to lose this weight and I'm off the wagon. And you know what? I didn't even think about it. I didn't feel guilty. I enjoyed every second – more than I've enjoyed myself in a long, long time."

"You have to live your life, petal," Daisy soothes, "and that feckwit has to realise that. Do you want me to slap him round the head for you? Or maybe give him a good steever up the arse, because I'll do it – say the words and any act of violence you choose can be enacted on him."

I laugh, even though the tears are still falling, and then I say, almost in a whisper: "If he is disappointed in me, that is nothing compared to how disappointed I am in him. I thought he was behind me on this, Dais, but he's only happy to support me as long as it's all going great guns. I can't live my life waiting for him to point out my faults, waiting for him to upcast at me every time I step out of line. I can't deal with this right now."

"What are you saying, Gracie?" Daisy asks.

I answer, and I can hardly believe I'm saying these words. "I'm saying, I suppose, can I come and live with you for a while?"

"Oh, sweetie! You don't mean that, do you?"

I nod a tearful response.

And then I sob again while Daisy mutters "I'll kill the fecker!" out to the lough.

\* \* \*

*Dear Aidan,*

*I hope you understand why I have to do this. I'm taking Jack and we are going to stay with Daisy for a while. I need to sort my head out. I know you don't believe that I'm trying, but I am – and it is hard work.*

*I can't live in a situation where you are waiting to chastise me for every mistake, because this is a long road and I'm going to make quite a few mistakes before I'm done.*

*I still love you, and I hope you feel the same for me, but I need to sort my head out if we are to come through this.*

*You can see Jack whenever you want.*

*Grace*

*x*

I put one kiss on it. I wanted to let him know that I loved him, but I didn't want him to read the note as some soppy love letter with Xs and Os at the bottom. Mammy and Daddy went round with the note and to pick up our things. Apparently Aidan was furious and swore at them. No one ever swears at Daddy and he was understandably taken aback. I had worried about telling my parents, but they didn't seem shocked. Mammy calmly told me that nothing I did these days would shock them and that they understood I needed to put me first at this time.

"Marriage isn't all plain sailing," Daddy chimed in.

"Sometimes it takes some time apart to realise what you have got."

Yes, well, Aidan Adams would have plenty of time to realise what he had, and what he had thrown away. I'd been with him now for eight years – eight years of playing the dutiful wife, being partner, friend and confidante, trusting him and making sure he never had any reason not to trust me in return.

From that first date, that first kiss, I had been obsessed with him. He was the first thing on my mind in the morning and the last thing I thought of at night. When we finally moved in together – when I could see him first thing in the morning and last thing at night – I was as happy as I had ever been. I forgave him his foibles – his fecklessness at keeping a job, his indecision, even at the age of thirty-two, as to what he wanted his career to be. I forgave that, because I loved him, and when we said our wedding vows and I had promised 'for better or for worse', I meant it. Perhaps therein lies my downfall – with all that in sickness and in health shite I should have added 'in fatness and in skinniness – and forsaking all barbed comments about the size of my arse, Amen'.

Is that what this is about though, me leaving because Aidan thinks I'm fat? (Which, for the record, I am.) No, it is because he lied to me. He promised to support me and he fell at the first hurdle. He promised that he still found me attractive, when he clearly did not. He promised that we could get through this together (I'm mentally hearing the big 'uuuh uuuuh' sounds from *Family Fortunes* here by the way). Wrong on that count too. So I can't trust him now. I can't trust his words, his actions, his loving support because it's all crap.

Lugging my suitcase into Daisy's spare room, I feel despondent. Jack is jumping around excitedly because he thinks he is on his holidays and Lily has a puzzled look on her face because she senses all is not right in her usually trouble-free world. Daisy is still swearing intermittently under her breath and I'm starting to feel dog-tired again.

"Have a lie down, Gracie," Daisy soothes. "I'll take the wains out to the garden to play and you have a rest. You look beat out."

I'm too tired, physically and emotionally, and too hung-over to argue so I sink into the sumptuous king-size bed and fall asleep almost immediately. This time I dream about Dermot again, but he is wearing a tracksuit and taking on Charlotte's role in Weightloss Wonders. "You've gained a stone!" he shouts at me, and the class erupt into giggles. "You needn't think I'm taking you to the BAFTAS looking like *that*, missy!" he says, raising his eyebrow in an almost menacing manner. I'm almost glad when the peeping of my mobile phone wakes me up.

**"I'll be round to see Jack 2morro @ 2"** it reads. No apology, no anger directed at me, just an instruction and I wonder if this is what my marriage is going to become. Sighing, I bury my head under the pillow and try and block it all out.

It hasn't rained in two weeks, so I suppose it had to happen sometime. The air had become sticky and hot – the kind of unbearable humidity where you want to take your skin off, wash it, wring it out, put it in the fridge for an hour to cool down and then put it back on again. Sitting in Daisy's living room, a cup of tea nestled in my hands, my feet curled up under me on the big squashy cream sofa, I watch big, fat raindrops beat against the windowpane and slide down to the sill. I can hear the grandfather clock ticking from the hall and Daisy is slumped on the armchair, her feet over the arms and her hand reaching down for the plate of chocolate biscuits on the floor. Amazingly, I've not had one yet – I seem to have found that the breakdown of one's marriage does wonders to curb your appetite.

For the last ten minutes I have been trying to find something to say, something to break the silence. Only one thought, that sums up how my life is panning out, keeps pounding in my head though.

"Feck this for a game of soldiers," I say.

"Indeed," replies Daisy and the silence resumes.

Fifteen minutes pass.

"You will be okay though, you and Aidan, won't you?" Daisy asks, staring at the window, not daring to let me see her face.

I think about it. I'm not thinking divorce yet but every time my brain starts to rationalise things – to move toward being together with him again – something screams at me to stop. He doesn't love me the way I am. My heart sinks each time I remember that silly little fact. I'm not good enough for him any more. Perhaps I never was.

"I don't know, honey," I say, and sip my now cold tea, watching the rain batter on the window and feeling as powerless as each drop.

The silence continues and the tiredness returns. These tablets, to be grateful for small mercies, leave me wiped out. I say goodnight and climb the stairs. Jack is asleep in his travel cot, but I lift him into bed with me. I need him beside me tonight. I need to feel his soft breath against my cheek, to look at his babyish, trusting face and to feel his pudgy arms and to be reassured that someone loves me.

I'm struck by the guilt though. The guilty realisation that I have taken my precious boy away from his daddy and he won't understand what the hell is going on. I'm tired, but I can't sleep. I have to cry for a couple of hours first, and then I will sleep on my sodden pillow and wonder how the hell things have gone so wrong.

\* \* \*

When Sunday dawns it is still raining. I can hear it beat off the window-panes and I feel colder than I have done in weeks. Jack is still sleeping and, even though I'm exhausted, I'm wide awake. Looking at the clock I see it is 6.45am. It's much too early to be this awake, but I know there is little chance of me getting back to sleep now. I roll out of the bed, leaving Jack in the centre – looking so very small – and pad downstairs to the kitchen.

Putting the kettle on, I stare out at the rain. It is dancing off the ground and the sky is dark and heavy. I notice Daisy hasn't covered the sandpit and that upsets me. All that sand, just gone to waste. If the weather improves later the children won't have their favourite place to play. I start to cry at the unfairness of it all and the sadness doesn't leave me, not even when I'm sitting on the armchair half-heartedly sipping my coffee and playing yesterday's events over and over in my head.

At around seven thirty, Lily toddles sleepily into the room, rubbing her eyes. "You look sad, Auntie Grace," she says. "Did you and Mummy have another fight?" Her dazzling blue eyes are wide with concern.

"No, sweetie," I reassure her. "I was just outside in the rain and my face got wet. Silly old me!"

172

"But your hair is dry, Auntie Grace," she says, eyeing me up and down suspiciously.

"Must be magic," I mutter before jumping up and setting about making her some breakfast. "I'd better go and check on Sleepyhead Jack," I smile, ruffling her hair as she tucks into her Cheerios.

"You'd better check on Sleepyhead Mummy as well," she says, giving me a knowing smile.

Climbing the stairs I hear Jack chattering to Daisy and walk into my room to see my friend sitting beside my boy sharing a cuddle.

"I was just getting a coffee," I start to explain, determined to let Daisy know I wasn't in the habit of abandoning my child in strange places.

"You look like shit," she counters. "Did you not sleep?"

"Not much. My brain wouldn't switch off. You know how it is. I spend half my life trying to switch the damn thing on and when I want it to desist it won't play along." I manage a half-smile. Daisy looks concerned and I reassure her that once my happy/ sleepy/ bokey pills kick in I will flake out and promise to take a long sleep.

"Okay then, chick. Do you want some breakfast? I think I have some soda farls in the breadbin."

"Funnily enough, I'm not hungry, Dais. I'll get something later. I've given Lily some Cheerios and Mr Fussy Breakfast Pants can have the same."

* * *

By the time two o'clock rolls around both the children are ready to climb the walls with cabin fever. The rain hasn't

173

abated any and my mood is still pretty grumblesome. Daisy has resorted to a DVD and bags of crisps to keep the children from wrecking her house and I'm sitting on the squashy armchair in the kitchen drinking my twenty-fifth cup of coffee.

"Are you nervous?" Daisy asks from her counter-top position.

"Naw, I think it's just the coffee giving me the shakes. I'm grand," I say, trying to find some kind of humour in the situation. My husband (or should that be ex, now that we are officially separated and all?) will be picking my child up in approximately five minutes for a visit. I have no idea if my marriage still exists or if I have just thrown away the last eight years of my life. Every time I want to forgive him, a wee voice roars at me to wise up and a quieter voice, a wee sneaky fecker of a thing, whispers in my ear reminding me that I have no idea if Aidan wants to be forgiven. Maybe this has been his breaking-point as well as mine?

Just then the doorbell rings and my heart jumps into my throat. I hear Jack run towards the door screaming, "Daddy, Daddy!" excitedly and I want to be sick.

"Do you want me to deal with this, Grace?" Daisy asks, jumping down from the counter.

"Nope, if there is one thing I've learned in the last two weeks it's that I need to start taking responsibility for my own actions, and Aidan needs to start taking responsibility for his too."

I walk to the hall and see him standing there, unshaven, with his hair wet and hanging limply around his face. I'm almost pleased to notice that he looks tired – there are distinct bags under his eyes – and his T-shirt is wrinkled as if he has slept in it. I'm almost about to get cocky when I realise I'm still in my pyjamas and my hair hasn't been brushed either.

"Hello, Aidan."

"Grace," he says, a one-word hello.

And he looks at me and I can't for the life of me read what is going on in his head. Usually his eyes give it all away but they are emotionless.

"Where are you taking him?" I ask, stepping a little closer to try and see him better, and if I'm honest just to be closer to him. I want so much to hit him now – to tell him he has hurt me but at the same time, God, I just want to be in his arms, to have them soothing me and making it all better.

"My mum's," he replies, reaching for the changing bag by the door. "We shouldn't be too late."

"Okay," I answer and feel my voice start to tremble. I'm about to melt, about to give in and beg him to stay but the door is already closed and both Jack and Aidan are gone. My family are gone.

"If you don't mind, Daisy, I'm a little tired now. I think I will go and have that sleep."

\* \* \*

I'm not sure if it was a good thing or a bad thing that I slept through Aidan returning with Jack. In some ways I wanted so badly to see him again, but at the same time I wanted to avoid him as if he had some medieval lurgy. All I know is that I have just woken up to Jack bouncing on the bed and shouting: "Wake up, Mummy! Time for din-dins!" I reach out and give him the hugest hug and then I get up because, let's face it, I don't really have much of a choice. I need to get up – to keep moving – or I fear I will spend the rest of my life in this bed in this lovely room until I die.

I walk down the stairs and Daisy has gone all out to lift my mood. In her dining-room (yes, she is very posh – she has a dining-room *as well* as a kitchen table), she has set out her best crockery and crystal glasses which are already topped up with wine. A traditional Sunday lunch, with all the trimmings, is waiting for me and while I know I should be hungry, and I know such a meal would normally have me salivating at the very thought, I find myself just pushing the food around on my plate and ignoring the wineglass for some water.

Yes, I'm chatting. I'm joking with Jack, making him giggle hysterically and as Lily joins in I find myself laughing – but behind it all I want to scream. I want to wind the clock back two weeks. I want to decide not to tell Aidan about Louise's proposals and then none of this will have happened. Aidan and I would still be moseying along at our usual rate – in blissful ignorance with our pecks on the cheek, our occasional fumbles and the insincerity of our 'I love you's'. I could be putting my son to bed in his own room tonight and sleeping under my own duvet (not that Daisy's isn't lovely, but the bed just doesn't mould around my body in the way my own does).

# 15

It's not surprising that when I go to bed I don't sleep well. I think my body clock has gone into some weird shock and I no longer know the difference between night and day. The only problem with the whole non-sleeping malarkey however is that today, Monday, I can't just go back to bed when the inevitable tiredness does kick in. Nope, I have a full day's work ahead – starting with the weekly editorial conference and ending with an appointment with Dr Dishy to check on my mental state.

In between times I am to phone Lesley at City Couture and reveal to my eternal shame and embarrassment my vital statistics so she can get prepared for next week's consultation. I also have an interview lined up with a Stay-At-Home Mum who will give me the low-down on how hard her life is and I will have to bite my tongue so as not to say 'Swapsies!' and list my own particular maternal gripes.

I've at least managed to put some make-up on. Lily informed me this morning that I looked very scary, and after a quick look in the mirror I agreed that the lack of sleep overnight was not conducive to a radiant complexion. I offer a silent prayer of thanks upwards that today is going to be one of the only days in the working month when Liam won't be tasked with taking my picture.

I nibble at the fruit salad I've brought with me for breakfast and sip at my water while looking over my emails and old files on the computer. I find a message from Jill, an old university acquaintance (one of the aforementioned five-foot bridesmaids) who I haven't heard from in ages. She asks after me, Aidan and Jack, and I mentally decide to leave it a month or two before replying to her email because, after all, I don't want to scare the poor girl when she was probably just sending the message to be polite and she no longer actually really cares what the hell is going on in my life.

Sinéad walks in, cursing the persistent rain (or "fucking pishing weather", if I'm to be accurate) and offers a quick glance in my direction before continuing to her office. I'm just starting to congratulate myself on getting away with looking, for all intents and purposes, half-normal when another email pops up from my screen – an internal memo from Sinéad.

"Get your arse in here now, Grace. You look like shit!"

I get up off my desk, bringing my bottle of water with me, and make my way into the office. Sinéad is already sitting on the sofa and I feel my eyes well up with this so very simple act of kindness. You see, by sitting there, by not facing me from behind her desk, she is showing that she actually gives a damn what is wrong with me.

"If it's none of my business then tell me to fuck off," Sinéad starts, "but I'm guessing the white face and the bottle of water aren't down to a hangover and you look like a bag of bones."

I raise a smile, if for no other reason than I'm happy to hear that I look like a bag of bones, and then I start to blub. I have no idea where these tears are coming from because I swear I can't actually have any left. All I have done is sob and snotter my way through the past two days. I wonder if that is why I'm so fecking thirsty?

"Sit down," she says and throws her arms around me.

I feel uneasy at her warmth, but unable to stop myself from giving in to it. I just need this hug, need to feel that I don't have to keep this a secret – not from Sinéad.

"I've left Aidan," I mutter, when the sobs have subsided. I don't know whether it is a good thing or not that she doesn't look shocked. "I don't think he understands what I'm going through right now."

"Do you understand it?" Sinéad asks, cutting through the bullshit in her own inimitable style.

"Honestly? No, I don't think I do."

"Then how can you expect him to?"

"That's the thing. I don't expect him to understand. I just want him to try," I say petulantly.

"I think you need to be easier on yourself, and on Aidan," Sinéad says. "I've read your first drafts, Grace. I know you are trying to make out this is no big shakes for you but I know it's a struggle. Don't forget I've been here a long time. I saw the ballsy young reporter who walked through the doors. I saw you wearing your designer clothes and dolling about here like a thinking man's version of Louise – and equally I've seen you

179

fade a bit. I'm not saying I'm unhappy with your work. You're one of the most valuable members of this team and you do whatever is asked of you, but I don't see so much of the passion any more. And I hate to state the obvious, and please, listen to this knowing that I have a fucking stupid habit of saying things the wrong way and sounding offensive when I don't mean to be, but I have seen you let yourself go. Grace O'Donnell would not have dared come in here without her hair styled and her make-up perfect. Grace Adams doesn't seem to care all that much any more."

I'm about to mutter my apologies – to promise to try harder – to book an appointment at the Clarins counter for that very afternoon when Sinéad continues. She is obviously on a roll.

"Now I don't want you walking out of here thinking all I've said is bad. Think about my words, take the positive out of it, and use it to your advantage. It's too fucking easy to get stuck in a rut, Gracie. I've been there." She sidles closer, lights a cigarette and takes a deep drag on it, exhaling slowly, and then she continues: "After Aoibheann was born I almost gave up, on me, on her, on my relationship. I can see that in you, Grace, and I wouldn't wish what I went through on my worst enemy. Say the word and we pull the plug on the Change Your Life feature. It's fucking brilliant stuff, but say the word and it's a non-starter. No one needs their life exposed in this way."

I take a deep breath and answer. "I do, Sinéad. I need this because everything you have just said makes perfect sense. The only difference is, I'm a lazy fecker. If I don't do something now, I'm afraid we will never see Grace O'Donnell again – not that she was perfect by a long shot – but she was better than this."

"That's my girl," Sinéad says, breathing a sigh of relief.

"Now, you are ordered out of the office for half an hour. Get yourself freshened up, reapply that make-up, get a cup of tea to steady your nerves and get back here and give 'em hell."

"I will," I say and something in me knows that I mean it.

Deciding Sinéad may have a point about me taking time out to compose myself, I walk to my desk to grab my car keys. Then I'm distracted by the shrill ringing of my phone. I know I shouldn't answer it. I know in my heart this call will bring no joy to my life, but I also know it's my job to lift the receiver and it could always be my Stay-At-Home Mammy telling me little Betsy has glued herself to the floor and they won't be able to come along for the interview and photo shoot. So I give in to curiosity and answer it and, just as predicted, it brought no good. It is Máire on the phone – the Mother-in-Law. No sooner do I say hello but she is ranting at me in a high-pitched squeak, talking about how she knew I was no good from the start and how I had broken her 'wee son's heart'. My mouth is opening and closing, trying to say something, but she is cutting me off at every opportunity. Her voice is increasing an octave approximately every ten seconds and I'm pretty sure that within the next thirty to forty seconds only dogs will be able to hear her.

She is wittering on now about marriage counselling, Relate, visiting the wee priest and then she says I'd better not fucking think that I can take Jack out of her life and I'm shocked at her swear-word but also mildly amused. She hangs up before I utter a single word and I take a deep breath. Yes, a drive would be just perfect around now.

Máire and I have a weird kind of relationship, one I usually refer to as mutual toleration. She thinks the sun shines out of her precious first-born's rear end. Aidan's sister, the lovely but ridiculously skinny Máiréad (they weren't very creative with names – Aidan's da is called Aidan Senior by the way) never really had a look in. She could win the Nobel Prize, the Pulitzer Prize and a fecking Blue Peter Badge and none of these would match the achievements of the Golden One – he who got six GCSES and two A Levels. Is it any wonder Máiréad, the other of the skinny bridesmaids, chose to move to London as soon as she could, where she has carved out a lovely little career for herself away from the interference and judging eyes of her mother.

Máire has never openly disapproved of me (not until now anyway), but she never really took me under her wing either. I suppose when I was younger I never thought about it much – after all, I had Mammy and that was all the mammy a woman needed – or indeed could handle. But after Jack was born I would notice her beady eyes examining everything I did with him, and how Aidan and I interacted together as parents. I became more and more aware that she was not going to found my fan club any time soon. I guess it wasn't exactly devastating to have my fears confirmed.

When I return, the editorial conference has been and gone. Louise is looking at me suspiciously because it is more or less against the law to leave the office when a conference is scheduled. Sinéad has left a doughnut on my desk with a wee note telling me to enjoy and when I check my email my daily message from *lifecoaches.com* says **'Don't forget you CAN make it happen'**. I suppose that's the point, isn't it, it's all down to me. So I offer the doughnut to Liam in the vain hope it will act as some sort of bribery when he wants to print some of those less than flattering photographs of me. I'm about to lift the phone to call Betsy's mother when it rings, half-scaring me and my sleep-deprived self witless. Again I take a deep breath and lift it.

"Grace," Aidan says and my heart starts thumping.

"Yes," I reply and I'm not sure how to play this.

"I hear my mum phoned you," he says and I smile because I can hear the embarrassment in his voice from here.

I'm almost about to laugh with him about it and tell him about her swearing. He would, I know, find that hilarious – but I'm not sure if it is appropriate to be joshing with one's estranged spouse.

"She did," I reply, choosing to keep my cards close to my chest.

"I'm just apologising on her behalf because if I know Mum like I think I know Mum then I'm guessing an apology is in order."

"'Sokay," I say. "She's pissed off. That's allowed."

"As long as you don't think that is coming from me," he says and sighs.

I can hear the tiredness in his voice and I suddenly long to soothe him, and make him feel better. Of course it doesn't take long for my brain to kick into gear and remind me that I'm the one needs soothing now, not him.

"I didn't, Aidan," I say.

"Grand. Well, I bet you are busy so I'll talk to you later."

He hangs up and I lift the car keys and go for another drive. Sinéad will understand.

*  *  *

By the time two o'clock has come around I have got myself together and have spent a joyous half hour listening to Betsy's mother rave on about how fabulous it is to spend all day, every day with her rugrat and how they never run out of things to do together. Betsy sits like a Stepford Baby in the corner and it crosses my mind that some form of Baby Valium must come into play to make Betsy's mother's day so painless. I've managed to get Liam to take some pretty lovely shots of the two of them together and I've even managed to make an article out of the train-wreck that was the Movement and Mood class.

I'm not sure said article is in English because the entire time I'm writing it I'm playing the conversation with Aidan over and over in my head and trying to find any hidden meanings, any hints that he is desperately sorry for his piss-poor treatment of me and ready to welcome me back into his arms and kill a fatted calf in my honour. My brain really does not feel that it can deal with much more of this today.

I'm just about to step out for lunch when the email icon pops up on my desktop and, being incredibly nosey I, of course, can't leave it until after lunch. I open my mailbox and there it is, an email from Máiréad, Aidan's sister.

**To: grace.adams@northernpeople.co.uk**
**Subject: My mum is a fruitcake.**

**Sweetie                                                                    ,**
**Mum has been on the phone spouting some shite about you and Aidan heading for the divorce courts.**

**I'm not sure what the fuck is going on but I know how Mum loves a drama. Don't be fooled into thinking she is genuinely annoyed about this. This is like an episode of *EastEnders* to her where she is the star of the whole thing.**

**This will keep her going in the martyr stakes for the next year. She is in her element. Ignore her ranting. I always just block it out by singing to myself.**

**Seriously, sweetie, I'm not sure what is going on but I know you won't have walked out without good reason. I also lived with Aidan long enough to know what a gobshite he can be and to be honest I'm surprised you haven't kicked his arse to the kerb long before now.**

**You know where I am if you need to chat. I hope the pair of you sort things out, but I don't blame you if you decide you've had enough.**

**M**

**x**

Bizarrely I'm exceptionally annoyed by Máiréad's email. The first thing that annoys me is that she equates the cesspit that my life is becoming to an episode of *EastEnders*. I could have handled a reference to *Desperate Housewives* or even *Coronation Street* but my life is depressing enough without putting it on a par with Albert Square.

The second thing that annoys me is that she is right. Máire will be in her element. She will be sidling up to the ladies in the Chat'N'Chew and telling them how her feckless daughter-in-law has gone and left her wee son. She will probably be telling them that I'm 'bad wi' me nerves' and on tablets and everything and totally unable to look after that baby of mine.

The third thing is that she has attacked Aidan and while I know he is a useless bastard at times, he is still *my* useless bastard. It is okay for me to be annoyed with him – I accepted the 'for better or worse' part in my marriage vows – but I can't bear other people implying that I've made a mistake and that he is no good. I click my email shut, vowing to reply later, and I'm just about to walk out the door again when my phone rings.

A sing-song voice chirps at me: "Helllloooo, is that Grace Adams? It's Lesley here at City Couture. Are you ready for your telephone consultation?"

Fuck. I had forgotten about that. "Yes," I reply half-heartedly, sounding like an ungrateful baggage not one bit interested in the oodles of free clothes and junk jewellery she is going to heap on me.

"Great!" she says, bursting with enthusiasm I was sure she would have lost by now.

You see, the first time I encountered Lesley was two years ago when I was pregnant with Jack and feeling blooming awful as opposed to blooming marvellous. As a treat to my fat and pregnant self, Sinéad had sent me to a Mummy-To-Be-Makeover at City Couture and bubbly Lesley had fussed about me, trussing me up in all sorts of the over-the-bump, under-the-bump and skimming-the-bump creations which made me look like a manic combination of Mr Blobby and Humpty from *Playschool*.

In fairness to her she was fairly new to the game then and finding her feet in the whole image-consultant basis. She was of the opinion that expensive or designer automatically meant tasteful.

A brush with bankruptcy and a night class in Body Image had, so her reputation would have you believe, made her buck up her ideas. She was now exceptionally sought after by the local LWL (Ladies Who Lunch).

But, I now realise, while the years have sorted out her

business sense, the hyperness has obviously lasted.

"What do you need to know?" I ask.

"Well, just your vital statistics, your basic lifestyle issues."

Lifestyle issues? I suddenly feel as though I should be confessing that I like to swing from the chandeliers at the weekend or dress up in leather.

"What exactly do you mean by lifestyle issues?" I ask.

"Oh, you, are you a fitness freak? A business lady? A yummy mummy? What do you do in your time off? What is practical for you?"

I'm tempted to reply that my current penchant for trackie bottoms and semi-fitted T-shirts is practical for me right now but I decide I need to be gracious. "I'm not sure, Lesley. I suppose I could do with some smartening up for the office."

"Yes," she enthuses, "Louise did say that might be on the cards."

"And I'd like to look smarter when I'm out and about with my son," I add.

"All good," says Lesley and I can hear the tip-tapping of her keyboard in the background. She is obviously taking notes. "What about trying something a little sexy for the man in your life?" she adds, and I just agree because I don't think I can take some overly enthusiastic sympathy from her just now.

After the ritual humiliation of revealing my dress size (18 on top, 20 on bottom) she informs me she will see me next Wednesday for the grand transformation and that we will have the "most fun ever". I'm not convinced but I lie and tell her I'm looking forward to it anyway and then, finally, at two thirty-five, I get away for my lunch. Only now I'm not so hungry any more.

Despite it now being considerably colder and wetter, the thermostat in the doctor's waiting room still seems to be set at 'Tropical Heatwave'. I'm trying to fan myself with a battered copy of *Woman* but it isn't really doing the job. I feel, and probably look, exceptionally tired and I know my make-up is now residing somewhere around my knee-caps. All I want to do is go home (well, Daisy's home, as mine is strictly out of bounds) and go to sleep again.

I'm a little annoyed at Dr Dishy for making me see him every week. I mean, does he really expect a week to have cured me? Fecking men! They think they can shake their magic wands and it's all better.

The buzzer goes and the light tells me it's time for my consultation. Gruffly I walk to the room, open the door without knocking (I'm not in the mood for being polite) and plonk myself down on the chair beside his desk like a petulant schoolgirl. I've had a shite day. I figure I deserve the right to be petulant.

He looks at me, or rather over my shoulder, and smiles. "Is 'Daisy who comes for moral support' not with you today?" he asks and I suddenly get yet another case of the 'sorry for myselves'.

Yes, I'd rather be home than here but why is it that *my* doctor would rather see my *friend* than me? Am I not sick enough? Or worthy enough of his time?

"No," I mutter, "she's minding my son."

"Right," he says, a look of disappointment dancing across his face. "I'm sensing you aren't feeling too great today, Grace."

"Ten out of ten for observation, doctor," I reply sulkily. "I feel a little out of control at the moment."

"In what way?"

"I've left Aidan," I say, sighing because I just don't think I physically can cry any more.

Dr Dishy leans forward, looks me in the eye and tells me he is sorry to hear that. "Do you think it's for keeps?" he asks.

"I don't know. That's the problem. I just don't know anything at the moment. I don't know my arse from my elbow. I don't know if it is a shite or a haircut I want."

He smiles, not in a patronising way, but in a warm and caring way and I have to resist the urge to ask him for a hug.

"So, the Movement and Mood didn't really help then, did it?"

"We got thrown out," I say, suddenly embarrassed, and he starts to laugh.

"Good for you," he says. "It shows you have a bit of fight in you still."

"I probably have a bit too much fight at the moment."

"No such thing when you are battling depression, Grace," he says, "no such thing."

We talk through my options. He says it is too early for me to feel the full benefit of the happy pills just yet and I'm to keep taking them for another week before we reassess the situation. He says I need to rest more and I offer to introduce him to Jack and Lily. He tells me that I need to be good to myself – perhaps pamper myself a bit – and I offer to show him my bank statements. I am officially in Sulk Mode 10 – imminent meltdown.

"Okay then, Grace," he smiles, "I think it's time to think about working through whatever is making you feel like this."

"I thought that is what we're doing?"

"No, at the moment we're treating the symptoms. Your

mood is low and we are working to raise it a level where you feel stable again. That is when we have to look at what was making you feel low in the first place."

"Ah," I say, "you see, Shaun, you told me this already. You told me all about serotonin depletion and all that malarkey. It's a chemical thing, and the tablets fix the chemical thing so that should make me better, shouldn't it?"

He sighs. In fairness it's only a matter of time before he starts losing the rag with me too.

"In theory, yes, it should fix it. But you obviously have issues, Grace. You didn't run away to Donegal for the night because you had a chemical depletion – and don't tell me you thought that was the reason, because you are more intelligent than that. Likewise you didn't leave Aidan because the tablets aren't working yet."

"You are right there," I smile, "I left him because he is a feckwit."

I leave with the number of a counsellor – although I'm still not quite sure what I need to be counselled about. Dr Dishy has said he will pull some strings to get me seen soon. As the lady in question is a private practitioner, and as I'm going to be writing about her for a big magazine, Dishy doesn't see it will be a problem.

Dishy is concerned that I'm not making as much progress as he would have hoped – which seems in my eyes to contradict the notion that it is early days and 'all good' and all I have to do is mellow and wait for the proverbial sunshine to come flooding through. So I decide I'll humour him because, well, I've nothing to lose, do I? I'm not exactly overflowing with joy and luck right now.

\* \* \*

Pulling into the driveway of Daisy's house, I see the windows are open and I can hear the children laughing. I paint on my smile and go in and Daisy shouts from the kitchen that dinner won't be long.

Once again I'm amazed at her energy. I doubt very much that I would have the energy to cook after a day running after kids. I scoop a giggly Jack up in my arms and give him a huge hug – enjoying the smell of him. He wriggles against my arm, calling out that he wants to play with Lily so I let him and walk into the living room where Daisy is grating cheese into a bowl. I can smell the garlic bread warming in the oven and see the pasta bubbling on the stove.

"There's wine in the fridge if you are that way inclined," she says without looking up.

I decline – after all, tomorrow is weigh-in day at Weightloss Wonders and, if I'm honest, I'm thinking if I start drinking I might get stupid drunk and say or do something I regret. I pour a cool glass of water and add some ice cubes before starting to set the table.

"Everything okay?" Daisy asks and I reply that it is because I figure the fact that I've not cried in at least four hours has to be positive.

"How was Dr Dishy?"

"He asked after you," I smile and she blushes. It's not often you can embarrass Daisy Cassidy so I'm quite proud of myself for managing it.

"That's nice to know," she smiles, "but I was more wondering how you got on."

"He wants me to see a counsellor."

"That's good, isn't it?" Daisy asks.

I shrug my shoulders. "Not sure I have anything I need to be counselled about but I'll give it a go."

"Grace, we all have things we need to be counselled about. We just don't realise it half the time. Anyway, it will be cool. You will be in therapy – it will make you sound all windswept and interesting."

"First time for everything, eh?" I grin and call the children through for their tea.

Jack clings on tightly at bedtime. He asks for Daddy and I fob him off with a lie that Daddy is working. I don't think a two-year-old would really understand the intricacies of marital strife. He looks at me suspiciously – his innocent blue eyes trying to suss me out and then he clings on tight to me and his Fifi doll and whimpers a bit before falling asleep. I should go downstairs and keep Daisy company, but I decide to lie there and just fall asleep myself. For the most part dreams are a lot more enjoyable than real life at the moment.

# 16

It's Tuesday and the rain has lifted a bit. I landed into work this morning to an email from Máiréad – just the same as yesterday with an extra note saying she wondered had I got the first one. I made a mental note to answer it today, but it's four thirty now and I've not managed it. I am really experiencing a full-on case of couldn't-be-arseditis.

Sinéad walked past my desk this morning and gave me a knowing wink. I could see Louise's gossip and paranoia antennae pick up the vibes and she looked very disconcerted by it all. It dawned on me, about that time, that she hadn't plonked her skinny arse on my desk in two whole days. Would it be too much to hope for that she was giving me a wide berth?

I've spent the day writing up my 'Stay-at-Home Mummy' feature on Betsy's mammy and searching the internet for advice on what to expect from a counsellor.

I really should have made that phone call for the

appointment. Dishy had even emailed me to remind me of the number – just in case I would have forgotten or thrown it in the bin or something typically 'me' like that.

I had lifted the phone a couple of times. I'd even dialled the number but I just couldn't bring myself to make the appointment. I felt that even by talking to someone over the phone I would be branding myself a mentalist. I didn't want to be judged – well, not more than I had already been of late. I mean tonight I will have to face the dreaded scales again. Surely that is enough judgement for any woman to take on a Tuesday evening in August?

Aidan is picking Jack up from Susie's today. I had a curt email informing me of the arrangements where he said he was sure I wouldn't mind as I had my 'slimming club thingy'. I am to pick Jack up after class, something I'm not overly happy about because I know taking him out of his house at bedtime will only serve to confuse him further. Nonetheless, with Máire breathing down my neck like a crazy woman, I'm not sure I can do anything at the moment which could possibly be deemed as obstructing the relationship between father and son – if for no other reason than not to give herself more fuel for her gossipy fire.

The phone rings and I already know it is going to be Daisy before I answer it. Breathlessly, as if the hunger pains are claiming her life as we speak she mutters: "After this weigh-in we are stopping at the chipper and getting the biggest, dirtiest, greasiest pile of food you could ever imagine. We are going to eat it straight out of the wrapper and wash it down with Bacardi Breezers and enjoy every last morsel until we are as fat as pigs and have to get a stair lift jobby to take us up to bed."

"C'mon, Daisy," I tease, "that is not in the spirit of transforming yourself to the You you want to be."

"Fuck that!" she laughs. "The Me I want to be right now is a big full-up lard-arse who has chip-fat dripping down her chin. I'm berluddy starving. I've only eaten an apple and a yoghurt all day to try and trick the scales."

"You're mad," I say. "You know Charlotte says we have to be sensible about this whole thing."

"Aye, well, Charlotte doesn't know about my biscuit-fest over the weekend thanks to your trauma."

"Don't blame me for your indiscretions," I laugh.

"going to blame you. I'm hardly going to take the rap myself, am I?" she laughs before arranging to meet me outside the school hall at six thirty. "We want to be there before the uber-dieters arrive to make us feel like big lumps."

* * *

The school hall is quiet when I arrive. Remarkably Daisy is already there and has a face like thunder on her.

"Two pounds on," she grumbles. "Two fecking pounds on, and I'm still bloody starving!"

"But you did eat nearly a full garlic bread to yourself last night," I soothe gently.

"I know, but still, God, I hoped for something. It was a Healthy Eating garlic bread after all."

I smile at her, trying to ignore the wee voice in my head that tells me 2lbs on top of Daisy's weight is still a lot lighter than my eventual goal.

Charlotte smiles at me from across the room. "Grace, lovely to see you! Let's get you weighed."

I take my jacket off, drop my bag on a chair and breathe in, as if that will make me lighter, and then I step on the scales and look straight ahead of me until Charlotte says I'm safe to stand off. Sitting down, I compose my face into an expression of complete nonchalance to avoid the outbursts of last time and Charlotte takes my little purple chart and starts to write down my vital statistics.

"Well, whatever you have done this week, Grace, it's worked. You've lost 7lbs! Keep it up."

Realising it is highly unlikely that I will leave another spouse between now and next week I realise this is probably a one-off fluke, but nonetheless I'm delighted. I'm no longer a 15-stone frump! I'm 14 stone and 12 lbs of gorgeousness.

"How have you found the diet?" Charlotte asks, interrupting my thoughts.

"Well, to be honest, I've had a lot on my mind so I've not been thinking about food all that much."

"Great," she replies, "and what about exercise? Have you managed any?"

I think about it. I've slept a lot, and had a good long walk around Glenveagh but I've not really been inspired to feel the burn. "Not really," I say.

Sensing my unease, she replies: "Look, it doesn't have to be an exercise class, or a swimming lesson. All you need to do is move about until you are breathless. Even a good session in the sack could do wonders," she laughs, winking at me.

"I'll remember that," I say wryly and go to take my seat beside Daisy, who still has that disgusted look on her face.

"Two fecking pounds," she mutters, grabbing her non-existent spare tyre and trying to pinch a non-existent inch.

I sit down, saying nothing, and look ahead of me. A wee

bubble of excitement is starting to build. I've lost seven pounds. Half a stone. Fourteen packets of sausages. I smile, despite myself. I smile even though there is no prospect of me going home and burning off some calories with a session of hot, passionate lovemaking with Himself.

"Gah!" Daisy mutters, crossing her legs in a huff. "Well then, how did you get on? Are you raging too?"

"Not exactly," I reply. "I lost seven pounds," grinning ear from ear.

A momentary look of jealous shock dances across her face before she grins, hugs me and tells me she loves me – then we settle down for our motivational talk on how to keep at it for another week.

Of course, the bubble of excitement doesn't last long – or to be more accurate it is replaced by a bigger and scarier bubble of dread at having to pick Jack up from Aidan. I'm sitting outside my own house, looking at my own front door, and I'm wondering whether it is okay for me to use my own keys to open it. I'm so not *au fait* with the manners surrounding a relationship breakdown that I've been sitting here for ten minutes. This is the house I pay for – the house I first saw on a property website and was immediately drawn to owing to its promise of original cornicing and a marble fireplace. This is the house I moved into with barely a stick of furniture to my name – where we spent our second night as husband and wife. This is the house we bought new flooring for and felt simultaneously childish and grown-up as we looked at the shag-pile carpets in the showroom and giggled at the name. This is the home we brought Jack back to – where we both lay awake all night listening to make sure he was breathing. This is where Jack took his first steps, where he fell for the first time, where Aidan and I smiled proudly on his first birthday.

This is the house where Aidan told me I was pathetic and I felt something in me give up.

Taking a deep breath I ring the doorbell. It seems the best thing to do. I hear tiny footsteps battering down the hallway, a little voice calling, "Mammy, Mammy!" excitedly and I hear Aidan laugh and tell Jack to calm down. It sounds like so many other days when I come home, except that I can't escape the fact that it isn't. This may never be my home again. The door opens and Jack jumps into my arms before I've had time to catch my breath. He snuggles close, patting my back with his pudgy hands, reassuring me in my own words: "I'm here. I'm here!" And he licks my face in his attempt at a kiss.

Aidan is standing awkwardly behind him. I'm both pleased and worried to see that he still looks like shit. He is desperately in need of a shave and he clearly hasn't been sleeping all that well.

"Hi," I say and he nods in response.

"How did you get on tonight?" he asks.

I reply that I did okay without revealing the details. He tells me I'm looking well and I smile back at him, unsure how to tell him he looks like he needs a good wash, a good feed and some clean clothes.

"Do you want to come in for a cup of tea?" he asks, making for the kitchen before I have the chance to answer.

I was going to say no. I was going to just leave, put Jack in the car and drive back to Daisy's to avoid any more weirdness, but since the kettle is on I feel it would be rude to say no. Walking into the kitchen I notice that it looks different. The same things are there, but just not in the order I would have had them. There are dishes by the sink and the washing-machine door is open. I push it shut and start running water in the sink to do the dishes. It's automatic – I'm not trying to make a big gesture, I'm just being the creature of habit I've always been.

"You don't have to do that, Grace," Aidan says, placing his hand on mine as if to stop me.

I shrug him off. "It'll only take two minutes," I say and carry on.

Jack is playing on the floor at our feet, pushing his toy truck up and down the floor and chattering to himself.

"Seriously, Grace," Aidan says, his voice still calm but insistent, and he turns the taps off. "Don't you think we should talk?"

I'm shocked. Aidan Adams has never in his entire life looked to talk about anything. He is a man. He does not *do* talking. Occasionally he listens (or pretends to, I notice the glazing of the eyes), but he does not talk. His excuse has always been that he is not a great conversationalist. So he must be serious about things now if he is actually instigating a chat.

"I'm not sure we have anything to say," I reply honestly, my voice trembling at the words.

He looks hurt.

"Aidan, I just don't know what is going on at the moment, with us, or with me, but I know that you let me down." My voice cracks and Jack looks up at me concerned so I compose myself long enough for him to turn his attention back to his toys.

"How?" Aidan asks and I'm amazed that he seems genuinely confused by this.

"You said I was pathetic. I had a drink and ate some fecking toast and that made me pathetic," I whisper and it sounds stupid now to my ears. It sounds like I have walked out on eight years of relationship over a slice of toast.

"I didn't mean it," he replies.

"Well, what did you mean, Aidan? Because it really sounded to me like you did. I'm trying to change and you promised to support me but you didn't. You let me down."

"I'm sorry."

I feel like sniping at him, like telling him that damn right he is sorry and so he should be, or telling him he doesn't even know the meaning of the word sorry. Internally my brain is singing a little chorus of 'Just you wait, Aidan Adams, just you wait!' but then I look at him and I want to believe he is sorry. I want this to work.

"Come home," he says and I see tears in his eyes, mirroring the ones in my own.

"I can't," I say, using every ounce of strength in me, "not yet. I'm not saying never, but I need to be sure you won't hurt me again."

"I won't, I promise."

"You can't promise that, honey, not at the moment."

"Can I see you again?"

"Of course," I reply.

"Can I take you out for lunch on Saturday? Can we talk?"

"Yes," I reply because I simply don't have the strength to say no to him any more. I have hurt him, and myself, enough for one day.

# 17

I'm barely in the door at Daisy's when Mammy phones demanding to know how the big meeting with "the ex" has gone.

She has taken to calling Aidan "the ex" now in a bid to sound perfectly okay with my crumbling marriage, when all the time I secretly know she is pinning all her hopes on a romantic reunion and the birth of at least one more grandchild. Sometimes I swear she has a secret camera trained on me at all times so that she can watch my every move – her timing with phone calls such as these, when I'm tired and emotional, is always perfect.

Daisy lifts a now-sleeping Jack from my arms, gives me a reassuring smile and takes him up to bed. I walk into the living-room and plonk myself down unceremoniously on the squishy white sofa.

Sitting beside my favourite seat is a bottle of wine cooling in an ice bucket and some Milky Way Crispy Rolls (a low-fat treat in the eyes of Weightloss Wonders). Daisy has scrawled a wee note saying *"Thought you might need these"* and I notice a box of tissues is sitting on the floor – proper soft balsam tissues, not the rough stuff that hurts your skin after a good cry. The tears start to fall at this kind gesture.

"It was okay," I tell Mammy through muffled sniffs and occasional sobs. "He said sorry and he wants me to come home."

"Do you want to go home?"

"I don't know what I want," I say, realising at this stage that I sound like a broken record.

I decide I'm not going to tell Mammy about the big date on Saturday – I don't want to get her hopes up that we are going to fall madly in love again and help her fulfil her dream.

She soothes me with her usual sage words of advice. "This too will pass, pet," she says. "I know it feels very scary now but it will pass and, you never know, you could come out the other side stronger for it."

I know Mammy is speaking from personal experience. I know that she believes love can overcome everything because it overcame her and Daddy splitting up when I was just a bit of a wain. It was after she had lost that last baby – when she spent a lot of time crying and staring into space.

\* \* \*

One day I came home from school, my Auntie Kathleen having picked me up, and I found that Daddy wasn't home. I assumed he was working late but things started to slip into place slowly over the coming hours. When I brushed my teeth that night I noticed there were only two toothbrushes in the chipped blue-and-white mug that sat on the window ledge. Daddy's shaving brush, the one with the stubby bristles that tickled and jagged at the same time, was gone and when I went into their bedroom, to cuddle up on the bed for my night-time story, Mammy didn't usher me into my own bedroom when the book was over.

I slept there, in their bed, confused. I waited for my daddy to come home. I couldn't figure out just where he was and when I woke in the morning, just me and Mammy there together, I wondered had he gone to the same place as all the babies.

"Has Daddy gone to get my wee brother?" I asked innocently over my Weetabix and Mammy started crying.

Needless to say I was even more confused when I went to school with Auntie Kathleen who told me not to worry about things but still would not explain what had happened. It was only when I started sobbing at break-time that my daddy was dead that the teacher called a rather shamefaced Mammy up to the school who looked eternally mortified as she explained Daddy has simply moved back home to his parents for a while and was, last time she saw him anyway, still very much alive and kicking.

I was allowed home early that day and Mammy took me into the Chat 'N' Chew for a gravy ring and a glass of milk while she explained that while they both still loved me with all their hearts, Mammy and Daddy just weren't so sure they loved each other any more.

I nodded as if I understood, but I didn't because mammies and daddies were supposed to love each other and be together always. I guessed this was just another one of those times when I would have to be brave.

I saw Daddy that weekend. He looked tired and worn out – the same kind of look Aidan has now, I suppose. His trousers were ironed funny, with a strong crease up the front that let me know that Granny Adams and not Mammy had ironed them.

He pulled me into his arms and held me so tight that I thought I might actually suffocate and then he told me he loved me and handed me a Crystal Barbie as a present. As the most coveted Barbie among the girls of Primary One, and a present usually only brought by the likes of Santa as it was so expensive, I figured this whole separation lark couldn't be so bad after all.

The pair of them over-compensated for their own confusion by spoiling me with treats like trips to Fiorentini's ice-cream parlour and days on the train to Portrush or the bus to Buncrana.

It was only when they handed me back to one another, when their eyes met and one of them had to leave, that I saw the hurt creep in and on those days I would always, without exception, cry myself sleep.

They were reconciled eventually, of course. I came home from school one day and noticed the toothbrush back in the mug and the shaving brush sitting by the sink. Daddy and Mammy were both smiling and it was around that time Mammy told me we were now the Three Amigos.

In my childlike brain I guessed they had been separated for about four weeks. I was shocked as an adult to learn it had been six months and that they both met with solicitors at one stage to discuss legal proceedings.

\* \* \*

As Mammy goes to end the conversation, something in her clicks that tonight was the big weigh-in.

"How did you get on?" she asks and I tell her I'm half a stone closer to the goal. In that unique mammy voice, in the way only mammies can, she tells me she is proud of me and wishes me sweet dreams. "Your dad sends his love, Grace," she says and I hear him shout that he loves me on the other side of the phone.

"Tell him I love him too," I say and hang up before pouring myself a massive glass of wine, and one for Daisy too. I then proceed to retell the whole sorry story again, but this time I tell her about the big date.

"Are you nervous?" she asks, sipping from her glass.

"Of course, I am. I don't know what he can say to make it better even though I'm not quite sure what he did to break it up in the first place. I know we didn't split up over a couple of Bacardi Breezers and a half a loaf of toast. Did we?"

"Grace," Daisy says, staring me straight in the eyes, "I'm saying this as a friend. You split up because you need to sort yourself out before you can sort out anyone else or your relationship with anyone else. I wish I had a magic wand, but I'm as baffled as you by all this. If you ask me, this has been building for a long time so that something as stupid as a couple of drinks and some buttery toast pushed you over the edge. But it could have been anything."

"Did you see this coming?" I ask, not sure if I want to hear her reply.

"Yes and no," she says and hands me the box of tissues

205

because she knows as well as I do that whatever she says next is going to make me cry again. "Grace!, don't you remember me asking if you were happy and you shrugged it all off?"

I nod in response.

"Well, I knew things weren't perfect. I can't say I knew just how unperfect they were. I suppose I didn't want to accept that life wasn't all sunshine and roses for you because you and Aidan have always been my idea of a happy ending. And you, my dear, have always seemed so in control of your life that I couldn't really accept that perhaps you were spiralling."

I smile at the notion that someone has thought I was in control. My whole life I felt like a spectator – pushed along by some mysterious force but certainly never in control. And as for me and Aidan being anyone's idea of a happy ending . . . well, words fail me to be honest.

"I didn't know I was," I say, but a wee seed of doubt is there now. Had I known all along but just chosen to ignore it, to push it to the back of mind and hope it will go away? I think back to the last few years and I find it hard to remember a time when I was truly happy. Of course there are moments of happiness, of pure joy, but the general feeling is of nothingness – not sadness, not anger, just nothing. Just that spectator watching my life go on around me and not caring that I wasn't playing an active role in it any more.

I drain my glass of wine. "I think I'll phone that counsellor in the morning," I say, kissing Daisy on the cheek and heading to bed.

"Grace," she calls as I leave the room and I turn to face her. "This too will pass. Love you, babes."

"Love you too," I say and head to bed.

# 18

"Hello, Cook Counselling, healing you today for a brighter tomorrow, Lisa speaking, how can I help you?"

I feel sorry for Lisa. Lisa has a lot to say every time she answers the phone and I'm guessing she has to sound cheerful every time she says it as it would not be good for business if she sounded pissed off. Happy voice equals healthy mind.

"Hello, Lisa," I say, trying to muffle my voice – which I realise is ridiculous as I'm about to give her my real name. "Is Cathy Cook available?"

"May I ask who's calling?"

"Erm, my name is Grace. Grace Adams."

"Are you a client, Ms Adams?"

"No, but I was wondering if I could be?"

Lisa takes a deep breath and still sounding quite chipper but with a certain jaded tone replies: "I'm afraid Ms Cook's books are full at the moment. There is a three-month waiting list. If you would like I could take your name and get back to you?"

"Actually," I say, feeling very daring because I know what I'm about to say is tantamount to a Z-list celebrity walking into a restaurant and doing the whole 'Don't you know who I am?' routine, "Dr Shaun Stevenson said Ms Cook would speak to me. I'm a journalist working for *Northern People* magazine."

"Oh, I'm sorry," Lisa says, "Ms Cook did tell me to expect a call from a journalist and to schedule you in. Would tomorrow at three suit?"

"That soon?" I say, suddenly nervous.

"Well, I did have you earmarked for next Friday, but we've had a cancellation. The appointment is yours if you want it?"

But do I want it? I mean, what would I talk about? The fact that I'm overweight? That my marriage is in tatters? That I'm constantly crying and hating myself?

"Yes," I say, "I'll take it."

"Grand so," Lisa says and I can hear her tapping my details into her computer. "You can bring a friend for support, but they will have to stay in the waiting room during the actual consultation. The fee is £30 per session, but Ms Cook has left a note to offer you the session at £20."

"That's more than generous," I say and hang up.

I then tap out an email to Dishy – we have become quite the pen-friends lately as he sends copy back and forth for the feature. Sinéad is so impressed she is considering taking him onboard as our full-time health expert. Daisy and I have had hours of fun imagining the shoot for the photo byline – perhaps we could get him wearing a stethoscope and not much else?

**To:** <u>shaun.stevenson@doctors.org</u>
**Subject: Thanks**

Shaun,
I want to thank you for pulling some strings. I have my first session with Cathy tomorrow. I'm very nervous, but I'm trusting you on this one.
Daisy (who is there for moral support) will be coming with me for moral support. I will let you know how it goes.
Grace

**To:** <u>grace.adams@northernpeople.co.uk</u>
**Subject: re: Thanks**

Grace,
Glad to hear Cathy could fit you in. She owes me a few favours, but that aside she knows her stuff.
Hope you find it beneficial. Tell Daisy I said Hi.
Shaun

**To:** <u>onefunkymamma@ntlworld.com</u>
**Subject: He's horny, horny, horny, horny**

Dais,
Dishy says Hi.
G
xxx

To: <u>grace.adams@northernpeople.co.uk</u>
Subject: So am I!

Grace,
Tell him I said Hi back
The Daister
xxx

To: <u>shaun.stevenson@doctors.org</u>
Subject: The joy of moral support

Shaun,
Daisy says Hi back.
Grace

To: <u>grace.adams@northernpeople.co.uk</u>
Subject: Give me your answer do . . .

Grace,
Has he answered yet? Has he said anything else? Don't keep me in suspenders.
Desperate Daisy

To <u>grace.adams@northernpeople.co.uk</u>
Subject: re: The joy of moral support

Grace,
Is Daisy single? I'm just curious, you know. Would she be free perhaps to offer me some moral support on Saturday night, do you think?

If you feel awkward about that scenario let me know. It might be weird for you, but I would like to take her out for a drink.

Shaun

(Eternally embarrassed)


To: onefunkymamma@ntlworld.com

Subject: She shoots – she scores


Whaddya doin' Saturday night?

G


To: grace.adams@northernpeople.co.uk

Subject: Does this mean what I think it means?


Grace,

If you are winding me up I will give you the biggest steever up the arse ever!

D


To: onefunkymamma@ntlworld.com

Subject: This is no wind-up


He wants to take you out on a date. I'll mind Lily. Say you will! Gw'an, ya will, ya will, ya will!

G

xxx

**To: grace.adams@northernpeople.co.uk**
**Subject: I have just shat myself**

**Okay then. If you don't mind.**
**D**
**X**

I grin to myself as I pass on the two phone numbers and let them do the rest of the planning themselves. Of course, I should be jealous – I should be heartbroken that two people are finding romance when I'm heading for Divorceville – population me – but I'm excited.

This feels right. This feels like it could work for Daisy and, as I've met Dr Dishy already in the flesh (and what glorious flesh it is too), I'm pretty sure he won't turn into some skeleton from her closet that she would rather forget.

Oh yes, I love it when a plan comes together.

By the time I reach Susie's to pick Jack up my mind is in turmoil. I'm stupidly excited by Dishy's date with Daisy (you see it even sounds right), but I'm nervous about my own impending dalliances with destiny. I'm not sure what to expect from the counselling but, all that aside, I'm even more nervous about my own 'date' with Aidan on Saturday afternoon.

As I ring the doorbell, Susie appears, looking more frazzled than ever. Usually an expert at keeping cool, calm and collected in the face of even the most violent temper tantrum from her charges, today there is a distinct throbbing of the vein in her temple which tells me life is not all rosy.

"Everything okay?" I ask, seeing Jack walk towards me, his

wee eyes red raw from crying. He is clutching his favourite Tigger toy and taking gulping breaths as if he has just sobbed his heart out.

"I'm sorry, Grace. I just haven't been able to settle him all day," Susie says, tears springing to her own eyes. "He hasn't wanted to let me out of his sight and, well, I have Molly and Zach to look after too and I had to put him down sometimes."

Jack is cuddled into my arms now, nuzzling at my neck, stroking my hair.

"I don't know what's wrong with him. I tried Calpol and taking him out for a drive, but he just cried the whole time. Have you any idea what might be upsetting him?"

Of course I know what is upsetting him. He misses his daddy. He is confused. He doesn't know what the hell is going on in his wee life and the goalposts keep moving. I know how he feels, because I feel the same myself and I'd love to spend the day clinging to someone's legs and crying until I made myself sick – because maybe it would make me feel better.

I can't tell Susie that though. She doesn't know about the big split – we decided not to muddy the waters by telling her – and I don't want to tell her now, despite her obvious upset.

"I'm sorry," I mutter. "I imagine he's sickening for something. I'll see how he is in the morning and if he isn't improved I'll let you know. Don't take it to heart!"

I leave, feeling utterly wretched.

And feeling utterly wretched there is only one place I can go – to see Mammy. We pull up outside and Daddy is beside the door of the car before I can put the handbrake on. He is waving at Jack, lifting him out and chatting to him nine to the dozen about *Bob the Builder* as I lock up and head into the house.

213

Mammy sticks her head through the kitchen door and enquires if everything is okay and I just shake my head and cry.

"I'm messing up my child's life," I say, flinging myself onto the sofa for dramatic emphasis.

Being Mammy she waits for me to continue before humouring me with her hushed tones and soothing remarks.

"He cried all day at Susie's. I don't think she ever wants him back and it's all because I've left his daddy and destroyed his sense of security."

"Oh Grace," Mammy says, sitting down beside me and taking my hand in hers. "Children are resilient. He'll be fine, and as for Susie, well, she is more than able to cope with this – and well, if she isn't, you can always call in a few favours with that Daisy one."

"I think I'm calling in enough favours with her as it is," I say, sighing loudly.

"Pish," Mammy says, "Daisy knows what side her bread is buttered on. That is what friendship is all about and sure as eggs is eggs there will be some time when she needs you and you will be there – like that time with The Dirty Bastard or whatever his name is."

"The Mighty Feckwit," I answer, begrudgingly. Typical of Mammy to bring her no-bullshit approach to my life when I'm trying desperately to feel stupidly sorry for myself.

"Now," she says, getting up and putting on the kettle, "stuff happens to children that you can't help but they get over it. Gracie, you survived all that happened to us when you were wee, didn't you?"

I nod, and keep to myself the fact that I've earmarked it to talk to Cathy about tomorrow at my counselling session.

Which reminds me, tomorrow – counselling session – feck!

"Balls!" I proclaim, sitting forward with my head in my hands. "I'm so unceasingly fucking stupid."

"Language, Grace," Mammy says matter-of-factly while setting the cups out.

"Sorry, Mammy, I've just remembered I've as good as told Susie she can have time off for good behaviour tomorrow and I've got an appointment I can't get out of."

"Good thing you have Daisy then," Mammy retorts, putting the Fondant Fancies onto a plate. "Now get this down your neck."

Pushing the Fondant Fancies away (they make my teeth hurt anyway) I take a sip of my coffee and relax. Mammy is right, I'll cope and Jack will cope and, as she always says, this too will pass.

"Oooh, I forgot to tell you," I say sitting up excitedly. "Daisy has a date with Dr Dishy!"

"That sexy young thing we saw that time I took you?" Mammy asks, sitting down beside me once again.

"Yes," I reply. "On Saturday night. He wants to take her out for a drink."

"Grand," Mammy says. "It's about time she got laid."

And I nearly choke on my coffee.

* * *

Jack goes to sleep after three read-throughs of *Bunny, My Honey* and a large cup of warmed milk. The exertion of his day of crying has obviously taken its toll – usually it would take five read-throughs. He was in remarkably good form all evening with his grandad. The pair of them had lain on the floor of the living room and played races with the stock of toy cars kept in Granny and Grandad's house for such occasions. I had heard them squeal with laughter while I talked with Mammy about the big date between Daisy and Dishy. Mammy has already said that Daisy Stevenson works as a name and I've had to tell her to get a hold of her senses. I kiss my boy on the head, softly stroking his gorgeous curls, and head out to the back garden where Daisy is sitting browsing through the *Next Directory* – desperate to find a new look for Saturday night.

"Hey, babes," I say and plonk myself down.

"Grace, I literally think I'm going to vomit with nerves," she says, sipping a glass of wine.

"No, you won't, hon. You deserve this. You can manage and you know there won't be any nasty surprises this time."

"I suppose," she says, sighing, "but that still doesn't tell me what I'm going to wear."

"Let's have a squizz then," I say, pulling the book towards me and we sit looking at sparkly tops and fancy shoes for two hours, pleasantly ignoring my impending counselling session and the date with disaster that my meeting with Aidan is bound to be.

By the time we roll into bed we have agreed to make a sojourn to the Foyleside Centre after the counselling session to pick up the outfit of choice. Niamh, Daisy's assistant at Little Tikes, has agreed to hang on to both Jack and Lily until six so we get a free run of the shops. As I drift off to sleep, it's nice to feel that life can be carefree–almost – sometimes.

# 19

Switching on my computer, and drinking the first of my requisite eight glasses of water a day I see my daily email from *lifecoaches.com* is telling me to clear out the clutter of the past to move on with the future – how appropriate for the day that is ahead! There is an email from Dishy, with research on 'Depression – the Curse of the Working Woman' and another from Charlotte at Weightloss Wonders reminding me to set an exercise goal. (When am I going to fit that in, I wonder? Does traipsing round the shops count?) Lesley at City Couture is reminding me to wear my most supportive underwear for Tuesday's makeover and Louise has sent a curt email outlining her ideas for the feature – which she has also copied to Sinéad in a bid to look efficient.

I look across the office at her and she is giving me a death stare from her desk as she talks on the phone – no doubt to Briege, her partner in crime – about what a god-awful bitch I am.

Sinéad walks down the stairs into our office area – known to all who work here as The Pit. You see *Northern People* is very glam and 'with it' and our salubrious surroundings reflect just that. We, the lowly hacks, are situated on a low-level floor so that all those who enter the building look down on us – the performing monkeys –  as they go about their business. I'll admit it looks good, but I'm always just waiting for someone to spit on me from on high or drop something on my head.

Sinéad smiles her hellos, puts her doughnuts on the central desk and sits a bag of grapes on mine – winking and walking on through to her own office. I can hear an audible huff from Louise, who puts her phone down and saunters over towards my desk.

"Mind if I have a share?" she asks and sidles her skinny arse onto the side of my desk.

"Help yourself," I mutter, turning my attention to answering my emails, and filing the remainder of my copy on Child Tax Credits.

"Are you feeling better then?" Louise asks, biting a grape in half and putting the remainder in the bin. I'm guessing her calorie count is now fulfilled for the day.

"Just peachy, thanks," I say.

"Grand," she replies, "because I have the mother of all treats lined up for you this afternoon. We've arranged an induction for you at the local gym."

"That's very thoughtful, Louise, but I have something planned for this afternoon. You should have checked the group diary for my appointments."

"I'm sure you can reschedule," Louise says. "This is the best gym in town. They don't give just anyone an induction."

"I'm sure that is the case," I reply, "but I can't reschedule.

This is very important."

"I'm Health and Beauty Editor, Grace," Louise fumes, "and what I say goes."

"Not this time, it doesn't. Take it up with Sinéad if you have a problem, but I can tell you now I won't be going this afternoon – or any afternoon – to your gym. I'll decide what humiliation I want to heap on myself next, not you."

Louise stands up, turns on her designer heels and storms towards Sinéad's office. I'm not concerned, I've told Sinéad all about the appointment – in fact, if anything I'm proud of myself. Three weeks ago I would have put Louise first, cowered under my desk and sent a hundred panicky emails to Daisy asking how the hell I was going to get myself out of this one. I sip my water, smile to myself and wait to see a kowtowing Louise walk back out of the office to her desk. It doesn't take long for Sinéad to give her the flea in her ear I was hoping for and then an email pops up on my screen.

**To: grace/editorial/northernpeople**
**Subject: Well done!**

**I don't what has got into you, Grace, but I'm glad Louise has been put in her place. Saves me having to give her skinny arse a kicking myself. Keep up the good work. Sinéad**

By lunch-time Daisy has texted to confirm she will meet me at Cook Counselling. She has also informed me that Jack is having a whale of a time in the toddlers' room and already has a girlfriend. Yes, he is still a little clingy and has been giving Auntie Daisy loads of cuddles, but he is as happy as a little piggywinkle in poop apart from that.

Louise is still giving me the Evil Eye from across the office, which I'm trying desperately to ignore. I try to put myself in her place. If I was still Health and Beauty Editor, would I like it if some wee upstart (not that I'm wee, or an upstart for that matter) came along and started making demands? In fairness it was Louise's idea, initially, for the feature. She did approach me and ask me to lose weight. She did set up the makeover at City Couture, the sessions with Charlotte and the yet-to-be-experienced manicure and pedicure treat at Natural Nails. Okay, she seriously overstepped the mark with the Botox and face-lift suggestions. She has run roughshod over my feelings as regards what I feel comfortable with and she still seems more obsessed with making me look good than feel good – but I'm guessing she deserves a little credit after all. I look up and see her chewing the top of her Biro, staring out the window at the sunshine. She looks every inch the professional. Her kitten-heel shoes look perfect at the end of her long, tanned legs. She is wearing a pinstripe pencil skirt and a white, scoop-necked top which shows off her assets. Her blonde hair is twisted into an effortless chignon and she looks as though she has stopped off at the Clarins counter for a makeover before coming into work. No doubt her look is somewhat helped by the reams of freebies which arrive on her desk on a daily basis. I look again at my collection of samples – today including a non-spill sippy cup and some herbal teas to calm the most overstressed of mothers – and I feel a little jealous. It's not Louise's fault I went off and got pregnant – not her fault that she was appointed Health and Beauty Editor in my absence. Perhaps I've been too hard on her all this time. So I stand up, in my RBTs and fitted blue T-shirt, and make my way over to her desk. "Look, Louise, I want to apologise if I was snappy with you earlier. I appreciate all the work you've put in and I think you've had some brilliant ideas, but this is very personal for me."

She raises her hand to stop me from talking. "Don't worry about it," she drawls. "I've read the proofs and I can see your life is much more of a mess than even I gave you credit for. Do whatever you want. Don't worry about me – I've enough on my plate. I've heard the new manager of Jackson's is single again and that's more than enough to keep me busy."

I want to grab her by her perfectly preened chignon and swing her around my head until her bony body smashes into a wall. I want to say something that will destroy her so utterly that she dares not darken my personal space again. I want to slap her silly. In essence, I want to turn The Pit into a modern-day arena and challenge her gladiator-style to a fight to the death – but I don't, of course – I just turn and walk back to my desk. Suddenly I'm fifteen again and back in class while Lizzie O'Dowd tells everyone I made a holy show of myself. And just like then I can't think of anything to say that doesn't make me sound like a complete feckwit, or a total bitch, or just a weak, pathetic person. So much for feeling victorious at the New Me – Louise is obviously a much tougher competitor than I thought.

Just then an email pops up on screen.

**To: grace.adams@northernpeople.co.uk**
**Subject: Good Luck!**

**Hi Grace,**
**I hope you got the copy earlier on depression and the**

working woman. Give it a read. Apart from that, good luck for today. Don't expect miracles, but give it a chance. Let me know how it all goes,
Shaun

**To: shaun.stevenson@doctors.org**
**Subject: re: Good Luck!**

Thanks, Shaun, I'll think I'll need it.
G

Cook Counselling is based in a building close to Brooke Park and, as a result, Brooke Perk. Daisy and I have just enjoyed a coffee there in almost stunned silence and I just feel too nervous to talk. The nerves are such that I have not even told her about Louise's latest onslaught – or perhaps that is because I have simply been too embarrassed to reveal all. The building is old, one of those terraced houses that smell of varnish and wood. The reception area is painted in pale creams with a selection of stylish prints on the wall. An oil burner is alight on a shelf and the smell is comforting, but still my nerves are jangling. I'm on my second cup of water from the cooler and have just returned from my fourth trip to the toilet. We are sitting on a comfy sofa, listening to a radio in the background blare out a discussion on the state of the city's schools. There are two other people in the room – one is Lisa, the cheery receptionist who has asked me at least three times if I need anything. She has told me there is a veranda to the rear of the building where I can get some air if I need to.

The second person is a man in his forties – dressed in a suit and looking as if there is no way he could possibly be in need of any kind of counselling – but then I'm not exactly sitting here wearing a T-shirt proclaiming myself to be a nutter either. To the outside observer I probably look relatively normal – whatever that means.

A clock is ticking on the wall and Daisy is reading one of the magazines laid out to amuse you while you wait for the big appointment. Today she isn't cracking jokes and laughing at the Top Ten Hints and Tips, today she just keeps darting a look in my direction as if to make sure I've not chickened out and run off.

Just then a woman, middle-aged with soft curly hair, walks into the room and holds out a hand in my direction.

"Grace?" she says and I look to Daisy for reassurance that I am in fact Grace before standing up and shaking her hand. "Would you like to come with me?" she says, turning and walking up the first flight of stairs, passing a large mirror in which I see myself – looking perhaps more scared than I ever have done in life. In fact I look even more scared than when I shuffled to the labour ward to give birth and faced the prospect of excruciating agony.

She opens a door and I walk into another cream room, with abstract paintings on the walls, and an aromatherapy burner on a shelf. Crystals hang by the window and a squashy cream sofa with opulent burgundy velvet cushions sits in the corner.

"Go on," Cathy says, "have a seat."

There is no chaise longue, no ominous desk for her to sit behind. A small desk sits in the corner, but Cathy sits opposite me on an equally squashy armchair. On a small table beside where I sit I see a glass of water and a box of tissues. How I wish the water was wine!

"With your permission I've been talking to Shaun about

your case," Cathy says.

I nod, wondering what he has said. At the end of the day our few short appointments and chatty emails can't have revealed everything.

Cathy continues: "I want this to be led by you. It's not my place to tell you what is wrong, just to help you find the answers for yourself."

I nod again and realise I've yet to break breath to this woman. I wonder how it will be possible to be counselled if all I seem able to do is keep my mouth shut and nod like a wobbly-headed dog.

"What we do is called person-centred counselling," Cathy continues. "In other words we will be looking at what has happened to you and looking at how you can find a way to examine, in yourself, what has happened and what it means to you. Would you like to tell me what you feel is the most important thing that you would like to deal with in these sessions?"

I answer just as I have answered every question about this breakdown before now.

"I don't know," I say and this time I don't nod my head, I simply shrug my shoulders.

Cathy sits back and crosses her legs. She has a little spiralled notebook resting on her knee, the kind I use when interviewing people. I think to myself how weird it is to be on the other side of the fence for once.

"How do you feel?" she asks, and again I answer that I don't know, but she doesn't interject with another question. She is waiting for me to speak – she knows there is more to come.

Not one to disappoint, or to sit in an uncomfortable silence,

I start talking.

"I'm not sure where to start," I begin. "I suppose I'm here because three weeks ago I had a wee nervous breakdown and ran away from my family overnight."

Cathy raises an eyebrow, scribbles something down into her notebook but doesn't talk.

"You see, I had this argument with Aidan, he's my husband by the way, and he said I was 'fucking unbearable'." I pause, aware that I have just used a swear-word and ask Cathy if that is okay before I continue. She nods that it is. "The thing is, I didn't think I was 'fucking unbearable'. I knew we had grown apart a little but we have a son, Jack, and we both work long hours and I had no idea he was feeling this way. On top of that, I found out they were all talking about me in work and wanted me to take part in this great experiment to change my life – and, well, I'm naturally paranoid anyway, but this made it worse."

"But you are doing the experiment, aren't you?" Cathy asks.

I nod. "But I wasn't going to do it at that stage."

"So what changed?"

"Nothing, I think that is exactly what changed – nothing. You see, I realised that nothing was going to change unless I changed things myself."

"But you said before you thought things were okay with yourself," Cathy says, and I nod again, taking a deep breath.

I keep talking myself into circles. "Then, I suppose I did, but now I realise things were very not okay. I'm not happy. Nothing makes me happy, not even my son, and how dare I not be happy when he is around – because he is so precious and lovely . . ." I realise I'm rambling and that I'm talking far too fast and most probably boring the tits off Cathy who will see me as nothing more than a timewaster. After all, my problems aren't real, Are they? I'm not grieving for a lost love. I don't hurt myself and I've never seriously considered killing myself. I'm just yet another sad and grumpy twenty-something who has lost her direction in life and can't find her way back.

"Tell me more about you," Cathy says. "What was your childhood like?"

I think about this, about all the things I had – all the things money could buy including a Crystal Barbie. I think about how precious I had felt having my parents all to myself but then I think about the brothers and sisters I wished away and even though I know it wasn't my fault – could never have been my fault – I start to cry.

I'm not sure how to put my feelings into words, however, so I stumble through my jumbled thoughts as best I can.

"I'm an only child," I start. "I have an amazing relationship with my parents. I felt loved my whole childhood but," and trust me this comes as a surprise to me as the words pour out of my mouth, "I don't think I ever really felt good enough."

"Why do you think that is?"

"Well, if I was good enough, why did they want another child so badly? My mammy lost four babies that I know of. She was devastated. We were to become the Three Amigos – that's what she called us – but I know she longed for a fourth, and I didn't. I wanted things the way they were and sometimes I felt as if I wished those babies dead."

I expect Cathy to look shocked, horrified even, but she nods again and writes some more and lets me know it is okay if I keep talking.

"I mean I was four, but I never understood why they kept crying, when they had me. I was a good child, never talked back, but it wasn't enough."

"Do you still feel that way now?"

"I don't know. I suppose no, but there is a part of me wants to go back and tell that wee girl she was good enough – to mother her in the times my mother couldn't be there for her. And God knows, I understand, because if I lost my son I would be lost entirely, but I was there – scared and not sure what was going on."

I'm sobbing now, and I feel like that four-year-old. I feel like the child who thought her daddy was dead, who saw her mammy crying on the bathroom floor, who hurt her mother so badly by saying she would go and get her little brother again and make it all better.

"Do your parents know you feel this way?" Cathy asks when the sobs have subsided.

"God, no," I mutter. "I don't think it would do them any good to know. They did the best they could. They just couldn't be perfect."

"And parents should be perfect?"

"As near as possible," I say, "which is why I'm a fecking joke."

"Why do you feel you have to be perfect?" Cathy asks, an eyebrow raised. "Those are pretty high standards."

I know she is right – after all, Mary Poppins was only *practically* perfect – but explaining my need to do things right is like trying to explain why the sun sets and the moon rises. It is just the way things are – and the funny thing is I'm just about as far from perfect as it comes. I mean, look at me, sitting here, fat, with roots that need touching up, a marriage on the rocks, a work colleague who is threatening to chase after my estranged hubby and I'm in the middle of some big mad guinea-pig experiment because my life is so bad it needs professional help to make it better.

Even I can see the irony in that, so I smile, dragging my sleeve across my face to mop my tears – before spying the untouched tissues beside me.

"I kind of thought you might be able to explain that one," I say to Cathy and she sits back.

"Grace, you obviously have self-esteem issues. These relate back to your experiences as a child. You have frozen those experiences in time somewhere because even though you are an intelligent woman now with a good relationship with your parents you still feel slighted in some way. Part of you, an irrational part, blames yourself for your mother not having more children. You are carrying a millstone around your neck and you need to let go of this."

"You make it sound so easy," I sigh.

"It's as easy as you want to make it, Grace. Give yourself time. As I said before don't expect miracles, but we can work through this."

"Okay," I say.

"Do you want more children, Grace?"

"Yes," I answer. There is a need in me to feel that joy of pregnancy again, to hold a newborn again. To do it right this time – and that is exactly what I tell Cathy.

"How did you get it wrong with your son – sorry, what's his name?"

"Jack," I reply. "I never appreciated him. I only appreciate him now. I just did what I had to do. I never loved him, not enough anyway, and I know I will never get that time back.

It's gone because I was too wrapped up in myself."

"All that time, when you felt you didn't love him, what did you feel?"

"Scared," I reply and once again the truth hits me like a bolt out of the blue. "Scared that I would lose him because I deserved to. Scared because Mammy couldn't have boys and this would mean something had to be wrong with my son. I was waiting for him to die," I say, and Cathy scribbles some more.

"Do you realise that was irrational?"

"I think so," I say, "but that doesn't make up for what I threw away."

"Grace, I think you need to realise you can't rewrite the past. You can only shape the future."

*　*　*

I feel bizarre, naked almost, as Daisy and I go shopping. She is trying on an array of gorgeous clothes in Next and waiting for my approval but I feel I'm in a dreamlike state. I have a lot running through my mind, and boot-cut jeans and a beaded top with junk-jewellery combo just isn't catching my attention the way it normally would. Normally I would be sittting like Lady Muck in the corner of the changing rooms while Daisy paraded and I did my best Trinny or Susannah routine. Today I'm just nodding and smiling and feeling that everyone who walks into the room can see that I've been crying.

Daisy is kind with me. She doesn't make me give my opinion on too many outfits and we finish in record time. I buy a lovely butterfly-embellished handbag under the pretence that it is for me, when I know I will hand it to Daisy before her big date tomorrow night and wish her well. I'm glad to say I've not become the absolute worst-friend-in-the-world-ever.

By the time we pick the kids up I feel as if I haven't seen Jack in a month. I want to hold him and squeeze him forever and make up for my general crappiness as a mummy over the last two years. Cathy has told me not to be so hard on myself and I've promised to try. I've promised to start looking towards the future and that starts right now.

As we get home – normally it would be just in time to pack Lily and Jack off to bed – I set about making a picnic tea while Daisy lights the Chimnea in the back garden. We let the children run about, playing with their toys and paddling in the pool and I think to myself what a blessing children are. I'm immediately saddened that I've thrown away so much of Jack's life, but grateful to have had him in the first place. And I realise, God I realise, how much I love my parents and how I need to let go of my silly little hurt.

"You okay, babe?" Daisy asks, walking into the kitchen to get the plates and cups.

"Yeah," I reply, "I think I'm going to be just fine."

"You know where I am if you need to talk."

"I'm all talked out but thanks. Thanks for everything. You are a real star and I would be lost without you."

"Pish!" Daisy says, giving my back a rub. "You are the star and don't you forget it."

We sit outside, eating our ham sandwiches and drinking our cola while the children play and laugh. I make a sandcastle with Jack and roar with laughter when he knocks it down. I even dip my feet in the paddling pool and laugh when Lily splashes me.

As the sun goes down and the Chimnea flickers, the

children climb on our knees and Daisy starts to sing softly – 'Hush Little Baby'. Lily curls in her arms, looking young and fragile and perfect, and her bright blue eyes flicker before closing and she drifts off. Jack is not far behind and, for a while at least, we can't bring ourselves to move them and we sit there in companionable silence, enjoying every ounce of their perfection.

# 20

Today is BDD – otherwise known as Big Date Day. Of course, being married to (and estranged from) Aidan means I'm not actually sure if our meeting for lunch qualifies as a date.

Daisy's date with Dishy (DDWD) definitely does qualify in the date stakes however, so for the purposes of making life easier we have both officially renamed today BDD. I've slept blissfully – which was something I certainly did not expect – not after the turmoil of yesterday. As I wake today I feel lighter though. I feel as if I understand a little of what is going on in my life. I don't feel as inclined to say 'I don't know' if someone asks me what is wrong, because I'm starting to understand it myself.

Jack is still dozing, the exertion of the late night paying off dividends – but Lily is standing wide-eyed at my bedroom door, rubbing her eyes and scratching her tiny, gorgeous belly.

Her dark curls are all messed up from the night's sleep and her eyes are still a little droopy. In her pink pyjamas, with her pinkish toes peeping out from the bottom of her pants, she looks angelic.

"Can I come in, Auntie Grace?" she asks.

"Course you can, Schmoo-face, but be quiet – Lazybones Jack is still asleep."

"So is Lazybones Mummy," she says, her voice a delightful mix of the Derry and Scottish accent. She climbs under the duvet and curls up beside me for a Big Squishy. "I like having you here for cuddles, Auntie Grace," she says.

I tell her that Lily-cuddles are among my favourite too.

"How come Uncle Aidan isn't here?" she asks, her eyes wide with curiosity.

"Oh, sweetie," I reply, wracking my brains for a suitable response for a four-year-old, "he is painting the house and Jack and I are just having a wee holiday here until he is done."

"Okay," she says, "but he is taking a long time about it. He must be a lazybones too."

"He is, darling," I say. "He is."

"What fun things do you think we are going to do today?"

"Well, your mummy is going to take you and Jack swimming today while I do a wee message and then when I come home, I'm thinking I could take you babies to McDonald's for tea and then we could have a play together, because your mammy needs to do a wee message tonight."

"What does she need to do?" Lily asks.

"Oh, she has to see a man about a dog," I answer, giving the stock answer my own mother would have given a four-year-old me.

"Really, are we getting a puppy?" Lily answers, eyes bright

with excitement.

I've been well and truly caught out.

"No, sweetie, sorry. Auntie Grace was messing. I'm not sure exactly what she has to do."

"Can I not go, Auntie Grace?"

Doubting very much that Dishy would want a four-year-old playing gooseberry on her date, I shake my head. "Sorry, Schmoo, but hey, Dermot is on reading the news tonight and if you are a good girl you can sit up late and watch the news with me. We might even have a girly pampering session."

"Yippeee!" Lily shouts. "I'm going to tell Mummy!" She jumps off the bed and runs from the room shouting for Daisy to wake up and I'm struck by her enthusiasm and excitement.

I smile as I turn to Jack, who is stirring by this stage, and give him a kiss. "Morning, Stinkers," I smile and he curls into my arms.

I doubt there is a better way to start the day.

\* \* \*

There is a soft, warm breeze. I can see the swings move ever so slightly, as if echoing the children playing on them – only quieter now – much quieter. I take a few deep breaths in the hope it will settle my nerves and I wonder how it has come to the stage where I would be nervous about spending time with my own husband. He has seen the best and worst of me, so why I am afraid to show him the Me I have become? I'm realising now that I am changing, that I'm evolving and, dare I say it, I'm growing stronger. I'm not saying the urge to break down and cry is gone. I'm not saying I don't still feel somewhat powerless and shamed in the presence of the likes

235

of Louise and her barbed put-downs. I'm not saying I feel good about myself, but I realise I don't feel quite so wretched. That, in itself, is a revelation to me because it has been an amazingly long time since I've felt anything but wretched.

Wretched had become so much the norm of how I felt that I don't think I even realised just how bad I felt. Now though, coming out of the tunnel, I realise just how much I've thrown away. Determined not to be down-hearted – not to start this day on a bad footing – I force myself to smile. Running my fingers through my hair and letting the sun shine onto my face, I sigh contentedly.

The sounding of a car horn wakes me from my daydream. I recognise the distinct pattern of the hooting – Aidan is nothing if not a creature of habit. I lift my bag and keys, close the big red door, and make my way down the path to his car. He smiles nervously at me as I get into the passenger seat and I note that he has made an effort. Usually on a Saturday, after the late night in Jackson's on a Friday, he saunters about in his old trackie bottoms with a scruffy fleece top and an unshaven face. Today he is wearing a crisp white T-shirt (new? Or did his mum iron it?) and his faded blue jeans with chunky boots. He is clean-shaved and his hair is spiked – his dark hair has traces of blond where it has been bleached by the sun and I can smell that he is wearing 'Eternity' – my favourite aftershave. I'm not sure what to do. Should we just say hello? Perhaps we should kiss? Shake hands even? Awkwardly, I reach across and kiss his cheek and he smiles back.

"Good to see you, Mrs Adams," he says. "You look lovely."

I blush, and return the compliment and off we drive, down that familiar road to Donegal. "I thought we were going for lunch?" I say, gazing out at the fields as we pass by.

"Who says we aren't?" Aidan smiles, raising his eyebrow at me. I swear he has been watching the news just to learn a few moves from Dermot.

"Are we going to Mamore Gap?" I ask and he shakes his head.

"Nearly right, but not quite. I thought we would go somewhere a little quieter."

"Where's that then?"

"Wait and see," he teases and switches the radio on, singing along in his inimitable style to James Blunt. I almost forget that we are estranged. This is how it used to be, driving the highways and byways, the pair of us singing badly, carefree and chilled out. Neither of us can get away from reality though and soon Aidan quietens down.

"I know things aren't good, Grace," he says. "I'm not trying to ignore our problems."

"I know," I say, "and it's fine. Let's just enjoy this. There will be plenty of time for talking whenever we get to wherever the hell it is you are taking me."

The winding roads of Donegal melt into each other as Aidan drives along, faster than I ever could in such circumstances. I may well love to drive, but I'm still nervous in comparison to my husband. After a short time we find ourselves at Kinnego Bay – a wonderfully secluded beach which seems to have fallen off the end of a cliff. Only one other couple, and their dog, are here too. They are walking in the distance and I can hear their laughter carried on the breeze. Aidan tells me to wait on the sand and then he returns to the car, taking out first a picnic basket and then a checked blanket.

"Have a pew," he says, spreading the blanket on the ground.

I sit down, slip off my mules and slip my toes into the golden, warm sand – I love that feeling. It makes me feel that all is right with the world.

"Would you like some lunch?" he asks and I raise an eyebrow.

I'm always nervous when Aidan has prepared food. He is not renowned for his culinary skills – indeed I'm half-expecting to find some part-cooked chicken and mouldy cheese slapped between two halves of a stale bap. He surprises me though – taking out some crusty bread, carved ham and a selection of cheeses. With a bottle of Schloer grape drink and some fresh fruit. I can feel my taste buds go into overload. When he brings out a small of box of chocolates as well, I can't resist but deliver that world-famous line: "Why, Aidan, with zeze chocolates you are really spoiling me!" He laughs – a hearty belly-laugh and I smile back while he starts to carve up the bread, dolloping on real butter.

"Go easy!" I say. "Remember I'm on Weightloss Wonders." I have to resist the urge to make some comment about being a pathetic big gulpen who loves her bread. It wouldn't go down well.

"Sorry," he says. "You look great on it."

I reply with a quick "I know" and pour myself a glass of juice.

"I didn't mean what I said that day," he says.

I know this is the point when I usually interject and tell him never to worry about it and sure it's all in the past – but I want to hear what he has to say. I want to make him explain why he is sorry, why he won't do it again, why he was a prick. It's actually a bit like the toddler-taming techniques I wrote about last month for *Northern People*.

238

"I was pretty annoyed with you, Grace," he starts. "I still am."

What? Him annoyed with me! I don't think this was how the script was supposed to go. I'm the one annoyed with him – all his fecklessness, his messing me around. No, this was not in the script at all.

He sees the look on my face, "Before you go running off again, Grace, give me time to explain."

"I'm not running anywhere," I answer. "Whatever gave you that impression?"

He rolls his eyes to heaven, then looks at me square in the face, his dark eyes a mirror of Jack's, and he says: "Because that is pretty much what you have done lately every time the going has got tough or we have had a confrontation."

I start to tell him he is talking pish but I'm having a light-bulb moment. Yes, oh my God, how did I not pick up on this before? Christ, I have been running away! He challenges me about why I'm a grumpy fecker – and I run away to a hotel. Daisy gets cross with me for abandoning Jack overnight – something I always knew she would be annoyed about – and instead of fighting it out with her, I run away. Aidan tells me he is pissed off about me having a few (okay, seven) drinks – and I run away. I start to flush crimson. It all made perfect sense at the time – it all seemed to be the most reasonable response to the situation ever but now I realise I was being the world's biggest coward. I'm dumbstruck. No words will come from my mouth, so Aidan chatters on – apparently unaware that he has just given me more insight into the last three weeks than have Dishy, Daisy, Mammy or Cathy combined.

"I had been boasting about you all week at work," he blethers. "I told the girls, Ciara in particular, about the locket

239

and by Jesus wasn't I the most popular man at work for a week? The girls were all rooting for you. Ciara was even talking about giving the old Weightloss Wonders a whiz herself. Every day they asked and I told them how I was so proud of you – you were so damned determined – and then you come into the bar with Daisy, who you think is so much more supportive than me, and the pair of you drink yourself stupid in front of all of them."

His voice isn't angry; it is more resigned. I embarrassed him. Christ, I'd have his knackers in a vice and smoosh them to smithereens if he showed up and embarrassed me in front of the folks at the office like that. I can't believe I've been so fecking blind to all this – so caught up in *me* to realise what I was doing.

I took Aidan's son away – his baby – because of a few drinks and some fecking toast. I did that because I couldn't see that Aidan had a right to be annoyed. I didn't wait to find out what had happened – I just ran, like the silly little schoolgirl who never faced a single confrontation in her life. I'm the person who didn't deck Lizzie O'Dowd square across the jaw for being such a god-awful bitch and I'm the silly, stupid little girl who threw the letter from the dance school in the bin without even opening it, because I was damned afraid that it might tell me I was shite when I knew, I still know, I was bloody good.

I look at him. He has stopped talking now, and is looking out towards the bay. I can tell he is worried – worried that what he has said will make me run again, so I reach out and take his hand in mine.

"I'm sorry, Aidan," I say. "I never realised."

"I know that," he answers, "and I know I was still an arse. I know I'm not blameless and I'm not looking for you to take all of this on yourself, but as long as we both understand, do you think we could start trying to work things out?"

"I'd like that," I say, resting my head on his shoulder and looking out over the azure sea of the bay with him.

"Good," he says, kissing the top of my head and moving to pour me another glass of juice. "And by the way, Grace, would you fecking email my sister back? She thinks you have dropped off the planet."

\*　\*　\*

To: <u>Máiréad@ntlworld.co.uk</u>
Subject: I'm so sorry!

Hi Máiréad,

Aidan tells me I'm not in your good books. I'm so sorry for not getting back to you sooner. As you can probably imagine things have been crazy here. I think I've had one of those wee nervous breakdowns your mother is always threatening to have.

Thanks for your concern about our relationship and thanks for not emailing me just to tell me what a god-awful person I am for walking out on your brother and taking his baby son with me.

I'm sorting my head out. Rest assured, and tell your mum that Aidan did nothing wrong – well, nothing majorly wrong. He was a bit of a feckwit – as all men can be, but this is all about me and my brain.

I would try to explain it all, but I doubt the internet has enough memory to hear the whole saga. Needless to say I've been unhappy for a while, with myself and my life, and I'm trying to deal with it.

The doctor says I have depression – please don't tell your mother that one. She would probably take out an ad in the *Derry Journal* to tell everyone what a bad mother I am. I'm not saying Máire can't be a good Christian woman when she wants to be, but we both know she doesn't hold court with mental illness. (What was it she referred to depression as that Christmas? An excuse for laziness and dressing badly? Something like that anyway.)

You should know that Aidan and I met today and we are going to start working towards a reconciliation. I'm not moving back in just yet. We are going to try and recapture the magic for a bit – I don't know how possible that is – but at least we both know we aren't heading for the divorce courts just yet.

I'll explain the full story to you when you next come over. There is a bottle of wine with your name on it in Jackson's.

Take care, you groovy chick,

Grace

X

I press send, close the laptop. I stare out over the garden and take a sip of my water. My head is buzzing – doing that weird combination of feeling really excited about the prospect of getting back with Aidan and at the same time fighting feelings of shame and regret about how I treated him. Why could it not have made sense to me before? Why did I not realise I was behaving in a destructive manner? My God, I'm lucky. Lucky that he seems willing to try again. Lucky that he isn't totally fecked off at how I've treated him. My God, if my coming into the bar half-cut embarrassed him, I dread to think what the news of me moving out has done. I mean, this is Derry – nothing happens in Derry without everyone knowing about it. If Louise, who only seems to care about *Hello!* magazine and other celebrity rags, had heard about it then I've no doubt Aidan was hounded for the last week by his colleagues.

Ciara won't have let this lie. She will have been itching to know all the details and won't have bothered to think about how anyone was feeling. In fact, now that I think about it, it was probably Ciara who told Louise. After all, Ciara is Briege's sister and Briege is Louise's equally anorexic best friend.

I cringe at the very thought, but thankfully a screech of a car outside the house and the subsequent explosion of noise from the backseat is enough to distract me.

"Mammy, Mammy!" Jack shouts, running through the house towards me. "We went swimming and to the park," he declares proudly, showing me a scrape on his knee.

Lily isn't far behind, her face aglow with freckles from her day in the sun. Daisy looks remarkably fresh for one who has spent the better part of the day entertaining two hyper children. Shooing them indoors, she looks at me, hoping for some sort of clue as to how my day has gone.

Giving her the thumbs up, I raise a wry smile. There is no need to explain all the nonsense that is going on in my head when she is getting ready for DDWD. For tonight anyway I want her to believe, for once and contrary to her own previous experiences, that things can work out and love can have a happy ending without complications.

"Do you little ones want to watch the Barney movie?" I ask and the children almost combust with excitement. Settling them onto their beanbags in front of Daisy's widescreen TV, I walk into the kitchen, where Daisy has developed the pallor of a condemned woman, and I open a bottle of wine.

"Get this down your neck," I smile, clinking our glasses together. "To fun times, good-looking doctors and getting your freak on!"

She smiles back, gulping the wine down as if it contains some magic ingredient to steady her nerves. "So how did it go with Aidan?" she asks and I smile.

"Better than I thought, but there is no way we are discussing this right now when we have to beautify you for the big date."

"I'm starting to wonder if this is such a good idea," she says. "I mean, I don't exactly have an impressive track record when it comes to men."

She's right, of course. She doesn't have an impressive record when it comes to men, but by my reckoning that means she is in line for some good luck soon.

I can't pretend to really know Dishy as such, but I get the impression he is a far cry from TMF who had the audacity to walk out on Daisy and his own daughter all those years ago. TMF was the type, as it eventually turned out, to charm his way into your pants but use the time you were reaching to the bedside table for a condom to rob you blind. Dishy didn't seem like that. He seemed nice – like a Clark Kent to TMF's Lex Luthor.

"Daisy Cassidy, I will never forgive you if you don't go through with this. I mean he might fall out with me and not be my doctor any more." She looks momentarily horrified, and I grin. "I'm only joking. If you don't want to go, you don't have to go but I'll bet my bottom dollar that come ten o'clock tonight when the kids are in bed and I'm drooling over Dermot you will be kicking yourself."

"You're right," she says, sipping her wine. "Fuck it, if you can get weighed in public, I can go and get me a man."

If anyone else had said what Daisy had just said I'm pretty sure I would take great pleasure in putting their head through a wall, but she understands what an effort it takes for me to reveal my weight just as I understand the effort it will take for her go through with this.

"Go and get your clothes and make-up out," I order. "I'll run you a bath and top up your wine. The kids are fine with the TV, so enjoy this peace and quiet."

"Yes sirree, boss," she replies and we go our separate ways.

Once the bath is filled and Daisy is soaking her cares away, I load the children in the car and take them to McDonald's. The last thing anyone needs when preparing for a once-in-a-lifetime date is their four-year-old daughter demanding a makeover.

By the time we return, my normally chilled-out and casual friend has transformed herself into a sex kitten and I have to usher Jack quickly to the bath before he smears her new outfit with the remnants of his tomato sauce.

"Mummy, you look like a princess!" Lily enthuses, demanding that Daisy does a twirl for her. She rushes over, cuddles into her mother and kisses her cheek. "You are so pretty, Mummy!" she says and I can see a little tear pricking in my friend's eye.

"Don't even go there, girly," I say, reaching into the cupboard and pulling out the bag I bought just for tonight. "I've filled this with tissues, some lip-gloss, a mini-hairbrush, enough money for the taxi home and –" I add with a wink, "some protection. Now go and pour yourself a glass of water to freshen up and I'll get the children ready for bed."

She nods, hugs us, and heads for the garden table to sit and wait, just as I did several hours before. I know she is nervous. I would be too. I just wish she could see herself as others see her. I know she sees a short, young-looking girl with nondescript hair and bazookas that are on the buxom side. What others see is a youthful ball of energy, with silky hair we would kill for but would never be able to manage, dazzling blue eyes and a figure that most of the mothers at Little Tikes (to say nothing of Weightloss Wonders) can only dream of. When dressed to the nines, on occasions such as tonight, she is breathtaking.

I'm midway through conditioning Lily's hair when the doorbell rings and I hear Daisy shout her goodbyes. I scream a quick good luck down the stairs and set about settling Jack, before Lily and I take our place on the sofa with a selection of lotions and potions to beautify ourselves.

At ten thirty Lily is snoozing soundly on the sofa, her finger and toenails painted a pale pink with her peachy skin now moisturised to within an inch of its delicate life. I'm treating myself to a glass of wine when my phone beeps into life.

**"All going well. Dishy very dishy. X"**

I smile and text back saying I won't wait up. When the phone beeps again, I'm sure it's the next instalment of Daisy's life but instead I see it is from Aidan.

**"Loved seeing you today. See you tomorrow. Always yours, Aidan x"**

His words give me hope, especially as I know he has taken time out of a busy night at work to send them. I wish I could go to Jackson's now and show Louise and Ciara and anyone else who wants to see that we are not defeated yet. We might be bruised and battered and a little bit scared. I might feel as though I may vomit when I think of what I've put him through this last week, but he loved seeing me and tomorrow when we go for a family drive  together he will love seeing me again. I'm sure of it.

# 2I

I'm just drifting off into a rather saucy dream where both Aidan and Dermot Murnaghan are offering to service my every need when the door of my bedroom creaks open and I hear Daisy try to grab my attention without waking Jack.

"Are you awake?" she says, a little more loudly than she should, and I blearily open my eyes. She is grinning from ear to ear and she has the look about her of someone who needs to talk before they self-combust with excitement.

"I am now," I say, struggling to open my eyes. "Put the kettle on, I'll follow you down."

I sit up, rubbing the sleep from my eyes and trying to resist the urge to lie back down and lose myself in another passionate embrace with my favourite newsreader. Daisy looks happy. This can only mean good things. This could mean the curse of bad romance which has dogged her for the last six years is now a thing of the past. Looking at the clock I see it is three o'clock. With the average bar closing at around one thirty I figure that gives her plenty of smooching time before she got home.

Padding down the stairs, I find Daisy sitting on the worktop, mug of hot milky tea in one hand, chocolate digestive in the other.

"You are never going to believe the night I just had!" she grins. Catching a look of my haggard face she immediately apologises for dragging me from my sleep – explaining that she would not have felt comfortable discussing such matters in front of Lily in the morning.

I nod, explain that I'm only annoyed because of the passion that was about to erupt in my dream and curl up on the armchair, allowing myself a chocolate biscuit with my tea because – as we all know – food consumed during the night does not count towards your daily calorie allowance.

"Right, now that I'm sitting comfortably, you can begin," I say, taking a sip of the warm, soothing tea and feeling my body relax into the comfy cushions of the chair.

"Well, I'm not sure where to start," Daisy says and I give her a look which states quite clearly that as it is three in the morning, she better damn well start to figure the best starting point and quick. "He was lovely, Gracie! Oh my God, he was just a gentleman! I mean he was a sexy fucker too, but most of all I just thought that the whole time I was there he was really interested in me, and what I had to say."

"Where did you go?"

"Well, first of all we went to Quay West where we had the most gorgeous meal."

"Please don't talk about food," I laugh. "I'm ready to eat the scabby end of a donkey these days."

"Well, I'll not tell you I had the stuffed mushrooms then," she laughs, knowing they are my most favourite food ever.

I grin back, her enthusiasm catching me unawares and becoming almost contagious.

"We talked the whole time. I mean, I couldn't tell you what songs were playing or anything because we just talked about everything."

"Everything?"

I raise an eyebrow, wondering if Daisy has managed to bring up the subject of the wee woman in her life.

"Yes," she says. "We talked about the Schmoo and he was so okay with it, and I don't mean okay with it and then won't ever call again, because he made a point of telling me that he was not one bit phased by my being a mum. He guessed I must have been a bit keen on kiddies working in Little Tikes anyway."

"Right then, tell me more."

"After dinner we walked along the quay. It was so warm and romantic and he held my hand. I seriously couldn't decide if I would have an orgasm on the spot or faint."

"Did you do either?"

"No," she laughs, "I managed to keep my cool. Then we ended up in Jackson's of all places."

My heart beats a little faster. I'm not entirely sure why. Part of me is dog-jealous that she will have seen Aidan and part of me is panicking in case she has seen him and he has told her that the whole separation malarkey was actually my fault – well, partly my fault at least – and that we can't hate him any more – not that we hated him anyways. We just thought he was a twat, which even he admitted that he was. I realise that Daisy is chattering and I'm lost in my daydream, my feelings of guilt and love and weirdness, and I have to physically snap myself out of it and refocus on her words.

"Gracie, it was so nice. He bought a bottle of wine for us to share and found us a quiet booth so we could sit and chatter."

I'm nodding, listening now, and I realise that she is in fact talking about Aidan and, as she is not looking at me funny or throwing the chocolate biscuits in the direction of my head in a modern stoning-of-the-harlot fashion, he has not sunk me.

"That's nice," I say and she nods.

"It was. I know he has been a twat, but he seems keen to make it up. Which reminds me, Louise and Briege were there."

Oh yes, Louise – who was going to make a play for the newly single manager of Jackson's. I hope to God he put a flea in her ear or a toe in her hole. "Did he tell her to feck her skinny arse off?" I ask – suddenly alert.

"Well, not in so many words, but she kept wiggling her insubstantial fried-egg chest at him and he didn't so much as bat an eyelid. She left in disgust at about twelve."

"Ha!" I say, mentally preparing my vicious comeback for Monday morning, but then I look at Daisy and see a little pleading look in her eyes – one that lets me know she needs to finish this story. "Sorry, Dais, tell me more about Dishy – or should we officially be calling him Shaun, now that you two are better acquainted?"

"Dishy will do just fine," she smiles. "It kind of suits him." She sips her tea. "You know when you just are mad about someone and you want to find out everything about them in as short a time as possible? That is what we did. I told him everything – about TMF, about leaving to come here, about my mum and dad and their relationship with Lily –

everything."

"Ach, so you would have told him what an amazingly wonderful friend I am then?"

"Actually," she says, turning a little red, "we made a rule at the start of the night not to talk about you. It's not that we didn't want to but, with him being your doctor and all, well, we didn't want it to get weird."

"I understand," I say, only for the first time truly realising how strange it might be for my doctor – who knows the very dose of Cipramil I'm on – to spend a night chatting to the friend who is housing me while my marriage is on the rocks.

"I'm glad," Daisy replies. "I was worried you would be weird about it."

"Thinking about it, I probably would be weird about it if you did talk about me. I mean, Jeez, he even knows my weight! But enough of me, the real question, Daisy, is: did you kiss him?"

"Yes, well no, well, he kissed me! My God, it was amazing! I mean we were both a little tipsy and we were just laughing about Louise Her Flat-chestedness and he leant over the table and kissed me and before I knew it, we were snogging like a pair of sixteen-year-olds."

I wonder if I will be able to look Dishy square in the face again knowing that he has just snogged the face off my best friend.

"Is that all you did?" I say, raising my eyebrow at her, a sly smile across my face.

"I don't kiss and tell," Daisy laughs. "Well, obviously, I do kiss and tell, but I don't do anything else and tell." She winks, adding: "Although, between you, me and the wall, there *may* have been some touching in the breast area."

I look at Daisy, her face alight with excitement, and I'm sure already that she isn't going to sleep tonight. She is going to lie awake and play over this romantic scene time and time again. I'm almost envious – envious of her feeling that first flush of romance.

And then she stops smiling, looks at me, her eyes suddenly brimming with tears.

"Please tell me this isn't going to go horribly wrong. Tell me he isn't going to stomp on my heart and hurt me!"

I get up and hug my friend and let her sob. I know she is letting out years of hurt, years of feeling not good enough to be loved and I know that while she is truly excited to be at this stage of a relationship again, she is scared.

"I can't promise, Daisy," I say, "but it has to be worth the risk, doesn't it? You could walk away but I have a notion you would be walking away from happiness. And hey, if he turns into a total shitehawk, I'm sure that between the two of us we can come up with some heinous revenge plan involving castration or chest-hair waxing!"

She smiles, a snottery, watery smile and I rub her back.

"Right, missy, time for you to go to bed. I'll get you some of my Lush Dream Time Temple Rub to help you get to sleep. Have a nice lie-in the morning. I'll get up with Lily and Jack."

"Are you going to your mammy's tomorrow?"

"Is it a Sunday?"

"Yep."

"Then yep, but we won't be going until one so I order you not to get out of your pit until then."

"Yes, boss," Daisy says, saluting.

"No probs, chicken. Sweet dreams." I start running the

cups under the sink.

"Grace?"

"Yes?"

"I love you."

"Love you too, hon – now get to bed."

I wash up the cups from the tea and think about everything that has happened. I hope with all my heart this works out for Daisy because she needs a break. She needs someone to love her for the person she is. And then it dawns on me: all this time I've believed I have been relying on her. I've believed she has been the strong one and whatever Daisy says I hang on to it because I'm just so damn grateful to have her in my life as a friend.

But she needs me too. Perhaps she even needs me more. I don't know whether to feel smug about that, or very sad.

# 22

Sundays at my parents are a tradition as long-standing as the sun setting, the moon rising, the ebbing and flowing of the tides. They are what we do. We are not allowed not to do them, except in fairly exceptional circumstances like when I bugger off to Donegal to have a wee nervous breakdown to myself, or when I leave my husband.

It's hit and miss as to whether Aidan comes along. A lot of it depends on how busy he has been the night before and whether or not he has done anything wrong which I will have told my mother about.

If he has been a twat and she is aware of his twattage, then generally he'll stay at home feigning illness or talking about paperwork he needs to catch up on.

Today, given the obvious marital disharmony that is not yet 100% resolved, Aidan will not be joining us. Jack and I will see him later when he wants us to go for a walk along the beach. I think, actually, that, despite the revelation that my marriage breakdown may actually have been my fault and not Aidan's, he is scared to see my parents. I can't say that I blame him – after all, I'm not exactly doing my internal happy dance at the thought of next seeing Máire. That said, I'm strangely envious of the fact that about now Máiréad will be on the phone to her, gleefully telling her mother that she hasn't got rid of me that easily. Now *that* I would pay to see.

No, today is all about me and Mammy and Daddy. Cathy suggested, at the end of our counselling session, that I talk to them about my feelings of inadequacy as a child. I have, however, decided that this would not necessarily be very productive. My mother operates on Guilt Factor 10 most of her life anyway. She may seem like a canny, no-nonsense kind of gal but the truth of the matter is she is soft at heart. She may hide it well, because, I suppose, she has had to over the years but I know that she worries she may have messed me up. It would not help her, nor me who would only inherit her sense of guilt, to discuss my childhood issues. She did the best she could, as did Daddy. They were great parents – just not perfect. It's up to me to forgive them for not being so. I suppose while I'm at it I might as well try to forgive Daisy, Aidan and myself too. I won't try and forgive Louise though, because she is a pain in the hole.

I don't refer to my parents' house as home – simply because it is not the house I grew up in. Mammy and Daddy chose to move shortly after I decamped to university. One day I went up the road to Belfast and by the time I returned to Derry the following weekend the home of my childhood was someone else's home.

Instead Mammy and Daddy had moved to a house with

four bedrooms. You would have thought they would have wanted to downsize now that I had flown the coop, but no, they wanted more space. Mammy used to joke it was so that she could house the many grandchildren I would produce for her in the future for sleepovers and other such festivities. Being twenty and more concerned with not getting pregnant than producing the next generation of O'Donnell wains, I do believe I told her to fuck off and earned myself a clip around the ear for my trouble.

They have transformed their house into the perfect grandparents' retreat. They have a massive master bedroom which I was delighted, when the time was right, to realise had more than enough room for a crib to settle beside their bed. When Jack was tiny, and a fecking terrorist with the colic, I would on occasion fob him off on Mammy so that I would not kill him, or indeed myself.

As he grew older, and as my parents fell madly in love with Lily and claimed her as one of their own, they decided to transform a bedroom into a children's haven, complete with bunk beds (even though Jack is much too young to be allowed to sleep anywhere without bars on all four sides). Mammy is exceptionally proud of her nursery, and the children love playing there. I try not to take the huffs that the remaining two bedrooms have in turn become Daddy's study and Mammy's dressing room.

Should I ever want to stay over I'm left with the unenviable choice of the top bunk or the sofa – and therein lies the reason why I love Daisy and her king-size bed so much.

In the corner of their living-room stands a wicker basket crammed to breaking point with toys and books. When Jack isn't rolling his toy cars along with the floor with his grandad, he is climbing up on the sofa, book in hand, and demanding to be read a story.

Luckily his grandparents are only too happy to oblige him, pouring out years of pent-up love for the children they lost into the new life before them.

When Lily first called my parents 'Granny' and 'Grandad', I thought my mother would burst with pride. It's not to say that Lily doesn't have the most amazing relationship with her 'birth grandparents' (as Mammy calls them) but it would seem my mam and dad have slipped quite nicely into the gap left by TMF's family's rejection of the Schmoo. Mammy has threatened, with a few drinks in her, to mosey on over to Scotland and kick their arses but luckily Daisy and I have been able to talk her down from that particular ledge.

So it is fair to say, my parents' house feels like Jack's home, Lily's home, Mammy and Daddy's home – but most certainly not my home. That's not to say it isn't homely, but I have few memories of it. It was somewhere I dossed at weekends between shifts at the supermarket – it wasn't a place I felt akin to. I suppose that's another wee joy of growing up and getting more sensible – when you realise home is more about the people in a building than the building itself.

Pulling into the drive, Jack gets excited. He knows he will be spoiled rotten for the next two hours. I can't say that I blame him. I would be excited too if someone was going to force-feed me ice cream and provide all my favourite playthings for my amusement. My food-deprived gut is feeling both nervous and excited too. If one thing beats having parents willing to take a fractious two-year-old out of your hands for a couple of hours, it is the knowledge that they will feed you the finest of Sunday dinners while doing it.

When Aidan and I first started dating we had this incredibly stupid and juvenile argument one day over whose mammy made the best Sunday lunch. He argued that Máire was the talk of her bingo club with her spreads, while I said no one could beat Mammy's home-made apple-pie for afters. After an hour of batting our arguments back and forth, it was decided the only way to really find the answer was, as the ad says, to suck it and see.

It was my turn first. I showed up at Máire and Aidan Snr's at three o'clock one wintry afternoon. I had brought a bottle of wine and immediately Herself looked down her nose at me. I could tell she thought I had a drink problem – why else would I need to drink wine *at three in the afternoon*? She didn't say the words but they hung there in the air like a bad smell and when dinner was served I was offered milk or juice – as if I was an errant toddler. Aidan later told me that wine was not consumed in the Adams household before 8pm. (Indeed he had a major battle on his hands with the She-Devil Who Must Be Obeyed over whether or not we should offer alcoholic punch as our guests arrived at our wedding reception. Máire thought we were encouraging drunken buffoonery – we thought we were being sophisticated.) I'll admit the food was nice – Máire certainly knows how to cook. And, being of the same gene pool, Aidan knew quite well how best to get on with his parents. I sat there throughout feeling a little lost. This was not how a Sunday lunch was supposed to go. It was much too refined and polite.

The following week Aidan had the joy of experiencing lunch O'Donnell style. The wine was cracked open at two thirty and we sat in the kitchen while Mammy busied herself cooking the roast and steaming the veg. Daddy entertained us with whatever naff jokes he had heard that week and by the time the apple-pie was laid out we were all a bit squiffy and our sides were sore from laughing. As we walked home that evening Aidan conceded that I was the winner but we agreed, for the sake of surviving into our mid-twenties, that we were never to speak of this issue again.

We walk in the door, Jack screeching "Allo!" at the top of his lungs before running straight into his grandad's arms. The smell of the dinner cooking is wafting from the kitchen and I walk in to see Mammy sipping from her glass, stirring the gravy and singing along to a Doris Day classic on the radio.

"Hey, love," she says, seeing me. "Join in!"

I can't help it, her warmth is infectious, so I start to sing along, reminiscing with her about the Black Hills of Dakota. When the song is done, she kisses me on the cheek and offers me a glass of wine. Sadly, owing to not having Aidan on hand to do the driving, I have to decline so I pour some iced water and sit down at the table, which has already been set.

"How are things, Grace?" Mammy asks, returning to her gravy-stirring. "Did Daisy get her end away last night?" Always straight to the point.

I laugh. "Not quite, but she will be seeing him again."

"Great, that wee girl deserves a lucky break. And how are things with you and yer man?"

After our separation Mammy began to refer to Aidan as 'the ex' but now has taken to referring to him as 'yer man' with increasing regularity. She's obviously unsure of how to refer to him and has decided 'yer man' is the safest option.

"Not so bad," I reply honestly. "We talked and I realise that maybe some of this is down to me."

"Pish!" she interrupts. "I'll not have him putting the blame on you."

"But he's not. We just talked and I realise, God, Mammy, I've been a fecking eejit lately. Maybe I've been an eejit for a long time but we just stopped talking and I kind of took to running away. You may have noticed that."

She has the decency to nod, but her arms are still crossed over her chest. Her body language is not that of a relaxed mother-in-law. In fact, I'm pretty certain she is mentally imagining what horror she can inflict on him with her rolling pin.

"Look, Grace, I don't want you taking all this on yourself. You've not been well. You have been depressed. The last thing you need is someone foisting the blame on you."

"But that's the thing, Mammy. I need to realise my role in all of this if I'm to get better. None of us has led a blameless life; we've all done things that have impacted on other people – whether or not we meant to."

Her face freezes. I know she thinks I'm talking about her, and I probably am a bit. I'm biting my tongue, because, as I've said, digging up past hurts isn't going to help anyone, but I can't let Aidan take all the blame for the mess my life has become. I'm to blame too, and Mammy, and Daisy, and Sinéad, and Jack and everyone else who ever spoke to me because they all influenced me in one way or another. Mostly they've been brilliant but sometimes, God, sometimes they have been a fecking nightmare.

"Are you trying to say I'm not blameless?"

I sigh and shake my head. "No, Mammy, I'm trying to say *I'm* not blameless. I have issues that have affected the way I've been around people. I need to take responsibility for those or nothing is ever going to change. Can't you understand that?"

She nods but she isn't convinced, and neither am I – but to say anything else would destroy her and she has suffered enough. I've seen her cry too many tears over the children she never had – I don't want to set her off over the one she does have.

There is a certain benefit to having children. The main one being that they can provide the perfect out-clause to any uncomfortable situations. Just as Mammy is getting ready to needle some more details out of me, Jack runs into the room waving a drawing he has just done. Daddy isn't too far behind him, his face a picture of pride.

Mammy swoops him up into her arms and buries her face in his thick curls. He giggles loudly and the pair of them dance around the kitchen, just delighting in spending time with each other.

How could I ever have been angry with this woman for wanting more? How, now seeing her and Jack together – joy dancing across their faces – could I ever have wondered why she wanted that feeling time and time again?

I get up from my seat and join them in their mad dance – Daddy taking me and swirling me around the room in the way he used to when I was a little girl.

Yes, there is a certain benefit to having children.

# 23

It's funny but between the months of October and May I never once find myself walking alongside the beaches of Donegal – but during the summer months I never seem to leave them.

Again we are here, Jack building a sandcastle, Aidan helping him and me observing this little family scene before me.

It was slightly awkward when Aidan picked us up. Having decided to give it another go, I don't think either of us really understands why we are not living together under the same roof again yet. At the same time we know, we both know, that this time apart is doing us good. It is helping us to realise what we have, what we want and how we are going to get it.

Seeing Aidan now, playing with his son, I realise that I'm one of the lucky ones. I realise, of course I do, that he is still a lumping great feckwit who drives me to distraction but that his heart, foolish as it is, is in the right place. He tries so much for me, and he does bloody well with Jack.

"Look at this, Mammy!" Aidan cheers as Jack makes a nosedive for the elaborate sandcastle they have just built, sending the sand scattering in the light breeze.

Jack sits up, his perfect two-year-old smile now hidden behind a mouthful of sand, and he laughs heartily as Aidan struggles to clear the sand from his face. I lift myself off my little perch and walk towards them to join in the fun.

I don't think I can remember the last time we did this. Yup, Aidan and I have gone together. Daisy and I have taken the kids, but it's hard to remember the last time we, as a family, did something like this.

Feeling daring, and more upbeat than I have done in weeks, I challenge Aidan to dip his toes in the icy Donegal waters. Walking towards the waves, with Jack threatening to run on to beat us to the shoreline, we hold hands and I'm starting to think this can work out.

Dare I say it, but I feel happy – so I'm hoping against hope this is not one of the typical Grace Adams things when I feel happy only to have it all blow up in my face afterwards.

As we drive home, Jack sleeping soundly in his car seat, Aidan and I sit in companionable silence – and therein lies the key – because it is not an awkward silence – it is a fine silence, perfectly fine. I'm not waiting for him to tell me I'm fecking unbearable again.

As we reach Daisy's he looks at me and I look at him. I feel as shy as a seventeen-year-old. I mean, what is the protocol right now? Do I invite him in for 'coffee'? Do we have a quick smooch at the garden gate? Do we run off home and have an almighty shag-fest?

I'm simply not sure. Aidan takes my hand, and places my locket in it – the locket he gave me to tell me that he believed in me, the locket I tore off when I left him, and I can feel happy tears threatening to trickle down my cheeks.

"I have another surprise for you, Grace," he says and I wonder just what he could possibly have in store. "I've booked you into a dance class. I want you to find your rhythm again."

And I can't speak for crying.

When Daisy sees me she wonders if things have once again gone drastically wrong. My eyes are red from crying and I'm speaking in gulping phrases – most of which are unintelligible to the average human. She stands, looking at me strangely, trying to make sense while between my sobs I'm trying to mime that I'm going to learn to dance. My arms are flapping, my toes are tapping and try as she might to look concerned, Daisy starts to laugh.

Luckily I do too. "Fuck!" I eventually manage. "He has booked me dancing lessons!"

"He has what?"

"Booked dancing lessons. He said he knew I could be good and he was going to make me prove to myself that I was."

"Oh my God, Grace, that's amazing! Are you going to do it?"

"I think so. I mean it's about time I faced my dancing demons."

"Didn't Abba write a song about them?" she says, her eyebrow raised and a sly smile creeping across her face.

"Very funny, lady, but you'll be smiling at the other side of your face come Thursday night."

"Why's that?"

"Oh Daisy, Daisy, Daisy, you have so much to learn! Don't you know I never do anything without you there to hold my hand?"

"I should have known," she sighs, while putting on the kettle to make a cup of tea. She is quiet for a while then turns to me, broadly grinning. "Does this mean we get to buy new shoes?"

\* \* \*

It's halfway through the month and it's about time the October issue of *Northern People* should be shaping up nicely. It's not quite panic stations – not yet anyway – but I know this is probably going to be the most important issue of my life. Worryingly, Louise is still in an almighty huff which makes it very difficult to co-write the articles with her.

I'm left to my own devices. My article plans are done. I'm focusing on different areas, on my emotional life, my physical life and my social life. I'm pretty much on top of it all. Dishy is all set to produce his health tips. Lesley at City Couture has offered to write a general piece on how not to dress like a buck-ugly eejit and Cathy is writing something on healing your heart and your head. When I think about it like that, there isn't much for Louise to do – but nonetheless as Health and Beauty Editor she should at least fake an interest – if for no other reason than for me to tell her about Aidan and me working things out. She can stick that in her pipe and smoke it.

Sinéad walks into The Pit in a fug of cigarette smoke. Throwing the doughnuts on the desk she does not even say hello before wandering into her office and slamming the door rather violently behind.

I sense, and call me psychic if you will, that she is not in a good mood. In fact as I look around me there seems to be a general attitude of feck-offedness in the office. Louise has her phone to her ear and is jabbering away nineteen to the dozen with an expression like thunder on her face. John is battering something on his keyboard so loudly that I can practically hear the words jumping onto the screen. Liam is sitting opposite John – having emerged from his sanctuary – and he is screaming down the phone that somebody had better fecking fix his camera before he shoves it up their arse.

I, on the other hand, am smiling to myself. Dare I say it? I'm even feeling smug. Perhaps if I had paid attention to these people over the last two years I would have realised that it is par for the course at the middle of the month when the pressure is just stepping up that wee bit. Instead I've hidden behind my computer screen, trying to be as invisible as possible. (Which, trust me, was no mean feat for a 15-stone woman, I can tell you.)

Within a few minutes Sinéad has barked orders from her office that we are to congregate in the inner sanctum for the weekly editorial conference. I make my way through, holding my notebook of ideas and feature plans to me. This month isn't just meaningless crap about bowls full of jelly and colic. This month has helped me find my way again – kind of.

Taking my seat, I wait for my colleagues to join me. Sinéad sits back in her chair, stubbing out her cigarette and putting her feet on her desk. "Impress me," she says and the younger staff take a deep breath before nervously listing their ideas and giving progress reports on page layouts, photo shoots and advertising tie-ins.

Sinéad reaches me and I start telling her everything. I'm dying to tell her about what has happened with Aidan and myself but I don't think this is the appropriate time. Sinéad, nods and even (half) smiles at times. When I finish, resisting the urge to bow, she turns to Louise for her approval.

Sitting there, a look of utter lack of interest planted firmly on her face, Louise is filing her nails.

"Well, Louise? Any ideas? Any input?" Sinéad asks.

"Oh sorry," she drawls, "I didn't realise this had anything to do with me. After all, I'm only the lowly Health and Beauty Editor." Her voice is thick with sarcasm.

I should be angry. I should be having my 'stapling of her head' fantasy again, but I'm not. I feel sorry for her. She is being sarky with Sinéad, who is obviously behind the feature 100%.

One thing I learned very early on with Sinéad Flynn was that histrionics don't work with her. She is not impressed with the tortured-artist routine. She doesn't care if you are feeling a wee bit put out by office politics. She didn't get to the top of her profession with the softly, softly approach. That's not to say she isn't there when you need her. Lord knows she has been there for me over the last few weeks, but that is because my problems have been genuine. I've not just had a severe case of the huffs.

"Oh, for fuck sake, Louise! Grow up! If you can't act like a professional then maybe you need to think about your profession."

With that Sinéad moves on to Erin and her ideas about the showbiz column. She does not wait to hear what else Louise may have to offer. She does not care. I look at Louise and she is dumbstruck. I can tell she is trying to think of a witty put-down – some barbed remark to put Sinéad in her place. She needn't bother. No one could put Sinéad in her place. That's another thing Louise would need to realise.

The meeting ends and nothing is resolved between Louise and me. As I walk back to my desk she follows me. Sitting down the edge of my desk, she narrows her eyes – glares at me and whispers – in a voice not too dissimilar to Don Corleone's, "I've your card marked, Grace Adams. You think you're something special. You think you're some big shakes with your counselling and your piddling weight-loss, but don't ever forget you would *never* have got where you are without me!"

She is almost snarling. If she were a Rottweiler, her top lip would be curled and saliva would be dripping down her designer white blouse.

"I was the one who suggested you would be good for this. I was the one who felt sorry for you. I was the one who saw your pathetic fat arse waddle in here day after day. I was the one who came up with this idea. I mean, Grace, seriously – do you think you would have done anything about your sorry excuse for a life if I hadn't pushed you in the right direction in the first place? You were the office joke, Grace. A big fat joke. Don't forget *that* when you go into editorial conferences all full of yourself, licking Sinéad's arse!"

I look at Louise and suddenly she isn't pretty any more. She is ugly. Dog ugly. Nasty and vile. I realise all this time that I've felt sorry for her, that I've been ignoring the fact she is a god-awful bitch. She is the adult version of Lizzie O'Dowd and her barbed put-downs. And my God, I might be fat. I have issues. I might be wondering what will happen in my life, but I'm not a bitch. I'm a good person. Fuck it, I'm a talented person.

I look Louise straight in the eye and tell her exactly what I should have told Lizzie O'Dowd all those years ago.

"Fuck off!" I say, turning my back to her, picking the phone up and getting on with my work. I'm shocked when I find that I'm smiling as I carry on with my writing. This is an achievement worthy of an entire page of editorial in itself.

*  *  *

I am smiling broadly as I walk into the doctor's surgery. I'm pretty sure the receptionist behind the counter doesn't recognise this smiling, cheerful version of me before her and she looks at me suspiciously when I tell her my name. I can tell what she is thinking. She is thinking, "Grace Adams doesn't look like that. Grace Adams scares me. Grace Adams looks as though she is 5.3 seconds away from taking a rifle to the watchtower and gunning us all down."

With a spring in my step, I make my way down the corridor for my weekly appointment with Dishy (Daisy's boyfriend – how Daisy and I have giggled over the fact she now has a 'boyfriend' – at twenty-eight! It sounds so decadent and youthful). The waiting room is filled with its usual mix of sick children, grumpy-looking pensioners and surly schoolchildren annoyed that their summer holidays have been interrupted by a serious case of the lurgy.

I take my seat and watch for the buzzing of the light which will invite me into Dishy's inner sanctum. Daisy has informed me that I'm not, under any circumstances whatsoever, to discuss her date or Dishy's feelings towards her. Instead I am, she says, to focus this precious ten minutes of Himself's time on making me feel better. Pah! Daisy is a killjoy.

The light beeps and I walk to his office, my smile not hiding the excitement I feel at the latest development in his life.

Must. Not. Talk. About. It.

"Hi, Grace, please have a seat."

I plonk myself down, cross my legs and look at him with a silly grin on my face.

Must. Not. Talk. About. It.

"How are things?" he says, looking at me intently, the usual look of caring and compassion belying any feelings he may have about my best friend.

Must. Remember. He. Is. A. Professional.

"Fine," I say, pausing before my brain finally kicks in to tell me that I'm supposed to be talking about me right now. "Things are going well. I'm starting to see the light at the end of the tunnel – and it's not an oncoming train." I giggle girlishly. Remembering that Dishy kisses like a sixteen-year-old.

"And did you see Cathy?"

"Oh yes, she was great. I mean, it was hard. I realised that the things I didn't think were annoying me were driving me to distraction."

"Are you going to see her again?"

"Yes, this week. This week we get to talk about Aidan."

"And how are things there?" He pushes a box of tissues toward me ever so slightly. A movement most would not even notice but which lets me know I've done an awful lot of crying there over the last month.

Pushing them back again, I smile. "Fine," I say. "We are talking. Really talking." My hand moves to the necklace I'm wearing, my locket back where it should be. "And he has booked me dance lessons."

"Yes, Daisy told me," he says, and my eyes widen and I have to fight every urge in my body not to shout 'I win, I win! You broke the rules first!'.

He blushes slightly, so I decide to keep schtoom. We say our goodbyes, agreeing to maintain my dose on the Cipramil for another two weeks and I leave the office – for once smiling as I leave. I can tell the receptionist is confused. Very confused.

# 24

Tuesday morning. I'm lying, dozing comfortably, while Jack does tiny baby snores beside me. The sun is battling its way through the blinds, and the room is already warm. I'm relaxed. I'm chilled out, I'm smiling to myself and then I remember it is Tuesday. The day of the makeover. The day when a woman I have met but once before will put an array of clothes out for me to wear. She knows my size. She will most probably open a curtain while I'm midway through changing and see me in my bra and pants looking like a refugee from the Roly Polys, that old comedy troupe of tap-dancing fat women.

Liam is going to be there too. Not in the changing room of course, that would be going too far, but he will show up for the great transformation and see me in whatever combination Lesley has chosen for me. My heart sinks slightly – but only slightly. Yes, I will have to show someone me in my best pants, but I should also become a beautiful butterfly emerging from a cocoon – the ugly duckling transformed to a beautiful swan. I sit up, stretch and walk to the bathroom where I run the shower. Stepping under the hot streams, I gasp. Sometimes I forget just how strong Daisy's shower is. Each time I step out I check the plugholes to see if my nipples are floating down there somewhere.

I get out, dry off and make my way downstairs where Daisy has gathered the troops and is serving up the required Weetabix/Cheerio combo when all they really want to do is to play outside. The coffee is ready and she has the bread all ready to pop down in the toaster.

"How are you feeling?" she asks, turning towards the fridge to fetch some freshly squeezed juice.

"Not so bad. In fact, I'm looking forward to it. I only wish you were coming too."

"Unfortunately, I do have to go to work sometimes. I'm only the boss," she laughs, rolling her eyes. "But if you see some classy wee designer numbers in my size, please stick them in your handbag and bring them home for me."

"Yes, boss," I say, saluting her as I take a bite of toast.

✳ ✳ ✳

City Couture sits in the Craft Village – a gorgeous little retreat in the centre of town where traditional shops, aimed at the tourists, mix with the very finest in designer boutiques. It's quite bizarre that in one shop you can buy a tacky '*Kiss me, I'm Irish*' plastic hat and in the next you can buy the latest creation from Donna Karan.

As I walk through the door to City Couture a little bell

pings. On the walls there are tasteful pictures of the LWL (ladies who lunch) dressed by Lesley. To my surprise the article I wrote while pregnant has pride of place over the counter. I wonder if she has put it there just for today? The front of City Couture does little to show what goes on behind the much-talked-about gold curtains which run behind the back of the counter. This is merely a waiting area, with squashy sofas, a fridge with the finest designer water, and vases of fresh-cut tulips and lilies. A low coffee table is strewn with the latest glossy mags. I get the impression no one actually reads the magazines – it would disturb the display too much.

A CD player is on one side, some relaxing classical music playing. All in all, it looks like the kind of place I'm usually terrified to go into in case I break something, or leave a dirty mark or am asked to leave à la Julia Roberts in that infamous *Pretty Woman* scene.

Spotting the old-fashioned bell by the counter, I press the button and it rings. A voice echoes from behind the gold curtain that its owner (whom I'm now imagining to be the Wizard of Oz) will be out shortly to help me.

I take a seat and look at the covers of the glossies – last month's *Northern People* is there, complete with a strapline about my Messy Play feature. Has it really been only a month since that day when I was up to my elbows in jelly and thinking that losing weight was something I would never achieve? I take a deep breath and steady myself. Everything happens for a reason – even nervous breakdowns and separations.

The curtain pulls open and Lesley is there, all 5'2" of her – skinny, blonde, perfect. She could well have been one of my bridesmaids.

"Grace," she says, cheerfully, "I was just putting the finishing touches to your ensembles. How very lovely to see you again!"

There is a warmth in her smile that I was not expecting. In my experience fashion folks don't deal with larger ladies all that well. They tend to give us a wee look up and down before directing us to the back of the shop – somewhere I have dubbed the Corner of Shame – where all the hideously shapeless clothes hang, almost falling off the hangers that are designed to show off clothes no bigger than a Size 14. For some reason the Corner of Shame always seems to be dimly lit as well. I'm sure the powers that be would tell you this is to create a slimming silhouette but I think it is more so that passing customers can't see that this shop caters for the (gasp!) obese.

I extend my hand and smile at Lesley. "I'm a little nervous," I admit, the words dripping from my mouth before I've had time to engage my brain. I hope she doesn't think I'm nervous because the last time she dressed me I looked like a Fimble on acid by the time she was done.

"No need to be," she smiles. "It's only us girlies."

Deciding humour could be my best defence, I say, "Yep, but some of us are the size of two girlies!"

She smiles, shakes her head. "Nonsense, Grace! I promise you I will have you feeling like a million dollars by the time we are done. You have a lot of assets we can show off. My God, I would kill for a cleavage like yours!" She pauses, putting the closed sign on the door and locking it, then she turns back, stares down at her own small but perfectly formed chest. "I would kill for any kind of a chest at all."

Just goes to show, we women are never happy.

It is then I am invited behind the gold curtain, which I have decided now to dub the Curtain of Dreams. I wonder if by the time I come out of it I will have undergone a mad transformation à la the folks on *Stars in their Eyes*.

"Tonight, Matthew, I'm going to be Mrs Adams again!"

The inner sanctum of City Couture is, I'm guessing, a shopper's dream. Directly ahead of me is a full-length mirror. I can see another one angled behind me, so that when I stand before this imposing sight, I will also be able to see how large my ass looks as well. There is a small podium, somewhere I imagine I will stand to have my photo taken and have Lesley decide if her choices are suitable or not.

On one side there is a changing room, complete with yet another Golden Curtain of Dreams. Facing it there are some more squashy sofas, and a small table with a couple of wineglasses ready and primed to give me the Dutch courage I so need. A large clothes-rail is crammed, totally crammed, with clothes, and beside it sits a plethora of accessories. I am tempted to phone Daisy to tell her about the accessories if nothing else – but it would be cruel to tease her.

"Right, Grace," Lesley says matter-of-factly. "You told me you want more of a yummy-mummy look, as well as something to feel more comfortable in at work – so I've put together a work wardrobe and a weekend wardrobe. There are some nice day-to-evening pieces in here as well if you fancy getting dressed up."

I nod, my eyes glancing at the fabrics and colours, dazzled by the array of clothes – and then I spot the shoes. I gasp. Really, I should phone Daisy. Would it seem unprofessional?

Seeing that my gaze has been drawn towards the pair of

green Mary Janes, Lesley smiles – looking ever so proud of herself – and says: "There are fabulous, aren't they?"

I nod mutely.

"Let's get started. I've put a selection of workwear in the changing room, set out in different outfits. Go in and get changed and we'll see what works and what doesn't."

A bubble of excitement threatens to burst out of me. "Okay," I grin, making my way into this gorgeous little Aladdin's cave of nice, shapely clothes.

I take a deep breath, holding it in, pulling my tummy tighter as I look around me at the clothes Lesley has laid out. I breathe out, shocking myself that my spongy tummy doesn't spring back out just as far as it would have done several weeks ago.

I step out of my clothes – my tatty old exterior – and look at what is before me. I feel the fabrics, their rich, starchy materials feeling so cool and fresh in my hands. I pray they will fit. I pray this won't be one of those times I quickly dress back into my old duds before opening the curtain and shaking my head meekly in the international sign language for 'Sorry, I can't actually get this zipped up'.

First up is a skirt. A gorgeous, chiffony, black skirt which skims my calves. I slip it on and slide the zip up with ease. In fact, there is room, if I so wished, to put my hands inside my waistband without risking cutting off circulation. Beside it hangs a crisp white wraparound shirt. I pull it on, expecting the contrast of black and white to make me look like a nun or a penguin but find that instead of accentuating my gargantuan hips, the fitted lines of the blouse show off the fact that I have a waist. My God! I have a waist. When did that happen? I breathe in again, close my eyes and settle the voices in my head which are screaming with joy that the clothes fit. Slipping my toes into a sexy pair of kitten heels which Lesley has left by my feet, I feel myself stand straighter – my poise immediately changing from the slumped-over unconfident woman of my past. I can't resist a stupid grin.

"Are you okay?" Lesley asks.

"Fine, just fine," I grin, pulling the curtain across so that Lesley can see just how fabulous her work really is.

She pulls a face, puts her hand to her chin and juts just one hip out as if in deep thought. "No, no, no, Grace! That's totally wrong for you."

No, it's not! I'm saying the words internally but I can't bring myself to say them out loud. No, I look good. I know I look good. I am tall and gorgeous. You will not make me feel bad today.

"The skirt," she mutters, stepping closer.

What about the skirt? I want to scream. The skirt is fine. I can fit both my hands in the waistband. I want to show her, to dance around the shop with my hands flapping in the side of my skirt in gay abandon. Of course, I just start breathing in tighter, hoping she realises it looks as good as I think it does. It falls down. I'm standing in my pants and Lesley is looking at the crumpled skirt on the floor.

"You need a smaller size, Grace," she says and I don't argue with her.

As I step back out of the changing room, in a skirt that fits, that looks even better than the previous outfit, my heart swells.

"Fabulous!" Lesley screams, clapping her hands with excitement.

Normally such a display of enthusiasm would annoy me but

today I want to join in, so I grin a happy 'I know', and dash back in to change into work outfit number two. Slipping on a pair of gorgeous black hipster boot-cut trousers, I feel glamorous. When I slip the knee-length black and white wraparound dress over the top I see my reflection appear before me and I know I have a decent figure. Okay, I'm not going to give Kate Moss a run for her money and yes, there is definite room for improvement but this looks good. Zipping up some knee-length boots under my trousers and swinging some chunky beads around my neck I look – can you believe it – I look like a professional.

"Perfect!" Lesley squeaks, readjusting the beads and pulling my hair back in a glossy chignon. "I have just the perfect accessory for this," she adds, pulling out a black leather handbag of such beauty that I fear I may swoon. It is big enough for my requisite notepad, and also has room for a spare stash of nappies just in case. Hanging from the strap is a little leather butterfly and my heart soars. Daisy would approve and I can't wait to show her.

I don't want to change out of this outfit. I love this outfit. I feel like Mrs Adams dressed this way, but Lesley is pushing me back into the changing room and I'm trying on trousers and skirts and dresses like never before. Some fit, some are too big, none are too small. This feels amazing.

Two hours later I emerge in a smart pair of boot-cut jeans, the funky green Mary Jane wedges on my toes and a layered top in green and cream. The requisite beads are slung around my neck again and I have a comfy cream cardi by my side in case it gets cold. I'm grinning from ear to ear.

Sinéad has joined us and is sitting on the big sofa, glugging wine and smiling broadly. "My God, Gracie, you look fucking amazing!" She sits back and applauds me (and Lesley too for good measure).

"I do, don't I?" I say, twirling on the podium like a movie star. "When is Liam coming for the photos?"

"He's not," Sinéad says, a smirk creeping across her face. From the look on Lesley's face I can tell she is in on whatever is going on.

"Why not? What's happening?"

"You don't think we would take your picture without full make-up and hair, do you?" Sinéad asks, her smirk now a grin. "Grace, next Tuesday you are booked in for a total transformation. Hair, make-up, nails, the works. Then you get these clothes. Then you get your photo shoot and then we put this edition to bed."

# 25

I don't feel nervous tonight. I know I've been a good girl. I know I've shunned wine and chocolate for water and fruit. I know I feel better, look better even and so I'm not as scared at the prospect of the scales. Daisy looks sick, however. She hasn't been so good. She has been eating and drinking like there is no tomorrow – although she argues she should get away with more because her job involves running around after children while mine involves 'sitting on your arse salivating over pictures of Dermot Murnaghan'. (Her words, not mine.)

I'm standing in the queue, waiting my turn at the scales. I see a few familiar faces. We nod, grimacing or smiling depending on the kind of week we have had, and each of us does a fake fingers-across-the-throat sign to signify we might get a shock. It's not good form, you see, to admit to being *über*-good at the start of a meeting. We might all be here to support each other, but secretly we feel sickened if someone loses more weight than us. I know I definitely got some half-hearted applause last week with my half-stone loss. I see a new lady enter the room. Her head is bowed. She doesn't want anyone to notice her and as she fills in her registration details she keeps her arm protectively around her clipboard – much like you would when trying to make sure no one copies you at school. I notice her shake her head as she fills in the details and I know what she is thinking. I know how low she feels and I want to run over and comfort her – to tell her that she is thinking the exact same thoughts I was two weeks ago but that it can and will get better. I want to tell her to be confident in herself. I want to tell her she is attractive and *can* do this. I also have a notion to tell her not to eat half a loaf of toast on Friday night in case her significant other takes the wobblies and her marriage falls apart. Instead I just sigh to myself and realise that I, myself, no longer want to hide away and while I can't fix everyone else's woes, I'm doing an okay job of fixing my own.

Daisy tries to shove me in front of her as we reach the top of the queue. "Go on," she grimaces. "I'm not sure I want to do this."

"Don't be daft," I chide. "C'mon, the sooner this is over the sooner we can treat ourselves to a sausage supper for our efforts!"

We have made a deal, you see, that if the scales are good tonight we will go all out and buy chips on the way home. We have promised to share a bag, mind. I'm not going to do the usual Grace Adams thing of beating a full bag down my neck and feeling sick and bloated the rest of the night.

Throwing me a defeated look Daisy steps forward for her chat with Charlotte. She breaks into a smile and before long walks towards me, giving me a sign I at first mistake for the fingers but then realise she is letting me know she has lost 2lbs. She is now back to where she started and she couldn't be happier.

I step forward now. I'm suddenly nervous even though I shouldn't be. Stepping on the scales, I force myself to glance downwards and see that the reading stops at 14 stone and 9 pounds. I have lost three pounds. That is 10 in total – which is nearly a stone. I can't help but break into an excited grin.

"Well done, Grace!" Charlotte says, writing down my new total. "You really seem to be taking this on board."

I nod, enjoying my moment as teacher's pet.

But then Charlotte looks directly at me, crossing her legs and leaning back in her chair. "And exercise? Have you done much?"

I could lie. I've written enough about aerobics, pilates and yoga to fake a class or two, but what would be the point? I'd only be caught out when the article was printed anyway. Shaking my head, I realise I've lost my teacher's pet position and I start to apologise. I'm waiting for Charlotte to tell me she is very disappointed in me, that she wants me to report to the headmaster to decide my fate but then I remember what she said last time. It doesn't have to be a traditional exercise class, does it?

"I'm going to a dance class on Thursday," I pipe up, my voice probably a little too overexcited. The only thing missing from my sentence was a triumphant 'So there!'.

Charlotte smiles. "That's great, Grace. Dancing is amazing exercise. Good luck with it. I can't wait to hear how it goes."

"I'll email you on Friday morning," I say, confident I'm now in the good books again.

Daisy and I grin at each other as we walk out of the school hall towards our cars. "I'll get the chips," she shouts. "You get the wains!"

I nod and set off in the direction of Mammy's house, where Jack and Lily will be waiting. I can't wait to hug them and to tell Mammy the news of my weight loss. I would love to tell her about telling Louise to fuck off too but she doesn't really appreciate foul language. I'll have to edit the story to suit her sensibilities.

I park the car and see Daddy is cutting the grass. I smile at him and he turns the mower off, and comes over to kiss me on the cheek and say hello.

"The kids are inside running your mother ragged," he laughs, wiping the sweat from his brow. "You look well, Gracie," he smiles and I smile back.

"I'm feeling good, Daddy."

"You know how we worry."

"There is no need, not now. I'm getting through this."

"I'm very proud of you, darling," he says. "I know it's not been easy. I know we've given you a lot of grief over the years. I just want you to know you have always been enough – more than enough – for us and I'm sorry if we didn't show it."

This feels surreal. Daddy doesn't do emotion. He doesn't talk much at all apart from telling silly jokes at the dinner table or saying the occasional rosary. And yet, here I am, standing in the front garden with my father – tears in his eyes – apologising for the one and only thing my parents ever did wrong. I'm almost tempted to ask him to repeat himself because I'm not sure if I've actually heard him right, or just heard what I wanted to hear.

I hug him, holding him tight and he lets me. He pulls me

closer and we stand there – in the garden – in front of the neighbours and anyone who wants to look or cares to see, and hug until I hear Jack and Lily come running into the garden looking for their share of the action.

Driving home, I can't help but smile. Lily and Jack are chattering in the background like a pair of cute baby birds. I know their excitement will only increase when they find out we have proper chip-shop chips waiting at home.

"Auntie Grace," Lily chirps and I look at her through my rear-view mirror. "Granny Mammy says we are the Six Aminos – what's an amino?"

I laugh, her childish mispronunciation making me feel warm and fuzzy inside. I answer, "An amigo is a special friend. You, me, Jack, Grandad, Granny Mammy and your mummy are all special friends."

"Yes, we are," she grins, "and Uncle Aidan too!"

"Yes, Uncle Aidan too."

✳  ✳  ✳

The music is thumping in the background and I'm struggling to hear Aidan over the noise.

"Is everything okay?" he shouts down the phone as I press the receiver tightly to my ear in the hope of hearing him a bit clearer.

"Just fine, Aidan!" I shout. "I just wanted to say I love you."

"Are you okay?"

"Perfect!" I shout and hang up.

Daisy is staring at me from across the room, a silly grin on her face. "Grace is in lo – ove!" she sings. "I love it when things go right."

# 26

I can't remember the last time I went shopping in my lunchtime for something other than nappies, Calpol or a wilted ham sandwich and yet here I am, standing in the middle of Debenhams – at the Pineapple concession – looking at the self-same dancewear I mocked Daisy for buying two weeks ago.

I pull out a black, off-the-shoulder, slouch top with the Pineapple logo emblazoned in pink across the front. Next I pull out a pair of funky boot-cut tracksuit bottoms and make my way to the changing rooms. Before now the changing rooms in Debenhams have been my least favourite place in the world. Yes, I'll have sat there happily advising Daisy on what looks fabulous on her (almost everything) and what looks naff on her (virtually nothing) – that much I was fine with. What I could never stand though was stepping into the teeny, tiny changing rooms with their huge mirrors, which I swear they bought at one of those fun-house places because surely no one is *that* fat?

Now I don't mind. Every curtain on every changing room is now my Golden Curtain of Dreams, and while I know not everything will fit and I know that I'm still on the wrong side of a Size 16, I know that I'm getting there and I have nothing to fear any more.

I slip out of my RBTs and into my new ensemble. I scrape my hair back in a shaggy ponytail and turn 360 degrees slowly to check all angles. Not bad for a fat bird. I get dressed and start to make my way out of the changing rooms, making my mind up that I will buy one of those fancy designer water-bottles all to myself before tomorrow night's dance class.

Head held high, I head to the counter to pay for my purchases and straight into the path of one Lizzie O'Dowd. The years have not been kind. I always wonder if I look like a woman hurtling towards her thirties and now I realise I don't. I'm quite a youthful-looking twenty-nine in comparison to Lizzie, who now looks closer to her forties than I would have thought possible. She looks fatter too, fatter than me anyway.

This is my moment. My chance to shine, to tell her she did not defeat me. This is where I tell her just how fabulous my life has become, where I play out years of fantasies, where I shove my business card in her hand and let her know I am somebody. This is where it all ends – where I let go and move on. This is perfect.

I look at her, noting a faint glimpse of recognition in her eyes, and I smile at her, moving closer towards the queue and muttering under my breath, just as I did with Louise, "Fuck off!"

I am free.

\* \* \*

Dressed in my Pineapple ensemble, with my Pineapple twin Daisy beside me, sipping from our Pineapple water-bottles I feel excited. There are no nerves – no sense of impending doom. I am wearing a pair of rather fetching dance shoes, not dissimilar to the ones they wear on *Strictly Dance Fever*. They even have a little smattering of diamanté on the T-bar.

I feel as invigorated as I did at sixteen when I was imagining I was that backing singer for Bros. All that is missing is Matt Goss dropping his kecks and revealing his American-flag boxer shorts. I've been having imaginary conversations in my head all day where I reveal 'I'm a dancer'. I find myself standing taller, pointing my toes and thinking about poise.

There is a strange sense of irony that I'm here, in my old dance school – the school to which I never allowed myself to go – aged twenty-nine and more confident than I have ever been. I let a little squeak of excitement leave my lips and I ask Daisy to pinch me.

"Are we really here, Daisy? Am I going to do this?"

She nods, putting her arm around my waist, "We are and you are."

Two women walk to the front of the class and tell us it is time for a warm-up. This week we are dancing the merengue, I'm told – a dance from the Dominican Republic.

"Loosen your hips and get ready to feel the music," the short blonde teacher shouts, turning on the stereo and letting the sexy Cuban beats fill the room. "Now sway your hips!"

She steps from side to side in a fluid and sexy movement. I join in, instinctively knowing what to do. My body seems to pick up the rhythm. I should be self-conscious but I'm not. I don't care. I'm good at this. My body is good at this – spare tyres and all. I want to walk to the front of the class and show them all how to do it. I'm lost in this music and it feels amazing.

* * *

I don't feel this appointment is necessary. I was having quite a great time sitting at my desk, writing, editing furiously – putting the finishing touches to my article, enjoying the buzz of the office, the banter with Sinéad and Erin. Louise has been behaving. She has left me in charge of the layout of the Life Change spread but has stopped doing her spoiled-brat routine. She managed to tell me I looked as if I had lost weight yesterday, and the compliment didn't choke her.

Nonetheless I made a commitment to be here for at least four weeks and I suppose I'd better keep it. The room is as calm as it was last week, the chimes are tinkling softly in the breeze and the fresh jasmine smells permeate the room. Cathy sits opposite me, her notebook poised, her ear ready to listen and she waits for me to start.

Today we are supposed to talk about Aidan. Apparently it's all about discussing the symptoms and the problems to find the cause but not the blame. Or something.

But there is so much just waiting to bubble out that Aidan seems like one small fish in a very big pond. There is Jack,

Daisy, Máire, Louise, even Lizzie to talk about. I want to tell Cathy how they have shaped me, affected me, changed me. I'm just not sure how to start.

"Don't worry," she says, as if sensing my thoughts. "In your own time.

I stand up and start to walk around the room, walking being the only way to keep up with what is racing through my mind.

"I'm getting better," I say. "I don't feel like crying. In fact I haven't cried since Tuesday and even then, those were happy tears."

She nods.

"I feel as if I'm seeing the world for the first time in a long time and it's bright, and colourful and full of hope. When I see Jack and his excitement for things, I feel it too. I allow myself to feel it. I don't push the emotion away. I don't have that wee voice telling me I'm making an eejit of myself any more."

"What do you think has changed?" Cathy asks, and it's a good question.

I find myself repeating that oft-used phrase of last month.

"I don't know. Maybe it's the happy pills, maybe it is these sessions, or singing 'The Wheels on the Bus' with a room full of strange adults."

"That's good, Grace. It's good to know you feel better. And how about your relationships?"

"Aidan and I are trying again," I say triumphantly. "We are taking it slowly but surely, and talking a lot." (I'm guessing Cathy would approve of us talking a lot.)

"And your parents?"

"It's all good."

"Did you talk to them?"

"Yes and no."

She raises an eyebrow (in a manner not too dissimilar to the delectable Dermot).

"I didn't chicken out," I protest. "I just don't see what good it would do. We've all made peace with it now."

She looks as if she doesn't believe me. "You don't put a sticking plaster on an  amputated leg," she says, avoiding my gaze as I stare at her in bewilderment.

I sit down, deflated by her belief that all is not right with my world.

It is her turn to walk, and she does. She stands up and walks to the window, opening it just a touch more so that the wind chimes rattle together. The breeze is still warm though and, as I watch the gentle billowing of the voile curtains, I have to force myself to focus on the task in hand.

"My leg isn't falling off," I say, gesturing at my extremities, struggling to find a clever put-down and failing.

"What I'm saying, Grace, is that you feel good now. You've had a counselling session. You are taking tablets. You have lost a little weight – but you won't get better, really better, until you have laid your demons to rest."

"I'm not stupid and I'm not sick either," I say, a note of anger in my voice. God, why when I'm doing well does someone have to try and knock me down again? I tut and put my head in my hands. I'm tempted to cover my ears to block out this waffle.

"Don't get angry," Cathy says, sitting down again opposite me.

Immediately I jump up again. To any observers this must look like one fucked-up version of Musical Chairs.

"angry!" I bark. "I'm telling you I'm doing okay and you are as good as calling me a liar. I feel alive this week. I've not felt this way in such a long time. I don't have a fecking amputated leg!"

"I'm not saying you haven't come a long way," Cathy counters, "but don't make the mistake of thinking you've completed the journey." Here she is with her metaphors and flowery language again. I wish she would call a spade a spade, or a mentalist a mentalist.

"Why do you want me to hurt my family?" I ask, sitting down defeated.

She doesn't get up this time. "I don't want you to hurt anyone, but I want you to help yourself. Get the feelings out there. You don't have to tell them, but you need to clarify this for yourself. Think about what you are feeling and why. Write it all down and then you can decide what to do. Hang on to it or let it go. You're a writer, Grace; you know how to use words. Use them to your advantage." She pauses, sitting forward, looking me straight in the face, waiting for my response.

I sigh, head in hands again.

She reaches for my hand, gently touching it, pulling it from my face. "I've seen too many people think they've dealt with their problems when all they've been doing is sweeping them under the carpet. I don't want that to happen to you."

"I went to see them the other night, my parents," I say, in case she doesn't realise who I'm talking about. "I watched them as they played with Jack and Lily. I watched the joy on their faces. I saw the happiness those two children brought and who am I to be so selfish as to have wanted that all to myself?"

"You were four," Cathy says, as if that is an excuse for acting like a spoiled brat.

"I was spoiled and selfish," I say, "too spoiled and selfish to realise how much they did love me."

"You have told me you were scared."

"Of course, I was. Mammy is pregnant one day, the next she isn't. The baby is gone and no one tells me why. They just cry and Daddy disappears and I can't make it better."

"You were four," she repeats, as if that is an excuse for not being able to make it better.

"I was glad of it. I didn't want another baby. I wanted Mammy and Daddy all to myself. I wanted them to stop trying because every time they tried, and every time they failed, they stopped being my mammy and daddy for a while and I needed them."

"You were four."

"I was only four," I say, and start to cry big gulping tears.

I can't believe I'm still here, stuck in this childish moment. I get up again, these damn thoughts racing and I walk around, sniffing and weeping periodically.

"Twenty-five years," I say, "Twenty-five fecking years of feeling like a consolation prize!"

Cathy poises her pen over her notepad. I sense she feels she is getting somewhere now. She is getting to the crux of the matter. She has made me cry. As her pen moves across her paper I imagine she is writing 'CONSOLATION PRIZE' in bold letters with asterixes and doodles on the side.

"Are you only talking about your family here?" she asks.

And I scream, "Of course I'm fecking not! I'm talking about everything and everyone and never feeling good enough – not until now – and now that I do feel good enough I'm so damned angry that I wasted so much time not feeling good enough."

The writer in me knows that sentence was clumsy and

grammatically pish-poor, but there is no other way to express my feelings.

I've felt not good enough my whole life – and why? – because of something that was beyond my control and got locked in my four-year-old brain? How stupid was I? I have let it colour every experience, every thought for twenty-five years, and I've let what should have become a distant childhood memory become this colossal issue that has almost destroyed me.

"When I was in secondary school, I had a best friend," I start. "Her name was Eve and she was so cool. She liked Bros too and we would sit and chat for hours in each other's houses, listening to our tapes, making scrapbooks, planning trips to London where we would marry our idols. We had sleepovers at least once a week and of course we never slept. We just talked all night. Eve was like the sister I never had and we were inseparable. We both hated the school bully Lizzie O'Dowd." I pause, wondering briefly if Cathy knows or is indeed related to my arch-nemesis. I feel compelled to watch for any flicker of recognition in her face. There is none. I decide to carry on. "We would sit for hours and plot our revenge on Lizzie and her cohorts, thinking how much we would laugh and gloat when we were married to the Goss brothers and she was left on the shelf. When I was a teenager, I auditioned for the dance school. I loved dancing," I twirl around for effects, the tears still dripping from my face. "I thought I was pretty damned good. I *was* pretty damned good!" I stomp my foot and sit down. "The next day I went into school and overheard Lizzie tell her cronies I had made a holy show of myself. That hurt, but what hurt more was that sitting there, laughing beside her, was Eve. We never spoke again. She became part of Lizzie's group and the worst of it was that I can't say I blamed her. I mean, there was me, Grazing Grace, all on my own – and then there was Lizzie, with all the cool girls. I'd probably have done the same, but I didn't get the chance."

"And this renforced the notion that you weren't good enough?"

"I was there for Eve until something better came along," I sigh. "I was the consolation prize, the starter before the main course, the Tesco Value version of what a friend should be."

Cathy writes some more, and I talk some more.

"When I started at *Northern People* I thought I had laid my demons to rest, and when I was appointed Health and Beauty Editor, I was convinced I had left them behind, but they had just gone into hiding. When I got pregnant – and fat, and miserable – I got 'promoted'," I find myself making quotation marks around the word because the world and his mother knows a move to Parenting Editor was far from a promotion. "I wasn't good enough any more. I wasn't beautiful enough, or talented enough or presentable enough. I had baby-sick on my top and stretch-marks just about everywhere. They brought Louise in, 5'11" of sex appeal. She was good enough," I finish bitterly.

"But you've told me Louise isn't thought of that highly?"

"I know that now," I say, "but I didn't then. Just like now I realise that Eve was just trying to be liked, to be popular, but then all I could see was the rejection. It's like I've pushed people away my whole life because I'm waiting for them to move on. People like Jack, like Daisy, like Aidan."

I sit back, my hands resting on my legs, totally exhausted. It's hard work getting better.

"Have you ever explained to these people why you pushed them away?" Cathy asks.

Here we go with the fecking letters again.

# 27

I had left Cathy Cook's office, a snivelling mess. Every feeling of inadequacy had come surging through my body and I had forced myself to take a long walk along the riverside to calm the thumping of my heart. I'm sure I looked as if I was on day-release from the local funny farm. I cried, talked to myself and gestured wildly while walking as fast as my legs could carry me.

I had been walking for an hour when I finally ran out of puff. I sat down, staring at the gentle lapping of the Foyle against the quay and I let go of it. I let the pain go. I said goodbye to it and I decided to move on. At least now I understood why I had felt so wretched for so long. Surely it was a good thing that I was now in control of my own thoughts?

I still wasn't going to write those damned letters though. Fate had other plans, or should I say Mammy had other plans.

She and Daddy had had a chat – just after we left on the

303

night my father had told me I was always enough and they decided to take matters into their own hands. Mammy phoned Cathy and asked if it would be at all possible to arrange a family counselling session. Cathy in turn contacted me and asked me would I mind. At the time I was deleting the 126 th attempt at my letter to them and I was too weary to argue. If I'm honest, I'm always too tired to argue with Mammy. She always wins, and ninety-nine times out of a hundred it is with good reason.

So we find ourselves sitting in front of Cathy. Daddy is on one side and Mammy is on the other. I am, as always it seems, piggy in the middle and I sit there feeling about eight years old and as if I should still be wearing long white socks and my hair in pigtails. I may be mistaken but I am pretty sure Cathy has a certain smug look about her – as if she is dying to tell me that she told me so, that she was going to get me to confront my parents one way or another. I imagine throwing her a dirty look or maybe even the finger and then sit back, my arms crossed across my chest in an act of wilful defiance and feel just ever so slightly sick about what is going to happen. Daddy has a strange smile on his face. I think it's down to nerves. It's bizarre to see him looking like that – vulnerable, with emotion (albeit semi-hysteria) drawn all over his face. Mammy has her business face on. It is mildly scary. I recognise it from all the days she called me by my full Grace Anne O'Donnell name when I was in serious trouble, or from the day she marched up to my school to teach the bullies a lesson or three.

"I'd like to welcome you all here," Cathy starts.

Mammy smiles, replying in her best snobby phone voice that she is delighted to be here if it means she is helping me on my road to recovery.

I, on the other hand, roll my eyes and grunt a huffy, "Whatever!"

"I'm sensing a little hostility, Grace," Cathy says and I have to try very hard indeed not to make some sarky comment about her obvious powers of perception.

Instead I bite my tongue and answer with a simple: "I'm just not sure this is necessary."

"And why's that?" Cathy asks.

"Yes, and why's that?" Mammy echoes.

Daddy just looks at me and I remember his words, his hugs and assurances that I was enough and, instead of feeling calm, I feel trapped. My heart thuds that little bit faster. If I tell them why I'm not happy for them to be there then I would be opening a giant, ugly, painful can of worms that I'm not sure I will be able to close again. I don't want to hurt them, or blame them or do anything which will make their own grief and pain more unbearable.

"I don't think it's necessary," I mutter, staring at my shoes. They are pretty shoes. Not as nice as the green Mary Janes but nice all the same.

"Why not?" Cathy asks.

"Yes, why not?" comes the echo. Daddy just stares.

"Because," I answer, raising my gaze from my shoes to Cathy and giving her a death stare I pray she will understand to mean 'You know exactly why, Cathy. I've told you a jillion times'.

She looks back at me, eyebrow slightly raised as if to say back 'I told you I would make you talk this one out'.

"Grace," she starts, using my name in a lovely soothing tone of voice to try to pretend she is my friend, "I know there are things you need to say to your family. That is why I agreed to this meeting when your mum requested it. I can assure you that family sessions are very much a part of what we do."

"After two weeks?" I ask. "And when I told you I didn't want to talk about these issues?"

"Ah, so you have issues then?" Mammy jumps in, her face at first ecstatic because I have admitted I have issues and then, in turn, taut with worry at what those issues might be.

I drop my head to my hands. You see, I didn't want this. I never wanted this. This look of worry, this pain. I haven't even opened my mouth yet and there it is, written all over my mammy's face.

"Of course, she has issues," Daddy says, and Mammy looks at him – shocked to hear him use the word 'issues'. Daddy doesn't do 'issues'. He might be sensitive. He might say the odd rosary, but he's not really a New-Age-in-touch-with-his-feminine-side kind of a guy.

Her mouth opens and closes, no noise coming out.

The thudding of my heart grows louder again – drowning out the noise of the clock ticking on the wall. All I can hear is the thudding in my ears, my slow breath, my inner voice praying that what he is about to say isn't going to open that big old wormy can without my being able to stop him.

"Of course, she has issues," he repeats, this time loud enough for the whole room to hear. Loud enough even to drown out the beating of my heart. "We all have issues," he adds, staring directly at Mammy. "You know that, don't you?" He sits forward, forcing me to lean back so they can stare directly at each other. He takes her hand in his, rubbing it gently and I am transported back to that bathroom floor. Him sitting beside her, rubbing her hand, reassuring her. Emotion etched across both their faces.

"You wouldn't have insisted so strongly on coming here if you didn't think she had issues and if you didn't think those issues were in some way to do with us. Things were tough when she was wee. We weren't perhaps the best parents we could have been. We didn't do anything intentionally wrong but that's not to say that mistakes, and plenty of them, weren't made. I mean, how much of her life was spent dealing with us dealing with our grief? Childhood shouldn't be like that."

I wonder if I have actually died. Or perhaps I am just asleep and this is a nightmare, my worst nightmare. I am lying back as my parents practically lean across me, weeping sad tears about how they were rubbish parents.

This was not the way it was supposed to be.

I eyeball Cathy. "See!" I shout, sitting forward, breaking the moment and the handclasp. "I told you no good could come of this! So now everyone's upset. Who exactly is that helping?"

"It's okay to be angry," Cathy soothes, and I am glad to hear her say it, because I am fucking (and, yes, that is fucking and not fecking) furious.

"This is supposed to be a healing process," I say, my voice stronger, angrier than before. "Who exactly is being healed right now? Is *he*?" I ask, pointing my finger at Daddy's wan and tired face. "Or perhaps *she* is? Don't you think she looks full of health and vitality just now?" I point at Mammy's tear-stained face.

Cathy just stares back, a look akin to bemusement on her face.

"Well?" I demand, my finger pointing madly at Cathy.

"Calm down, love," Mammy mutters, taking my hand – my

pointing finger of doom – and bringing it down by my side. "Do you really think this could hurt us more than what we have been through already? We've been waiting for this. Hiding it away. I suppose we have been hoping it would never come out because then we would all have to admit that life hasn't been perfect – but, you know what, I'm glad it's out there because I don't have to tiptoe around you any more. I'm sorry, Gracie," she says, her hand still holding mine, "I'm sorry that we didn't make you the centre of our world and that other things – other babies – got in the way of what should have been a perfect childhood for you. But I'm even more sorry that we didn't ever really talk about it. We thought we were doing the right thing by keeping quiet. I think we persuaded ourselves you were too young to have known what was going on and when we realised you knew most of it, when you were twenty, it seemed too hard to talk about it then."

Daddy takes over, his monologue making me wonder if they have practised this speech. I even wonder momentarily if Cathy had helped them write it.

"You seemed so together," he says. "You had your great job and then you met Aidan and the pair of you seemed so happy. And Jack . . ." his face erupts into a smile when he thinks of his precious grandson, "well, he's perfect. We had no reason to think that you were anything other than happy. Until . . ." he trailed off.

"Until I ran away to Donegal and had a minor breakdown."

I've said it now. The words are out there and I've finished the speech. The speech Cathy wrote without realising. She looks pretty smug. I can't say that I blame her. It is a pretty touching sight, seeing the three of us hugging – forgiving each other.

# 28

"I need a drink," I say, walking through the door to an expectant Daisy.

She is sitting on the armchair in the kitchen, a book in one hand, a chocolate biscuit (which she tries to hide as I walk in) in the other.

"Was it awful?" she asks, her voice heavy with concern.

"Yes and no," I sigh, walking straight to the fridge and pulling out a bottle of icy-cold Pinot Grigio before rummaging in the drawer for the corkscrew.

I lift two glasses from the cupboard because whether she likes it or not Daisy will be having a drink with me.

"Is it warm enough to sit outside, do you think?" I ask.

Daisy looks at the slightly greying sky and announces it's better not to risk it. "Let's just go to the living room and you can tell me all about it," she says and I follow, bottle in one hand, glasses in the other.

"Did the kids settle okay?"

"No problem, although Jack has taken Muck, Scoop and Dizzy to bed with him," Daisy says, while claiming the squashy sofa closest to the window.

I pour the drinks before sitting down opposite her and drawing my feet up under me.

"You look remarkably calm," Daisy says.

"You should have seen me an hour ago."

"Did you cry?"

I nod. "And shout, and huff and then Mammy cried and then Daddy cried and then we all cried, apart from fecking Cathy Cook who just looked remarkably smug and pleased with herself."

"For making you all cry?" Daisy asks, sipping from her glass of wine and letting out a satisfied sigh as the cold liquid slides down her throat.

"No, for making us talk it all out. God, Daisy, they've been killing themselves with blame these last few weeks."

"So you've been able to sort it all out with them?"

"Sort of. We've put a few demons to bed, but it wasn't easy. I'm not sure how I feel."

"But it's good to get it out there and talk about it?"

"I don't know if good is the word, but yes, I can see it's going to be helpful."

Daisy nods. "Darling, you know I love the bones of you, and Mammy and Daddy, but you all needed this, you know. They need to let go of all the wee ghosties that are in their past and you need to feel loved for the wonderful person you are."

I blush a little. I'm used to hearing Daisy telling me that I'm wonderful, but it still makes me that little bit embarrassed. I still can't really believe anyone would find me wonderful.

"God, I need this wine," I say, bringing the glass up to my lips.

"Get it down your neck then."

"But it's not very Weightloss-Wonders-friendly, now is it?"

"You're allowed the occasional misdemeanour, babes," Daisy smiles, before adding with a wink, "as long as you don't eat half a loaf of toast afterwards."

* * *

Two hours have passed and the wine bottle is upended in the cooler. A second wine bottle is looking dangerously close to being empty. Daisy and I have talked through everything that happened at Cathy's, what's been going on lately in *EastEnders* and whether or not thong underwear is really more comfortable than belly-warming full briefs. We are now on the subject of why we really should do this more often and by this I think we mean sharing a few drinks and a laugh as opposed to the 'this' meaning me leaving my husband and moving in for a couple of weeks.

My head is in that slightly swimmy, lovely hazy state. The world has a Doris Day kind of glow about it and I grin to myself as the thought pops into my head that Daisy and I are like Calamity Jane and Katie all holed up in our wee cabin together. (Without the lesbian undertones, obviously.)

"You're grinning like an eejit," Daisy says, a smile on her own face.

"Jus' thinking how lucky I am, you know," I mumble drunkenly.

Daisy stands up, taking a second or two to balance herself before walking to the stereo and switching the radio on.

"If Mohammed won't come to the disco, then the disco will go to the mountain," she mutters as I splutter wine down my front. "Don't you fancy a wee dance?" She laughs, hauling me to my feet. "No point in wasting the drunk feeling by not dancing. We can practise our moves from class."

A generic dance song is playing on the radio and she stands there, one eye closed in concentration, trying to remember the routine taught to us in just one hour.

I try to follow, but within seconds I'm bent over laughing.

"Don't laugh," she grins, continuing with her hip waggling. "You couldn't do much better, could you?"

"Is that a challenge, Miss Caddisy?" I stutter drunkenly.

"Well, if you are too chicken . . ." she says before losing her balance and landing flat on her rear end.

"Oh, I don't think it'll be too much of a problem to beat that shameless display," I laugh, taking my position in the middle of the living room – toe pointed like an Irish dancer getting reading to perform at the Feis. My head held high, I wait for a change in the music and then I start to move my body, my hips swaying, my arms twisting and pointing.

"Holy fuck!" Daisy exclaims from her position on the floor. "Gracie, you can dance!"

Another hour passes and while we have at least been sensible enough to replace the now-empty wineglasses with full pint-glasses of water, I still feel hazy and spaced out. The radio has switched from generic dance songs to those slushy love songs from the seventies and eighties and I've now joined Daisy on the floor. As each songs starts, we girly-scream that we know this one and start to sing along, only to realise that, bar the first few lines and perhaps the chorus, we don't really know it at all.

And then The Carpenters start to play and I'm transported back to my childhood – to sitting on the stairs, the sound of Karen Carpenter's smooth and soothing voice almost, just almost, drowning out the sound of Mammy's tears.

"I love this one," Daisy says and starts to croon along.

I join in, but this time I know the words and the lyrics seem to reach right inside me and for the first time I know what it is like to feel my heartstrings physically pulled.

Although I don't usually sing in public – my tuneless warbling normally reserved for the car or shower – I start to sing along. The words of 'Rainy Days and Mondays' resonating with me now more than before, I start to cry, staring at Daisy and singing through my tears.

"Ach, babe, don't cry!"

"But you don't get it," I mutter. "This song is about me – and you – and I love you and you saved my life and you are the only friend who has ever loved me back and you make me feel like I belong."

Daisy starts to cry too. "No. You!" she says pointing. "You are the one who saved me. You are my bess-friend and I love you."

And she starts to sing along too.

And I realise the most important thing in the world is to know someone loves me – in fact, I'm lucky because lots of people love me. Even Cathy, in her own twisted little way.

\* \* \*

*My greatest fear in life has always been that I am not good enough –*

*that I have been life's great consolation prize – the human equivalent of a Blankety Blank cheque book and pen. It has taken me twenty-nine years, a nervous breakdown of sorts and two sessions with a counsellor to realise that, and while some may lie down under it I realise I'm one of the lucky ones. I have realised it and I'm doing something about it. When the powers that be mooted the idea that I change my life for* Northern People, *I laughed it off. (Well, if the truth be told, I cried for half an hour in the toilets and then I laughed it off). Me? Change my life? Step out of my comfort zone? Not a chance.*

*Like most working mums I was stuck in a rut. From the Weetabix-stained clothes I wore to work to slobbing in front of the telly in the evening, praying my son would sleep through and give me some peace, I had stopped living and started merely existing.*

*If I'm honest, I got pissed off. I had been promised it all. My generation had been told that we could have everything we wanted. A career? No problem. A fulfilling home life too? Why not? The joy of spending quality time with your child? Sure thing. Instead, I got a different version of it all. Stretch-marks? Yes. A headache? Yes, sirree! A life in freefall where I no longer knew who I was? I was your gal!*

*I've written this introduction one hundred times, and one hundred times I've deleted my silly little platitudes about being an every-woman super-creature who is perfection personified. In the end I decided to strike a blow for real women. I am not a yummy mummy. I am me and I am doing the best I can. I am a mammy and I am a wife. I am a daughter and a friend, but most of all I am me and I implore everyone who reads this to stand up and be counted for the person you are.*

*If you are feeling miserable, then the chances are something needs to change and although I would never have believed it myself a month ago, I now know we have the power, individually and collectively, to make those changes.*

*This is the story of my transformation.*

I type the word transformation with a flourish before closing over the laptop and taking a refreshing sip from my glass of wine. Looking over the garden, to where the children are playing in the sand, Daisy crouched beside them, I feel elated.

"Right, young lady, you would need to be getting ready for your big night out!" I shout across the garden to Daisy. "I've finished this blasted intro, so I can take over children duties and you can get yourself into the bath quick smart. You've only two hours to go."

Daisy grins, saluting me and kissing Lily on the head. Yep, tonight is another date with Dishy. (We had toyed with the notion of abbreviating that to ADWD, but we decided that was taking things a bit too far.) I'm on baby-sitting duty – something which I admit feels weird given my twenty-nine years on this planet. But it feels kind of cool also because my 'boyfriend' is coming over to help me. Now on a rare night off from work, Aidan was initially gutted I couldn't get out of my baby-sitting commitments to Daisy. I mean, the woman has basically kept me for the last two weeks, so I could hardly say no. In the end it was Daisy herself who suggested he come over to keep me company – reminding me of just how much fun 'baby-sitting' can be. I feel myself flush. Aidan and I are supposed to be taking things slowly. I am not supposed to be having lustful thoughts about him.

Jack runs over and jumps up onto my knee, sensing that my work is done for the day. "Mammy, come and play!" he giggles, grabbing my hand, jumping down and pulling me in the direction of the sandpit.

"Okay, darling," I laugh, plonking myself unceremoniously down beside him and Lily and starting a game of build and destruct with the sand moulds.

An hour and a half later, Daisy and I are sitting in the living room as the children run around in their pyjamas.

"I won't wait up," I grin, topping up a glass of wine for my friend who looks a lot less nervous than she did this time last week.

"Well, I'll make sure to phone before I come back. I don't want to be coming back and walking in on you and Aidan in the act."

I choke on my glass of water. "Daisy Cassidy, we are a respectable married couple. We don't do that kind of thing any more."

She raises an eyebrow. "Well, there is protection in my bedside drawer, just in case."

I throw a cushion at her, shocked that I'm actually quite excited at the notion of getting physical with Aidan again. Our sex life had become so humdrum – so predictable – that I could almost time our every move down to the second. But now it feels different. It feels a little like it did back in the early days of our relationship. I was nervous then too, of course I was, but, God, I loved the passion. I loved that we could barely keep our hands off each other – that we could spend an entire weekend in bed and not even notice the time pass. I'm not saying tonight will be the night the flames of passion re-ignite with Aidan, but I can feel the embers start to smoulder that bit again and there is nothing that I would like more than to spend time entangled in his arms, feeling his nakedness against my own.          •

Daisy laughs. "I just want you to be careful," she says.

"Well, I hope you have packed some of your little rubber friends too," I tease. "Because I don't want you to come round here with any babies!"

It seems such a transformation for us – we two friends sitting here and talking about functional relationships as opposed to those in freefall or those which actually do not exist at all. For as long as we have known each other we have both been longing for passion and romance. It mattered not that I was married. Aidan had his occasional moments, of course he did, or we would have been divorced a long time ago, but more often than not we acted like housemates who occasionally bumped uglies. And as for Daisy, her love life was a train wreck. The only man she had been associated with was TMF – well, there was also an unfortunate episode which never really took off with that Little Tikes accountant. We don't ever talk about that one. Some things are best forgotten. There were so many nights we talked about how we longed to feel that thrill of falling in love again and now, hey, look at us, doing just that!

Daisy leaves just as Aidan arrives, kissing me awkwardly on the cheek as he walks in. Jack runs to his arms with Lily not far behind. It feels weirdly comfortable. Here is my family, but in someone else's home with Lily thrown in for good measure.

Aidan and I work together to get the children settled and it occurs to me just how well we fit – how well we know each other and our habits. He kisses Jack tonight, but lets me say his prayers. I make sure Lily has gone to the toilet before bed, but it is Aidan who checks under her pink bed for monsters. As I serve up our dinner – a healthy salad and stir fry – Aidan lights the Chimnea and pours the wine. We sit together in the dusky twilight, enjoying the warm breeze of this late August night around us as it gently moves the branches on the trees.

"This feels good," Aidan says, breaking our companionable silence.

"Yes, it does. Doesn't it?"

"I've missed this."

"Me too."

And we both know we are talking about a hell of a lot more than the last two weeks. We are talking about the last two years.

He reaches his hand to mine, the warmth of his touch sending shivers down my spine.

"I've missed you too, Grace," he says and again I know instinctively this is about much more than our trial separation. I look at him across the table and I realise how handsome he is. Damn it, I realise how fecking sexy he is. He obviously looks older now than when we first met. He has more wrinkles, more grey hairs. He has a tiredness about him, but all this serves to make him look more like a man – a proper, grown-up, testosterone-filled man. He looks more like Harrison Ford in *Indiana Jones*, all stubbly and sexy, than Harrison Ford in *Star Wars*, all fresh-faced and boyish. I feel my heart beat a little faster.

"Will we go inside?" I say, lifting my wineglass and walking towards the door.

He stops me, catching me by the wrist, turning me towards him. He takes my wineglass from me, sets it back on the table, all the while never moving his gaze from me, and pulls me towards him. His hand slides behind my neck, pulling me closer to him. I am powerless to resist – even if I wanted to, which I don't. He kisses me, slowly at first – tentatively waiting for my reaction. I kiss him back, my need growing. I need to show him I love him, want him, believe in him, trust him and fecking fancy the arse off him.

He groans in response to my kiss, pulling me closer to him again so that I can feel every delicious inch of him against me. This taking things slowly is going to a be lot harder than I thought. In fact, I think it is going to be impossible.

* * *

Opening my eyes I try to get my bearings. Here I am on a cold, uncomfortable surface and yet I feel totally relaxed. Aidan's arm is draped across my waist and his lips are nuzzled against my neck. There is an intimacy in our embrace that hasn't been there for a long time – in fact, I'm not sure I can remember the last time I felt this blissful. I look to the display on the front of the DVD player and see that it is 11.30 pm. I can only have been sleeping for an hour, but I feel totally rested. There are cushions scattered around us.

I wrap the throw from the sofa around myself and pad to the kitchen for a glass of water, leaving Aidan lying on the floor, asleep and gorgeous. How could I have forgotten just how amazing he looks when naked? Amazing and mine. I grin as I walk to the fridge. Bringing two glasses back I sit on the floor, trickling a little drop of water on Aidan's bare chest, prompting him to jump awake.

"Wakey, wakey, sunshine!"

I laugh and he grabs the glass off me, threatening to pour it over my head.

"You can't do that!" I laugh. "Daisy will go mad if you soak the floor."

"It can be mopped up," he teases, tipping the glass slightly so that the water starts to drip from the glass.

I grab his wrist, and we wrestle together playfully before our eyes meet and we find ourselves locked in another kiss. I had forgotten how intimate a kiss can be – how powerful and sexy. I had forgotten how to show my vulnerability in that single meeting of lips, how to express my love in that tender moment. I had also forgotten just how much it could turn me on.

Pulling away, while every part of me wants to lose myself in the moment, I sigh: "I suppose we just get ourselves into a respectable state. Daisy could be home any moment."

"More's the pity," Aidan says, running his hand along the length of my thigh before sitting up and starting to dress. I kiss his back, his neck and hold him close.

"I love you, Grace," he says, pulling my arms around him and holding me close.

And I say, "I love you too."

# 29

Today feels like my wedding day, my graduation day and my birthday all rolled into one. No matter how gradual this transformation has been, no matter how long this month has been and how I have wanted to give up and walk away during it, today is the day where I see the me I am going to be. I'm not stupid or naive. I know this isn't done. I know this is just the start, but I'm not scared of it any more.

I wake to Jack prising my eyes open, his eyes close to mine and his tiny nose rubbing against my own.

"Morning, Mammy!" he cheeps. "Me wanna go get breakfast, and play with Lily and go to the beach and go to the park and eat ice cream and have fun."

He barely pauses for breath and his enthusiasm for life makes my heart swell with pride.

"Well, Mammy wants a kiss and a cuddle and a kiss and a cuddle and another kiss," I giggle, grabbing him close and tickling him until he squeals in delight.

At just that moment Lily pops her head around the doorframe, eager to find the source of the laughter.

"Morning, Auntie Grace, morning, Crazy Jack!" she shouts, running and jumping up on the bed. "Attack of the Babies!" she screams as she and Jack launch themselves at me, tickling and wriggling until we are all in danger of waking the whole neighbourhood with our laughter. Instead, we manage just to wake Daisy who pretends to be cross – which serves only to make the children laugh louder.

"Come on, children," she says, in her best Little Tikes manager voice. "Time for breakfast. Auntie Grace has a very busy day today."

Lily jumps off the bed. "Is today your Princess Day, Auntie Grace?"

I nod. Jack hugs me.

"Mammy's not a princess, Mammy's a bum!" he laughs and I tickle him again.

"No messing, Mrs Adams," Daisy says. "You have to get ready for your close-up."

Of course, she is right. Today is the day of my makeover and my photo shoot. I can hardly believe that I'm having a photo shoot all to myself – nor can I believe I'm actually looking forward to it. I've never looked forward to having my photo taken in my life.

While some people would spend a small fortune on finding just the right photographer for those wistful and romantic shots for their wedding albums, I wanted someone who takes pictures as quickly as possible and preferably of everyone else and not me. I opted for Liam in the end – he made he feel relaxed, but not relaxed enough to actually enjoy the experience. Liam is taking the photos today too, but this time I've promised myself that I won't bark, "Enough is enough!" at him before storming off for a glass of champagne in the hotel.

I shower and dress in jeans and a T-shirt before leaving Jack with Susie and heading into work. Everyone knows today is my big day and they know of the transformation, internally as well as externally, that I've undergone.

I handed my last proofs to Sinéad yesterday afternoon and by the time I had left the office at tea time, the mock-ups of the pages were almost complete. There was me, 15 stone and 5 pounds, looking glum and terrified at the start of my journey, surrounded by text telling my story. Four pages remain blank. They are for my "After" pictures in a variety of outfits and poses. I am the talk of the office, but this time no one feels sorry for me.

I walk into reception and Sheila smiles at me broadly from behind her desk.

"Morning, superstar," she grins and I smile back. "Are you ready for your close-up?"

"I was born ready," I grin, making for The Pit and the rest of my colleagues.

"Hang on a minute, missy," Sheila shouts after me and I turn to see her holding a massive bouquet of ivory roses, each stem studded with a glittering crystal. "Somebody obviously loves you," she says and I blush, reaching for the card. I don't need to check who they are from, I know already, but I long to see his words on paper – to hold a card in my hand that he has touched.

"*Good luck, Mrs Adams,*" it reads. "*I'm ready to carry you over the threshold any time you want.*"

I grin again – at least now there is less chance of his gaining a hernia from the endeavour.

"You know what, Sheila," I say. "Somebody really does love me."

Carrying my bouquet down the stairwell to my desk, I catch sight of Louise from the corner of my eye and can almost feel the green hue of envy from where I stand.

"Morning!" I shout. "Lovely day, isn't it?"

I sit down and switch on my computer, staring at that image of me from just four weeks ago. It is time, I decide, to put it behind me. I look at the selection of photos on my desktop. Dermot is still there – still as gorgeous as always, but there is a photo which immediately looks more appealing. Two gorgeous men, both with the same glint in their eye, the same smattering of dark hair, identical broad smiles – standing in the sunlight, waving at the photographer – someone they clearly love with all their hearts. Aidan and Jack are my new screensaver and, of course, I was behind the camera.

"Looking fucking cool, Grace!" Sinéad shouts, walking into the office. "Loving the flowers!" she winks, knowing this means things must be on the right track again with Aidan. "We leave in about half an hour. Hope you're ready to have some serious fun."

"You bet I am!" I answer and I can almost hear Louise's huff move up a notch. My phone rings and I pick it up, with almost no hesitation. "Good morning, editorial, Grace Adams speaking."

"Good morning, Grace-Adams-speaking, how are you?"

"Grand, Mammy, what can I do you for?"

"Just wanted to wish you luck, sweetheart. I can't wait to see the pictures. Can you call over after work so we can see the transformation?"

"I'll do my best. See you about five thirty?"

"Perfect. Have fun."

"Will do. Love you, Mammy."

"Love you too, darling."

Sinéad drives us to the town centre, where I'm whisked to a hair and beauty salon. I walk in and suddenly loads of skinny, blonde twenty-somethings are buzzing around me. They cloak me in one of those wonderful capes which stop you seeing the true horror of your spare tyres as you sit in the hairdresser's chair, and get to work.

Apparently, I'm getting highlighted, or is it low-lighted? While the colours work their magic I'm having a manicure, and a pedicure, and a facial, if they can manage it. A glass of wine appears by my side, despite it being just ten thirty in the morning, and Sinéad has taken a seat alongside me while one of the blonde twenty-somethings works on her perfectly manicured talons.

"We're really excited about this month's issue," Sinéad says, sipping from her glass, her mouth clearly needing something to help fight the urge to light up. "The advertisers are peeing their pants with the possible tie-ins and I have to say this is just the shake-up we needed at *Northern People*."

"Louise's idea was a good one," I say.

"Feck that. Jesus, Louise just wanted to humiliate someone. I'd like to say her heart was in the right place, but then that would mean admitting she had a heart in the first place."

I stay silent. I don't want to become the office bitch – no matter how tempting that might be.

The effort of biting my tongue must be showing, as Sinéad stares at me and drops her voice to a whisper.

"Don't feel sorry for her, Grace. *Northern People* has no

place for people who don't play to our team strengths. We have even less room for people who try to destroy us from within by creating bad feeling within our own staff. We can achieve a lot more by working together than by working against each other, and her display last week beggared belief. She'll soon learn though."

I raise an eyebrow, looking at Sinéad while icy-cold dye runs down the back of my neck, making me shiver.

"Just between you, me and the wall," Sinéad faux-whispers, "Louise is on her way out. She is being relocated to Belfast to work on a new title, and the word is if she doesn't up her game there she may find herself out on her ear."

"Does that mean my old job is reopening?" I ask, feeling ready once again to take on the mantle of Health and Beauty Editor – this last month relighting my passion for writing.

"Afraid not, Gracie, but I'm looking for a Features Editor if you're interested?"

I choke on my wine a little. Features Editor. Also known as 'Grace's Dream Job' (you know, if the position of Dermot Murnaghan's bed-warmer was all gone). This would make me Sinéad's right-hand woman. I would get my own office, with my own squishy sofa. I would help set the editorial tone for the magazine. I can barely contain my excitement.

"Damn right I'm interested."

"Damn right the job's yours then!" Sinéad smiles, clinking her glass against mine. "I'm delighted to welcome you, the real you, back to *Northern People*."

✳ ✳ ✳

All it takes is three hours. Three hours of dying, cutting,

painting, preening, dressing and some occasional tears and snotters, to make me feel like me again. This is the me I always wanted to be – only better because I never realised before I could be happy not being a Size 12. I have been twirling and smiling for the past two hours, changing outfits and allowing my lip-gloss to be touched up. Who would have thought that all this time there was a diva in me waiting to get out?

"You look stunning, Gracie," Liam says as he takes his final shot and I swear I see a glimmer of a wee tear in the corner of his eye. This truly is a day of miracles after all.

\* \* \*

I arrive at Mammy's house shortly after five thirty and ring the doorbell. I feel nervous and excited. I can't wait to see her reaction and to show off the spoils of my efforts. Knocking again I wait, and wait, and there is no answer. I'm about to give up when Mammy comes running to the door in a fluster.

She stops, looks at me and starts to cry. I hear the words "look" and "beautiful" between her gulping sobs. The rest I can barely make out, but I just hug her, as tight as I can. It takes a few minutes for her to compose herself.

"Darling, you look wonderful," she says. "Like yourself, only better. Come to the garden with me and we'll have a wee glass of wine to celebrate."

"God, I don't think I could touch another drop. I've still more weight to lose, you know, and everyone keeps feeding me wine these days. Have you got a glass of water I could have or something?"

I make for the living room, but she steers me away. "Come out to the kitchen to see your dad. I'll get you your water there."

I follow and when the doors open there they are: Aidan, Jack, Daisy, Lily, Sinéad, Susie, Sheila, even Dishy. There is a collective intake of breath, disturbed only by Jack's shout of "Mammy's a princess!". The garden has been transformed. Fairy lights twinkle from the trees and there are tables laden with delicious food and even more delicious wine. But I'm not hungry, or thirsty. I'm satisfied, for the first time in a long time.

Jack is dressed in his Superman costume while Lily is doing her best Cinderella impression in a blue satin gown. Everyone looks happy, contented, and I look around and realise that there is nowhere else on this planet that I would rather be right now than here with these people.

I realise I am loved and that I am worthy of that love. That one realisation, more than anything, blows my mind. This is how it should be.

Everyone laughs, then cheers and I find myself swamped by cuddles, kisses and good wishes. I can barely keep up with them, can barely see the people I'm cuddling for the happy tears.

I work my way around the garden until I get to Aidan and Jack. Holding them both tight, breathing them in, I realise I never want to let either of them go again.

Music starts to play softly and Aidan asks if he can have this dance. Handing Jack over to his granny and her warm, inviting cuddles, Aidan takes me in his arms and we start to dance around on the grass. As the guests at this little soirée cheer and clap for us, I realise this beats our wedding day, and that gorgeous fishtail gown, hands down.

"Aidan?" I say.

"Yes?"

"Can I please come home now?"

# The End